Marcus Hieronymus Vida

The Christiad

An Heroic Poem in Six Books

Marcus Hieronymus Vida

The Christiad
An Heroic Poem in Six Books

ISBN/EAN: 9783744716444

Printed in Europe, USA, Canada, Australia, Japan

Cover: Foto ©Andreas Hilbeck / pixelio.de

More available books at **www.hansebooks.com**

THE

CHRISTIAD:

An HEROIC POEM;

In SIX BOOKS.

WRITTEN BY

MARCUS HIERONYMUS VIDA,

And Translated into ENGLISH VERSE,

BY

EDWARD GRANAN, M.A.

Immortal VIDA! on whose honour'd brow
The Poet's bays and Critics ivy grew:
CREMONA now shall boast thy name,
As next in place to MANTUA, next in Fame!

POPE.

LONDON:

Printed for the AUTHOR,
And Sold by R. BALDWIN, in Paternoster Row.
M DCC LXXI.

T H E

L I F E

O F

MARCUS HIERONYMUS VIDA.

I Think it more eligible to uſher in to the Public this performance by prefixing to it the Author's Life, than endeavour either to palliate its inaccuracies, or to diſplay its merit ; fully perſuaded, that the one can no more be mended by, an obſtinate defence, than the other can be totally extinguiſhed by ill-natured cenſure.

Marcus Hieronymus Vida was born at Cremona, in the year 1470. He was the ſon of Gelelmus Vida, and Leona Ofcaſala, both Italians of

the

the neighbourhood of St. Leonard; and each was of
illuftrious extraction, Bonvefinus Vida being Conful of Cremona, in 1166. But, at the time of our
Author's birth, little of opulent fplendor remained
in the family, but its inherent virtue was ftill the
fame, unaltered and unblemifhed. To tranfmit it
to their child, his parents fent him early in life,
near home, to the fchool of the celebrated Nico-
laus Lafcarus, where his progrefs in the Claffics,
Philofophy, and Oratory, much exceeded what
might be expected from his years, though not
from his genius, which was found to be uncom-
monly bright and piercing,

Thus inftructed at Cremona and Mantua, he
went to Padua, where, and at Bologna, he applied
himfelf to Divinity and Poetry; the firft, his oc-
cupation; the fecond, his amufement. His fkill in
Divinity procur'd for him, when young, a Pre-
bendary's ftall among the Regulars of St. Mark's
of Mantua, a Community of royal foundation; and,
being foon after invited to Rome to enjoy the fame
dignity in the church of St. John of Lateran, he
took his laft leave of his parents.

When Vida went to Rome, Leo the Tenth filled
the Pontifical Chair. To him it is that the finer
arts owe their revival, as having extricated them
from the Gothic darknefs which for many ages
had

had obſcured their beauties : For which reaſon his
character drawn by Mr. Pope is minutely juſt, and
poetically elegant :

But ſee ! each Muſe, in Leo's golden days,
Starts from her trance, and trims her wither'd bays,
Rome's ancient genius o'er its ruins ſpread,
Shakes off the duſt, and rears his rev'rend head.
Then Sculpture and her ſiſter Arts revive;
Stones leap'd to form and rocks began to live;
With ſweeter notes each riſing Temple rung,
A Raphael painted, and a Vida ſung.

While Leo had in view the finding out of a Poet,
whoſe judgment could diſpoſe in order, and fire
animate the actions of Chriſt, Leſcaris, a King's
Legate, preſented him with Vida's Scacchio or
Game of Cheſs; which he no ſooner had begun to
read, but his looks were expreſſive of the ſatisfac-
tion he ſhould have in peruſing the poem.   Come
at length to the fictitious battle, he cried out. This,
this is the man, the only one I know of ſufficient a-
bilities to undertake, and happily to execute the life
and deeds of Chriſt ! Vida being immediately ſent
for to court, his Holineſs deſired, he would com-
poſe a poem to be call'd the CHRISTIAD ; and at the
ſame time conferred on him the priory of St. Syl-
veſter in Tuſculum, that now, at his eaſe, he
might purſue the work with proper aſſiduity and
ſpirit.

A 3

Retired

Retired to live on his benefice, he firſt frames the plan of the Chriſtiad, then works upon it, enjoying from Leo's munificence that independence which foſters and cheriſhes the vigour of every muſe. Yet even here he was not a mere recluſe ; for he ſo temper'd the ſolitary with the ſocial life, that he diſſipated the ſupineneſs that generally ſteals on the former, and avoided the diſtraction that attends on the latter.

His houſe was therefore open to men of taſte and elegance, where they were received with a plain generoſity, which freed him from paying dull compliments, and his gueſts from that reſervedneſs which formal ceremony is uſually productive of.

When Vida had finiſh'd the firſt Book, he laid it before the Pontiff for his peruſal ; who, on returning the copy, to expreſs his approbation, and compliment the Author, ſpoke the following diſtich:

    ' Cedite Romani ſcriptores, cedite Graii ;
    ' Hic ſcio quid majus naſcitur Æneide.'

Ye Bards of Greece and Rome reſign your bays ;
Something now loftier grows than Maro's lays.

                                                  But

But what place is fecure from uneafinefs ? If Rubens, in his perfpective view of Arcadia, placed, in a corner of the delicious fcene, a tomb infcribed with this motto, ET IN ARCADIA, EVEN IN ARCADIA; furely Vida could not expect an uninterrupted feries of happinefs in his Tufculum. During his refidence here, he loft both his parents, almoft at the fame time; and, to complete his affliction, his own fupport and the life of his mufe would have died away by the death of Leo, which happened foon after, had not Clement VII, in the fpace of two years (after the death of Adrian VI.) afcended the Papal Throne.

Clement, being fellow-ftudent with our author, and not ignorant of his genius, infifted that he fhould finifh the Chriftiad, which he had undertaken at the inftance of his uncle Leo. And here I hope the Reader will indulge me for obferving, that there is not one power in Europe the learned world is more indebted to, than the Houfe of Medicis ; which appears from the encouragement given to the Belles-lettres by Leo the Xth, Clement the VIIth, and Catharine of Medicis, Queen of France, all of the fame Houfe ; to the laft of whom we owe the famous Gallery of painting in the palace of Luxembourg in Paris. When the Chriftiad was finifh'd, Clement patronized it, and rewarded the Author with the Bifhopric of Alba, in the

A 4   Mar-

Marquifate of Monferrat, then vacant by the death of Antonius Molus.

Paul III. intended further to promote him to the fee of Cremona, as fucceffor to the Cardinal Accolita deceafed ; but his death prevented Vida's being inftalled there. His election, however, to Cremona by the Chapter of that cathedral is ftill extant in their regifter, where, after the ufual preamble, are thefe words :—" They have none fit- " ter than the Rev. M. H. Vida ; one fo excell- " ing in all kinds of virtues and true piety, as to " deferve much greater honours."—

This work, though intended for the moft noble purpofes, the promoting of Chriftianity ; and embellifhed with the charms of poetry, to court and fix the attention ; has not efcaped the pen of Scaliger, who fays the lines have often the tautology of Ovid, the bombaft of Lucan, and fometimes the words, but never the majefty of Virgil : But this is a cenfure on words, not on things ; and therefore not worth a refutation. But there is a ferious objection made by P. Frizon, and adopted by Mr. Bayle, which is, that the fpeeches of Jofeph and John the Evangelift, which take up the third and fourth Books, are too long. The force of this objection will foon vanifh, if we confider, that every tranfaction, related in either fpeech, was new to the

ears

ears of Pilate ; and consequently what may appear
tedious to a previous knowledge is generally short
so the raptured sense of novelty.   Again; unless
we make Pilate such a Judge as Shakespeare's,
" who would hang the prisoner, before he'd eat
" his mutton cold;"   we must suppose him to
have had a competent knowledge of all the parti-
culars necessary for the due discharge of his office,
and therefore to have disregarded the law maxim,
that ' nunquam longa est cunctatio, quando de
' vitâ hominis agitur ;'   as indeed, ✱ ✱ ✱ ✱✱✱✱,
the deliberation in some cases can never be too
long, when a man's life is in question.

Besides the Christiad, Vida's other genuine
works are divine Hymns, his Art of Poetry, the
Silk-worm, the Poem on Chess, three Eclogues, and
some Poems on various subjects.   These in his life
time were honoured with a place in the Academy
of Bologna, and translated into various languages.
To him are also ascribed a Treatise on regulating a
Common-wealth, and others on Religious subjects.

Should we pass in review Vida's sentimental
life, the prospect will appear as amiable as his
poetical is picturesque.   We observe in him the
tender heart join'd with the courage of the soldier ;
the clearest reason, submissive to Revelation ; the

wit

wit of the Scholar blended with the devotion of the Hermit : We see him humble in an opulent estate ; parsimonious to himself, munificent to others ; courted by the Great, attending the poor and infirm ; in short, the citizen and the christian happily united in his person.

The tenderness of his heart is obvious in the elegy he inscribed to the memory of his parents ; where filial piety weeps in mournfully-pleasing numbers.—When the war raged between the Emperor Charles V. and Francis I, the French troops so vigorously besieged Alba, that when the Imperialists saw the enemy gain the trenches and some enter the town, they instantly left the ramparts defenceless, and sought safety in the most fortified parts. Vida, laying aside the Mitre, and taking on him the General, rallied the citizens, and, marching at the their head, attacked, defeated, and put to flight enemy ; and thus saved the town from the impending plunder and carnage of the sword.

Add to this signal instance of his courage his humility, which made him as amiable to mankind, as his courage respectable. This appears by the postscript to his Christiad, where he assures the reader, that, if any line or thought should be found in the work contrary to the dogms of faith,

or

or the fanction of the ancient Fathers, it fhould be deemed as inferted inadvertently. This learned humility is fo peculiar to Vida, that few have endeavoured to become his rivals in the practice of this virtue: The chief rival of any note was Monf. Fenelon, Archbifhop of Cambray, and author of Telemachus; who, when his treatife on Quietifm was cenfured, mounted the pulpit, condemn'd it publicly, and caufed it to be burned before the door of his cathedral.

As he imitated Virgil in the majefty of his fentiments, fo he followed him in the modefty of his expreffions; for not one word is found in all his works that can offend the chafteft ear: And what the prefent Lord Lyttleton truly faid of our celebrated poet Mr. Thompfon may with equal juftice be applied to Vida:

Not one immoral, one corrupted thought,
One line, when dying, he could wifh to blot.

He was fent to the Council of Trent with an authority little inferior to that of the Pope's Legates; where, after having difcharged the duties committed to him, he retired to his Diocefe, whence he could not be withdrawn by the fplendor of a Court, or the preffing invitations of the Great; being employed in public works of utility, by erecting, repairing, or beautifying

fying Religious edifices; or confoling the uneafy, and relieving the poor, many of whom he daily fed at his own houfe, and was careful to have them ferv'd before he fat down himfelf to meat. Thus happy in the confcioufnefs of making others fo, and labouring for above thirty-five years in the feveral duties of a good and pious Prelate, until his death, which happened the 27th of September, 1566, after he had lived ninety-fix years; his body was, with folemnity, amidft the cries, lamentations, and tears of the poor, buried in the cathedral of Alba, and foon after the citizens of Cremona erected a monument in the greateft church of their city, with the following infcription, the tranflation of which I fhall give in the words of the Rev. Mr. Pullein :

To Marcus Hieronymus Vida, Bifhop of Alba,
A man well known to the world,
The City of Cremona, decreeing, at the Public expence,
A Sepulchre to its much deferving Citizen,
Performs its laft duties.
Who, being endowed by nature
With every great and worthy accomplifhment,
Seemed alfo to deferve immortality from her,
Were it not ordained
That all men muft die ;
Neverthelefs, he ftill lives among us,

And

And will live to lateft Pofterity
In the perpetual remembrance
Of his moft good and tender offices,
Who, having fulfilled all the duties which he owed
To the flock he was intrufted with,
Left us at a time rather fit for himfelf
Than others ;
Eminent for piety, charity, faith and conftancy,
Void of offence, dear to all ;
Who not only fo fincerely and devoutly ferved God,
But alfo fo celebrated him in fong,
As to gain a place ever to enjoy him
In Heaven,
And to the advantage of all mankind
A fame unperifhable
On earth.
Died Sept. 27. Anno. Dom. 1566.

He was tall of ftature ; his countenance open and elevated, and the air of his afpect grave, with a mixture of fweetnefs, that produced at once both love and veneration. There are fome Medals extant with his image and name on one fide, and on the reverfe Pegafus with this infcription :—Quos amârunt Dii— the Favourites of the Gods.   In other Medals the reverfe has this motto—Non ftemma fed virtus— not titles but virtue.   His picture has a place in
many

many public repofitories of learning, and among others in the Duke of. Tufcany's Library; his writings have been admired by men of the fineft tafte, and even commended by fome of the fevereft critics, being, of all the moderns, the moft refembling Virgil's, in elegance, harmony, and fimplicity.

THE

A

L I S T

of the S U B S C R I B E R S.

RIGHT Hon. Lord Arundel.
Rt. Hon. Lady Arundel,
Mr. Benj. Adams,
Mr. W. Adams.
Mr. John Alders, 2 Books,
Mr. John Alders, *Junior*,
Mr. Alleyn,
Mr. Alfley,
Mr. Archer,
Mrs. Arden,
Mr. Armifhaw,

B

Mr. Jeffery Babb,
Mr. John Babb,
Mr. Thomas Babb,
Mr. Charles Bagnall,
Mr. James Bagnall, *Senior*,
Mr. James Bagnall, *Junior*,
Mrs. Ifabella Bagnall,
Mr. Richard Bagnall,
Mr. Samp. Bagnall, *Senior*,
Mr. Samp. Bagnall, *Junior*,
Mr. S. Bagnall,
Mr. Thomas Bagnall, 4 Books,
Mr. Bagot.
Mr. John Ball,
Mrs. Bailey,

Mr. W. Bailey,
Mr. Edward Beaumont,
Mr. Francis Beaumont,
Mr. Beaunam,
Mr. Baker,
Mr. Willam Baker,
Mr. Henry Baker,
Mr. Bar,
Mr. Banks.
Mr. Ifaac Barber,
Mrs. Bartlet,
Mr. Barneby,
Mr. Barker,
Mr. Bates,
Mr. Barlow,
Thomas Beech Efq;
Mr. William Beech,
Mrs. O. Beirn,
Rev. Mr. Bentley,
Mr. Beckitt,
Mr. Nathaniel Beard,
Mr. James Bennet,
Mr. James Bentley,
Mr. Samuel Bentley,
Mr. George Beefton,
Mr. Robert Beefton,
———— Berkley Efq;
Mr. James Bent.
John Berrington Efq;

Thomas Berrington Efq;
Mr. Robert Bill,
Mr. Bill,
Rev. Mr. Bird,
Mr. Edward Birch,
Sir Walter Blount Bart.
Lady Blount,
Lady Dowager Blount,
Richard Blount Efq;
Mifs Blount,
Mr. John Blackwell,
Mr. John Blurton.
Mr. Jofeph Boone,
Mr. George Booth,
Mr. Hugh Booth,
Mr. Booker,
Mr. John Bourne,
Mr. William Bourne,
Mr. Samuel Boyer,
Mr. Thomas Boyer.
Mr. Thomas Brindley,
Mr. John Brent,
Lady Brown,
Mr. Samuel Brown *Senior,*
Mr. Samuel Brown *Junior,*
Mr. Breeze,
Mr. Bremare,
Mr. George Bromley,
Mrs. Brueton,
Mr. Henry Tichborne
    Blount, 2 Books,
Henry Blundell Efq; 2 *B.*
Mr. William Bratt,
Mr. Abra. Bracebridge,
Mr. Buckley,
Mr. Jofeph Bucknall, 2 B.

Mr. John Bucknall,
Mr. R. Bucknall, 2 Books
Mr. Chriftopher Bullen,
    10 Books,
Mr. Francis Burgefe,
Mrs. Buchanan,
Mr. Butcher,
Mr. Alban Butler, S. O.
Mr. Charles Butler,
Mr. Butler,
Mr. R. Butler,
Mifs Elizabeth, Bulock,
Mr. John Burch,
            C
The Hon. Tho. Clifford,
The Hon. Mrs. Clifford,
Mafter Clifford,
Mifs Clifford,
Francis Canning Efq;
Mrs. Mary Cach,
Mr. Capon,
Mr. Callon,
Mr. George Carr,
Mr. William Carr,
Mr. Charles Carpue,
Mr. Charles Chatterley,
Mrs. Chatterley.
Mr. Charles Clarke,
Mr. Clough.
Mr. John Child,
Mr. Ralph Colley.
the Hon. Mrs. Collingwood
Robert Cheney Efq;
Mrs. Cheney,
Mr. John Cobb,
Mr. B. Conolly,

Mr. —— Conolly,
Mr. Cooper,
Mrs. Coffen,
Mr. Colclough,
Rev. Mr, Copeland,
Mr. Richard Cotton,
Mr. Thomas Cotton,
Mr. William Cotton,
Mr. Edward Collins,
Mr. Adam Cope,
Edward Coyney Efq;
Mrs. Coyney,
Mr. William Caulborn.
Mr. James Cook,
Mr. John Cook,
Mr. Henry Crutchly,

D

Mr. Dadford,
Mr. Dale,
Mrs. Rachael Dale,
Mr. Thomas Daniel,
Mr. William Darley,
Rev. Mr. Davenport,
Mr. Davenport,
Mrs. Davies.
Mifs Demfey,
—— Doughty Efq;
Mr. Duffey.
Mr. Duxbury,

E

Mr. Eaftham,
Mr. John Elderfey,
Mr. William Edwards,
Mifs Erdefwick.

F

Mr. John Fallows,

Mr, John Faulkner.
Mr. Philip Fernyhough,
Mr. John Feaftone,
Mr. Charles Fielding,
Mr. Benjamin Fifher,
Mr. William Fifher,
Richard Fitzherbert Efq;
Tho. Fitzherbert Efq; 4 ö.
Sir Tho. Fleetwood, Bart.
Mr. Flyn,
Mr. Henry Fothergill.

G

Rt. Hon. Ld. Gormanfton,
Mr. Samuel Gallimore,
Mr. John Galimore,
Mifs Galimore,
Mr. James Genders,
Mr. Rupert Gettliffe.
— Richard Gibfon,
Thomas Giffard Efq;
Mrs. Giffard,
Mafter Giffard,
Mifs Giffard,
Mr. John Graham,
Walter Gough Efq;
Mr. James Godwin,
Mr. John Goflyn,
— William Goflyn,
Edward Green Efq; 2 B.
Mr. John Green,
--- Jofeph Green,
--- Thomas Green,
--- Thomas Griffin,

H

Mr. Hackwood,
— Halford,

Mr. John Hales,
— Thomas Hartley,
— Hugh Haffall,
— Charles Haffells.
— Harbet,
Miſs Harriſon,
Mr. Joſeph Harriſon,
— Robert Harriſon,
— Thomas Hart,
--- William Haſley,
Thomas Havers Eſq ;
Mrs. Havers.
Mr. James Hill.
— Richard Hill,
— Thomas Hill,
— Edward Haughton,
— —— Hawley,
Mr. Joſhua Heath,
— William Hammerſley,
— Holmes,
Captain Holme,
Rev. Mr. Herring, M. A.
Mrs. Hernon,
—rs. Hodgeon,
Mr. Hollins,
James Shuttleworth Holden Eſq ;
John Hornyold Eſq ;
John Hornyold Eſq ;
Mr. Hough,
Mrs. Howard,
Mr. Charles Howard,
— Edward Howard,
— Edward Howe,
— George Howe,
— Richard Howe,

Miſs Howel,
Mr. Thomas Howell,
— John Hughes, 2 Books,
— Hughs,
— Hunt,
— Hunt.
— Robert Hurſt,
— Hurſt,
— Hurd,
Francis Hutton Eſqr,
Mrs. Hyatt,
Miſs Hyatt,

I

Mr. Joſeph Jackſon,
Mrs. Jackſon,
Mr. George Jeffries, Senior.
— George Jeffries, Junior,
— Thomas jeffries,
Edward Jenningham Eſq ;
Mrs. Helen Jaffon,
Mr. Thomas Jones,
— Joſeph Johnſon,

K

Mr. Kaye,
— Keates,
— Keene,
— Anthony Keeling,
— Kelly,
— R. Kendal
— Jonh Kent,
Rev. Mr. Keyling,
Mr. Kingſtone,
— Kniften,

L

Rt. Hon. Lord Langdale,
Hon. Marmaduke Langdale,

The Hon. Mrs. Langdale,
Mr. Langdale,
— Lane,
— James Lander,
Rev. Mr. Samuel Langley D, D, Rector of Checkley,
Mrs. Latham,
Mr. D. Lawler,
— William Lowndes,
John Levet Esq;
Mr. William Laughton,
— Lindow,
George Lee Esq; 6. B.
Mr. Francis Lee,
— Francis Lees,
— James Leigh,
— Lightwood,
— William Locketts,
— Lockley,
— Arthur Lowe,
— John Lowe,
— Joseph Lloyd,
— Francis Lycett,

M

Mrs. Macclesfield,
Miss Macclesfield, 2 Books,
Mr. Richard Mahony,
— Mackarell,
— Mackniven,
Mrs. Malo,
Iohn Maire Esq;
Mr. Bailey Madeley,
Miss Margaret Mansell,
Mr. Mannock,
Mrs Mannock,
Mr. Iohn Manifold,

Thomas Manningham, M D
Mr. John Marstan,
— Laurence Martin,
Edward Markham, Esq;
Mr. Edward Massey,
Andrew Mathews, Esq;
Mr. Mathews,
— Peter Merchant,
— James Morgan,
— Andrew Morrell,
— James Morrell,
— Thomas Morrell,
Mr. John Moony,
Mrs. Molyneux,
Mr. Benjamin Mosely,
Lady Moyston,
F. Noel Clarke Mundy Esq;
Mr. Myatt,

N

Her Grace the Dutchess of Norfolk,
Mr. Nangle,
Rev. Mr. Nanney,
Mrs. Nelson,
Mr. Nelson,
— James Nelson,
— Henry Nelson,
— Nichols,
— Northen,

O

Mr. Thomas Osbourn,

P

The Rt. Hon. Lady Petre,
Mr. Humphry Palmer,
— Francis Parker,
— John Parks,

Mr. John Parrey,
— Thomas Parrey,
— Patteson,
--- Joseph Patteson.
--- Peard,
--- Tho. Wm. Perks
--- Joseph Pendrell,
--- John Partridge,
--- John Perry, S. O,
--- Perry,
--- John Philips,
--- Philips of hay Bridge,
Mr. Thomas Philips,
John Pitchford Esq;
Mr. Plunket, 2 Books,
John Porter Esq;
Mr. John Price,
--- Thomas Price
--- Charles Pyatt,
--- Powell,

R

Mr. Charles Rauthrell,
Mrs. Racket,
Mr. W. Rawlinson,
Captain Thomas Reed,
Mr. Robert Rhodes,
--- Rider,
--- Tho. Ridge, *Snior*,
--- Tho. Ridge, *Junior*,
--- Francis Richards,
Mrs Robinson, *Cheadle*,
Mr. Robinson *London*,
--- John Robinson,
--- Thomas Robinson,
--- John Robinson,
--- Thomas Robinson,

Mr, Robinson, 3 Books
--- O Reilly,
--- Robert Rogers,

S

Rt. Hon. Earl of Shrewsbury
The Rt. Hon. Countess of
   Shrewsbury,
The Rt. Hon. Lady Stour-
   ton, 4 Books,
Mr. Sant,
Thomas Savage, *M. D.*
Mrs. Savage, *Senior*,
Mrs. Savage, *Junior*,
Miss Savage,
Mr. George Saunders,
Miss Saunders,
Mr. John Shelley,
--- Thomas Shelly,
--- Scot,
--- Robert Sileto,
Mrs. Shipley,
Ralph Sheldon Esq;
William Sheldon Esq;
Mr. John Sherwood,
--- Samuel Sherwood,
--- Slaughter,
--- Shingler,
--- Sherrat,
--- John Shaw,
--- Thomas Shaw,
--- Slater,
--- Nicholas Sloan,
Sir Edward Smythe Baronet,
Lady Smythe,
Walter Smythe Esq;
Mr. Smith,

--- Iames, Smith,
--- Ralph Smith,
Mifs Smith,
Rev. *Mr.* Simes,
Mr. Amdrofe Smith,
--- Anthony Smith,
--- Samuel Smith,
--- Thomas Smith,
--- Iofeph Smith,
--- Iohn Smith, 2 B.
Iohn Silvertop Efq;
Mr. Thomas Simpfon,
--- Iohn Sparrow,
Mrs. Southcot,
Mr. Benjamin Stone,
--- Iofeph Stone, 2 Books,
--- Marmaduke Stone,
--- Thomas Stone,
---- Stonor, Efq;
Mrs. Stonor,
Charles Stonor Efq;
Mrs. Stonor,
Iohn Stonor Efq;
Mrs Stonor,
Mr. Iames Stephens,
--- Iofeph Stephens 2 Books
Mrs. Stephens, 2 B.
Mr. Samuel Steele,
--- Eenjamin Steel,
--- Sudell,
Thomas Suffield Efq;
Mr. R. Suffield,
--- Iohn Stocton,
--- Peter Stocton,
Mifs Therefa Stocton,
Mr. Henry Styche,

Mr. Iofeph Syers,
--- Swindall,
Thomas Stapleton Efq;
T
The Hon. Francis Talbot,
The Hon. ---- Talbot,
The Hon. Thomas Talbot,
The Hon, Mrs Talbot,
Mifs Talbot,
Mifs Bab. Talbot.
Mafter George Talbot,
---- Iohn Iofeph Talbot,
Mr. Alban Toft,
--- Iohn Taylor,
--- William Taylor,
Sir Thomas Tancred, Bart.
Mr. Taylor,
--- David Thompfon,
--- Iohn Tidmarfh,
--- Iames Tidmarfh,
--- Thornbury,
Sir Henry Titchborne, Bart,
Lady Tichborne,
---- Tuitte Efq; 3 Books,
Mr. ---- Tuitte,
Mrs. Trundley,
Mr William Trimer,
---- Trant Efq;
Marmaduke Tunftal Efq;
Iohn Townley, Efq;
Mr. Iohn Tyldefley,
U
Mr. Charles Vann,
--- Varley,
--- Vaughan,
--- Iohn Underhill,

Mr. Randle Underhill,
--- Iohn Underhill student
in medicine,

W

Her Grace the Dutchess of
Wharton,
Mr. Moses Walker,
--- George Wall,
--- Wake,
--- Wakeman,
--- Iacob Warburton, *Senior*
2 Books,
--- Iacob Warburton *Junior*,
--- Isaac Warburton, 4 Books
--- Iohn Warburton,
--- Ioseph Warburton,
--- Thomas Warburton,
--- William Warburton,
Mrs Ann Warburton,
--- Mary Whrrburton, 2 B.
Mr. Church Warden,
--- Abraham Ward,
--- Edward Ward,
--- Iohn Ward, 3 Books,
--- Iohn Walters, *Checkley*,
--- Iohn Walters,
--- Samuel Way,
Mrs. Walters,
Mr. Thomas Warrilow,

Mr. Thomas Warrilow,
--- Francis Ward,
Lady Webb,
Mr. Josiah Wedgwood Pot-
ter to her Majesty, 2 B.
--- Charles Weston,
--- George Weston,
--- Stephen Weston,
Francis Whitgreave Esq.
Mr. Thomas Weston,
--- Iames Whitfield,
--- Iohn Whitfield,
Mrs. Waters,
Mr. Whittingham,
--- George White,
--- R. Whitnall,
Mrs. Williams,
Mr. Winstanley,
--- Iohn Wooldrige,
--- Thomas Woolrich,
--- Aaron Wood,
--- Iames Wickins,
Anthony Wright Esq;
Mr. Philip Wright,
--- Sampson Wright,
--- Ioseph Wood,
--- Iames Wrigley,

Y

Mr. Yates,

THE
ARGUMENT

OF THE

FIRST BOOK

OF

VIDA's CHRISTIAD.

After the propofition and invocation, the poet, to furnifh
himfelf with epifodes arifing from the fubject, introdu-
ces CHRIST, his Hero, on the verge of life, repairing
to Jerufalem, where he is to fuffer death. As he purfues his journey, he is received by Zaccheus, at whofe
houfe a meffenger arrives, and announces the mortal
ficknefs of Lazarus. While CHRIST was going to
Bethania, to reftore him to life, SATAN calls a council to fruftrate the great defigns of the SAVIOUR.
Having left Bethania, he ftops at Simon the leper's
houfe, whither Magdalen comes uninvited, repents of
her fins, and is forgiven. As he approaches Jerufalem, he is met and conducted to the city by a band
of youths and virgins, hailing him with choral fongs,
the people ftrewing the way with their garments and
flowers. The poet then gives a defcription of the pool
of Bethefda, where the LORD reftores to Jairus the ufe
of his limbs; alfo a defcription of Solomon's temple,
whence the buyers and fellers are expelled. Next he
explains the myfterious figures fculptured on the tem-
ple-walls. Thefe exhibit the work of the creation—
the tranfgreffion of Adam—the general deluge—Abraham with uplifted fword to flay his fon—Jofeph fold
for a flave. Mofes's paffage through the Red Sea.—

B   Laftly,

ARGUMENT.

Laftly, Chrift, leaving the temple, faves Sufanna from being ftoned to death. He thence proceeds to mount Tabor. His prayer there, and transfiguration.

THE

THE

CHRISTIAD.

BOOK the FIRST.

O THOU, whofe Godhead fills fkies, earth, and feas;
    SPIRIT BENIGN! infpire my voice to praife
The twice-born KING, who from his Father's dome,
Gliding into the Virgin's pregnant womb,
In mortal form, inhal'd this vital air,   5
And fhed his blood to fave his human care
From the drear prifon of eternal night,
And waft the pious fhades to fields of light.
Earth fcarce fuftain'd, convulfive with a groan,
Her God in pangs, for vices not his own,   10
In ether's height, Sol veil'd in clouds his fhame;
And nature lower'd, fuffus'd with livid gleam.
THOU! once her guide, the Mufe fhall pleas'd furvey
The blue immenfe, and quaff eternal day;
Unfold God's counfel, and the caufe relate,   15
In ftrains immortal, of fo dire a fate.

Now Christ beheld the deſtin'd moments flow,
When death ſhould end, at once, his life and woe.
Full of his fate, Phenicia's bounds he flies,
And ſeeks the plains, where Salem's turrets riſe. 20
A band of youths and ſires around him throng
To view his deeds, which fame records in ſong:
Where-e'er he goes, new crowds his preſence draws
To ſhare his travels, and obey his laws:
The towns their thouſands pour to fill his train, 25
And numbers wound the deſert's ſilent reign.
So from Mount Veſulus, with pines imbrown'd,
In rills the Po creeps o'er the teeming ground;
Wide ſpread his ſtreams, as he victorious glides,
And Naids pour their urns to feed his tides. 30
Each bound foam'd o'er, his torrents roaring ſtray
In various beds, and burſt into the ſea.

Now from the throng his choſen Twelve he calls,
The true aſſertors of his deeds and toils
To a dark grove, where with a penſive look, 35
Beneath a cedar, thus in ſighs he ſpoke.
'Tis done, my friends; lo! time ſhall ſhortly bring
The day, that bears my fate on ſable wing.
Glad with my ſight no longer earth ſhall be,
But the bleſt Manes trim their bow'rs for me: 40
With joy to hated Solyma I go
To meet my death in all its pomp of woe;
So oft foretold: view how the Flamens flame
To caſt away that life, they cannot blame.
I dying ſhall each ancient crime deface; 45
Such are thy gifts, firſt Sire, of human race!

.Of all its fweets you drain'd the fruitful prize,
˙Mine are the woes, that from the fraud arife.
Yet free from flaughter fhall I mount the fkies
·E'er fable night the third day's luftre flies.   50
For you, who blufh not ftill to hear my lore,
Of cruel pain the fates referve a ftore :
Yet dare thefe ills ; and bold with me confpire
To fcorn, for heav'nly day, this life's defire.
No manfion here, to you no feat is giv'n ;   55
·Your home, your country are the fanes of Heav'n :
That realm with ftars, to light your paffage, glows ;
Where dwell calm peace, and labour's fond repofe:
Thither contend, tho' narrow be the road,
And fix with joy your permanent abode.   60
He faid ; th' attendants with his words confus'd,
Caft down the clouded eye, and penfive mus'd.
Then Peter, impotent to hide his care,
Thus rev'rend to the God addrefs'd his pray'r.
Offspring of God, can Heav'n thy Godhead move 65
To rufh on danger, and death's anguifh prove.
Since HIM, who whirls the ftars, you call your Sire,
Nature obedient moves to your defire ;
From harm fecure, perform your own decree,
Nor, fick of day, of life profufive be :   70
Pity thyfelf ; let us thy pity tell,
And from thy mind thofe dread refolves expell,
Nor fpurn, unkind, your helplefs train, who wait
Guides of your way, and partners of your fate.

Thus he ; with warmth the Hero thus replies ; 75
Too blind to blufh ! too heedlefs of the fkies !

B 3   Has

Has earth then charms to feize your groveling breaft,
And from her cares have you not learn'd to reft?
Did e'er fuch maxims from my labours pour?
Far other counfels wants the prefent hour;   80
Far other agents, pure from vile defire,
When prefs the mandates of the mighty Sire.
Let but the foul imbibe one heav'nly ray,
Then fhall this world unheeded roll away.
Labour fhall groan, without a fenfe of pain,   85
And human thoughts fhall ceafe the mind to ftain.
The groupe of ills (ills flie on ev'ry fide)
Tho' fad, yet bear, and fpurn with honeft pride.
The galling tongue, dark flander's pois'nous breath,
Difgrace, falfe crimes, and tortures big with death. 90
Myfterious ills! what joys attend your frowns;
Unfading glory, and immortal crowns.
Thus having faid; he gains the mountain's height;
The fad companions on their Monarch wait,
Refolv'd with him to feel fate's partial blows,   95
Touch'd with his bloom and foft'n'd with his woes.
Now come to palm-crown'd Jericho's fair feat,
Zaccheus gives the dome, and fpreads the feaft,
Who once to pleafe his wicked thirft of gold,
The mazes trod, that mifer's plans unfold.   100
But when his breaft confefs'd the prefent pow'r,
And grace defcended in a heav'nly fhow'r,
In diff'rent tides, quick rolls the fraudful ftore;
The fuff'rers one, and one relieves the poor.
In woe a Herald fudden here appears   105
And his fad meffage wounds the lift'ning ears;

Not far hence, Laz'rus held Bethania's plains,
Wealth fwell'd his gates, and regal blood his veins;
The Syrian realms once heard his Sire's lore,
And conquer'd cities bent beneath his power.   110
His welcome portals courted ev'ry gueft,
And poorly typ'd their Mafter's lib'ral breaft.
Hither the Lord difdain'd not oft to come,
And fhare th' indulgence of the feftive dome;
Here oft the clouds, that veil'd Him, fled away, 115
And pour'd his Godhead flaming on the day.
But when he heard the burthen of the plaint,
That Laz'rus feiz'd with ficknefs, pale and faint,
Refpir'd with painful throbs his gafping breath,
And feebly ftruggl'd on the verge of death;   120
The gufhing grief rolls ftreaming down his cheeks,
And to his fad companions thus he fpeaks:
Since death, e'er now, has fnatch'd our friend away,
Let's hafte our courfe to call him back to day.
If now, as oft, the Sire fupreme will hear,   125
And prove his pow'r by nodding to my pray'r.
He added not; but to Bethania tends,
Environ'd by his train of faithful friends;
Behind, in long proceffion, crowds proceed
To view the God perform the wond'rous deed. 130

Mean while the monfter, whofe tyrannic fway
The dark and wide ftretch'd coafts of hell obey,
With eyes tranfpiercing fate's myfterious gloom,
Sees the day rip'ning in time's pregnant womb,
Proftrate in ruin, when his drear realm fhall be 135
Himfelf a captive, and his manes free.

B 4

A crowd

A crowd of plans his anxious mind o'erwhelm,
T'' avert deftruction low'ring on his realm.
He burns with rage, that to his ardent eye,
Unfeen, came down this native of the fky,   140
Whofe death fpontaneous fhould at once deface
The crimes and vengeance due to human race;
Of various counfels Deicide feems beft;
This he revolves and fofters in his breaft.
Without delay, his Chiefs and train he calls,   145
A horrid Council! to his palace-walls:
And lo! the trump emits the piercing founds,
Which the huge dome thro' all its cells rebounds.
Loud roars each cavern from its gloomy feat,
And earth vibrates beneath its pond'rous weight. 150
Inftant the gate with various fpectres fwarms,
To day adverfe, and ftrange with monft'rous forms;
Their breafts exprefs the man, their waftes forfake,
And writhe with fpiry folds into a fnake:
Gorgons and fphynxes breathe an horrid air;   155
Some ftalk a centaur, fome a hydra ftare;
Thefe rife chimeras, fpouting livid fires,
And Scylla's barking image thofe infpires.
Fiends clad in harpies fwell the dreadful train
And realife the fhapes, that mortals feign.   160
Above the reft, the form of towring fize,
And flaming front of hell's grim tyrant rife:
With hundred hands th' ambient air he cleaves,
And his throat pours a hundred burning waves.
From all their mouths, and eyes, and noftrils ftream 165
Dark gales of fume, and fheets of fickly flame.

                                        Around

Around their heads fnakes bend into a wreath,
And dimpling down their necks in hiffes breathe;
Each wields a trident, each a firebrand fhakes,
That urge the guilty ghofts to burning lakes.   170
From earth's green margin fpectres hither fwarm
Who with oblivion fhade fair Virtue's form ;
In ev'ry clime, thro' which they vagrant ftray,
And dazzle men with fin's fictitious ray.
To thefe fucceed the wing'd infernal race,   175
Riding in clouds and ever changing place ;
Who tempefts rule, and ruder blafts inform,
And low'ring mount the horrors of the ftorm.
All come with fouls elate, in counfel ftrong,
And the roofs eccho to th' infernal throng.   180
Till in the mid the King majeftic rofe,
And while he fpeaks, his hand with thunder glows.

   Tartarean Chiefs, whofe births from ether fpring,
Sad victims, now, to Heav'n's inclement King ;
Who (proudly weak, thro' luft to reign alone,   185
To bear each Equal, rival of his throne)
Againft us roll'd his thunder big with fate,
And hurl'd us flaming from our native feat.
Should fame deny our conflicts to renew,   190
The woes that wait us, fhall prefent to view
What wars we kindled in th' etherial plain ;
What fury labour'd in each adverfe train,
But now the Victor boafts the ftars his prize,
And arrogates the fceptre of the fkies.   195
How dire his vengeance our difafters tell ;
Once brightnefs wrapt us, now the gloom of hell ;
                   Our

Our lot's to fhare, with human ghofts thefe fcenes,
In crimes once like us, now alike in pains.
Earth intervenes between our hope and Heav'n 200
And in reward, our thrones to men are giv'n.
But here end not our woes ; again, he frames,
Raging with war, his deep concerted fchemes ;
To drive us hence in ftratagems he low'rs,
And hell's the envy of the blifsful bow'rs :   205
For this defign, a youth forfakes the fkies
(His Son or Angel in a youth's difguife)
Prepares, relying on celeftial aid,
To pour deftruction on thefe realms of fhade ;
Withdraw our fubject-fpirits from our lore,   210
And leave us with the impotence of pow'r.
Perhaps (unlefs we bold fruftrate the means)
Ourfelves fhall feel the flav'ry of his chains,
Be led in triumph to the bleft abodes,
The glory He, and we the fcorn of Gods.
Think not this caution flows from fancy's fear ; 215
Experience has confirm'd tHe truth you hear :
To fay he's mortal, is to view his frame ;
To fay he's woundlefs, hear each baffled fcheme :
I have intrepid oft oppos'd his way,
And oft decreed him to my wiles a prey ;   220
Approach'd him various in each fhape and air,
That hatred can belye or malice wear.
But armlefs he, my keeneft arms defies,
And without ufing ftrength, my ftrength outvies ;
For by his utt'ring of the Prophets ftrain,   225
Arms blunt, deceits unmafk, and words are vain.
                                        But

But to my counſel now attention pay ;
To Salem's ancient tow'rs he bends his way.
Tho' odious there to all their hoary Sires,
And to the Prieſts, who zealous for their choirs, 23●
Their myſtic forms, and their paternal laws,
Reſolve to ſlay him in religion's cauſe.
For thro' the towns new myſt'ries he reveals,
Preſcibes new rites divine, and old repeals.
Now with occaſion let your aid conſpire   235
On him to pour the Rabbi's deadly ire ;
And left truth ſhould a gen'rous ſenſe impart,
Their anger calm and humanize the heart ;
Soft in their minds infuſe a pois'nous hate,
And to ferment it, lyes as truth relate.   240
Then blow it into rage by ſland'rous breath,
And never let it die, but with his death.
But could we gain by fraud or ſmooth applauſe, ⎤
One of his choſen twelve to 'ſpouſe our cauſe, ⎬
Then conqueſt's ours, and chilling fear withdraws. ⎦

    Scarce had he finiſh'd, when the wicked band, 249
Impatient to perform the dire command,
Impetuous pour diverſe thro' all the gates,
And earth the murmur feels thro' her retreats.
Now pois'd in air, they cut the darkſome ſpace, 250
And earth's expanſe with ſnaky pinions graze.
In greater myriads not the flower-fed bees,
(When Auſter rain not, nor fierce Boreas freeze)
In fields of ether war indignant wage,
Of rival Kings to vindicate the rage.   256
Sad is the place, on which theſe demons low'r !
How great the havock ! havock their ſole power !

                                            Near

Near to Bethania come, God's offspring ends
His pious march, attended by his friends;
There virgin Martha, Magdalena there,   260
(From Magdel's ancient town they nam'd the Fair)
With hair diforder'd, and with ftreaming eyes,
Performing at the tomb their obfequies,
He view'd : Whom when the mornful virgins faw,
They leave their friends, and from the rites with-
                draw :   265
Firft pay the homage to his prefence due,
Then pour their grief while tears their cheeks bedew.
In tender words, and looks o'ercaft with gloom ;
Are you then come to view our brother's tomb ?
Who to his aid oft call'd You, noble gueft,   270
While with death's chilling cold he lay opprefs'd.
Nor is there room to doubt, had you been here,
He would have now inhal'd the vital air ;
But fince your pray'rs àre realiz'd in heav'n,
To hope, that he fhall live again, is giv'n.   175

While thus they pray'd, grief melts the ftanders-by
And from their breafts refults one gen'ral figh.

The Chief forbids the crowd the youth deplore, ⎫
Intent to free him and to life reftore,   ⎬
Tho' rolls the fourth fun, fince he was no more. ⎭
The town foon ecchoes with the wond'rous fame; 281
And fends her thoufands to behold the fame,
The mountains, eager to detail his fkill,
Pour down their people and the valley fill.
                            The

The tomb approach'd, the youths there form a
    ring   285
Where ftands in filent pray'r the Heav'n-born King,
With hands ftretch'd forth, and with erected eyes
Invokes his Father to his enterprife.
The crowd in filence and furprife, attend
The op'ning of the wonder and the end.   290
Twice from his face the fhifting tincture flies ;
Nods fhake his head, and twice burft forth the fighs.
But lo ! the tomb fhakes with a quick'ning throe
The fight forbids the gazers' blood to flow,
On all their fenfes pours a dewy fear,   295
And from the Hero draws this vocal pray'r.

   Tho' ever prefent, O Imperial Sire !
To give relief and fecond my defire ;
Still thanks moft warm are for this favour due,
Which paints thy virtue to the people's view. 300
But hafte ye fervant throng, the tombftone heave,
Tear from the corps the drap'ry of the grave.
Without delay wide opes the yawning tomb,
And blots the ftiffn'ing crowd with horrid gloom.
With looks fhot down the vault, they trembling eye ⎫
The faded corps in foul difhonour lye,   306 ⎬
And heave with life's infinuating figh.   ⎭
Thrice, Lazarus come forth, the Hero cries,
When from the tomb he ftalks and breathes the fkies.
The circling train, with chilling horror wan,   310
With inexhaufted looks devour the man ;
Inhale with greedy ears his rifing breath
Which to them wafts the feries of his death.

                                      How

How the rack'd foul in fad and plaintive cries,
Her confort body with reluctance flies :   315.
What furies, in dread fhapes, difplay'd their pow'r,
And threatning rofe upon his dying hour :
With pain the fpirits of eternal day
Chas'd the foul demons from their prefent prey.
To this, the clufter of rewards fucceeds,   320
That terminate the blifs of virtuous deeds.
The pains, the guilty feel, conclude the theme,
Their wretched fate and hell's eternal flame.

   The wonder finifh'd, by requeft o'ercome
The God repairs to Simons' neighb'ring dome, 325
Whofe limbs diftain'd with leprofy's difeafe
The God refin'd, and bade the fury ceafe.
While at the board, with grateful viands preft,
Amid the Nobles, fat the welcome gueft ;   :
Unbidden, lo ! a maid invades the room,   330
Fam'd for her mien, and texture of the loom :
Her purple robe fwell'd, ruftling in each fold,
With filver cloy'd, and interwoven gold ;
Pond'rous with gems, the luxury of her veft
(Her fhoulders pride) a golden clafp compreft. 335
A cawl her treffes held in ringlets wreath'd,
Sleak with the comb, and liquid amber bath'd.   •
O'er which with ftudded jewels blaz'd her Tire,
And a large ruby fet her front on fire.
Big pearls and diamonds ftrung on fufile gold, 340
Around her neck their blended luftre roll'd.
So earth (her bofom bright with vernal fhow'rs)
Unlocks her gems and decks herfelf with flow'rs.

                                                    An

An orphan left by both her parents' death,
This maid became fole heirefs of their wealth. 345
Religion to her tender age beam'd fair,
And blufhing honour was her virgin care.
But by degrees youth revels in her veins
And Venus furious in her fenfes reigns,
Who in her bofom lights unlawful fire,   350
And the broad blaze confumes each pure defire.
Now loft to all, that grace a virgin's name,
Religion, coynefs, and a Veftal fame,
In pride of womanhood, fhe joys to roam,
A vulgar object, from her private dome.   355
Shines firft at banquets, and theatric fcenes
And giddy bears not admonition's reins.
So fome tall fhip, without a pilot's guide,
When the big waves upon the tempeft ride,
Subject to billows and the ftorm's domain,   360
A vagrant courfe purfues along the main.
Of her large ftore of ancient wealth now vain,
She meditates, among the youthful train,
To foothe him into love, whofe manly form,
Above the reft, fhall glow with ev'ry charm. 365
And now fhe hears, that one of beauteous frame
Hither arriv'd, and ftil'd a God by fame.
Her joy, impatient of a long delay,
To view the fame fhe bends her rapid way.
But when his mien exhal'd its breathing grace, 370
And fhe inhal'd the luftre of his face ;
When her breaft caught his eyes' love-feeding
    beams,
Her former paffion fudden fhe difclaims,
And feels her heart refine with chafter flames.

And

And now feven firebrands, horrid to behold! 375
Rufh from her lips benighted in a cloud ;
Dark as the fparkles, that in gafps afpire
From dying taper, and in fume expire.
Lo ! flies, exclaims the God, the fouleft Fiend,
Who prey'd upon her heart and warpt her mind.
Maria then (fuch was the damfel's name)   381
New in defire, nor now in thought the fame,
Who hither came, in confcious beauty bold,
Her bofom blazing with embroider'd gold ;
Tears off the glories, that her head furround, 385
And her bright bracelet twinkles on the ground ;
Her tunic fpurns, that cafts a golden gleam,
Rack'd with the fenfe of guilt and flufh'd with
        fhame.
Prone as the dog, beneath his mafter's board,
For pity, proftrate fhe invokes the Lord :   390
Clings to his knees, his feet with tears bedews,
And dries with robes, affum'd for other views.
Now from an alabafter urn fhe brings
The blended fragrance of Arabia's fprings.
The blufhing Cafia, Nardus' od'rous ears,   395
Amomum fweet, and frankincenfe's tears.
Faft on his feet the od'rous ftreams fhe pours,
And the air grows pregnant with the balmy fhow'rs,
Pleas'd he receives the homage of the Fair,
Her faults abfolves, and points to heav'n her care. 400

Mean while in mournful groupes the patients
        come,
From neighb'ring cities, and furround the dome,
                        The

The Blind for fight, the Lame for motion cry,
The Dumb for fpeech, the Deaf for hearing figh.
Hither the infane for relief are brought,   405
Unconfcious of their ftate, as void of thought ;
But God diftrefs'd with each peculiar pain,
Reliev'd and fent them back, a healthful train.
He feeks, departing hence, Jerufalem,
The mighty fabrick of thy fons, O Shem,   410
Planter of vines ! when earth fuperior ftood   ⎫
To the broad furface of the general flood,   ⎬
And the check'd ocean in his channel flow'd.   ⎭
With victor-arms the Jebufites then came,
And call'd the captive city by their name.   415
Here Juda's race with regal blood elate,
Subdu'd the neighb'ring vales, and fix'd their feat.
Here rear'd great Solomon, with foreign toil,
From of everted fhrines the copious fpoil,
An awful temple, of ftupendous fize,   420
Its airy fummit mingling with the fkies :
All other fanes their ornaments refign,
To drefs this temple out for rites divine.
Here, brazen cifterns, dazz'ling to behold,
Here tables fhone, compos'd of maffy gold :   425
Here fleecy robes drank deep the purple dye ;
And the ftiff veftments glitter'd on the eye :
Altars arofe devote to fanguine rites,
And pendent lamps diffus'd their awful lights.
Here tripods, cenfers, bowls blaze on the fkies, 430
And all the great parade of facrifice.

C   Jehovah's

Jehovah's ftatutes fculptur'd deep on ftone,
And fhrin'd in wood religioufly here fhone.
Before the king, and in the people's view,
The prieft, within the fane, the victim flew.   435
In this fole place, the holy pow'r is found,
With ritual gore, to ftain the blufhing ground:
For Ifrael's race, by cuftom hither led,
Thrice in the year the victim-homage bled.
The Lord oft to this temple bent his way,   440
To fhare the rites, and adoration pay.

When the Meffiah near Jerufalem drew,
The tow'rs and columns rufhing on the view,
The train of thoufands, who his labours fhare,
Boughs in their hands of palm and olive bear.   445
The foot precede, behind him move the horfe,
And in the mid, the Hero takes his courfe;
No prancing fteed, in pride of trapings dreft,
Nor foaming with keen life the Hero preft:
But to the poor his darling want to fhew,   450
An afs, beneath him, moves his dull feet flow.
(This deed once ftrung the Prophet's facred lyre,
And from the theme he caught celeftial fire)
Bare was his head; his robe (the work of love,
Which for his youth his tender mother wove)   455
Flow'd to his ancles, in a various fold;
Tho' worn, yet new, nor by duration old:
A pair of fandals on his feet he laced,
And in this humble pomp the city traced.
Before the gate in long arrangement ftand   460
A choir of youths and maids, a beauteous band:

Twin'd

Twin'd in the virgins' locks the rofes breathe ;
And with fhorn crowns the youths their temples
　　wreathe.
Large boughs of living palm their hands employ
And their glad hymns flow fparkling with their
　　joy.　　　　　　　　　　　　　　465
All vie, with holy emulation warm,
Who moft may view the God's delightful form.
Within the walls, the people form a ring,
And ardent prefs to hail the Saviour—king.
Spears grace their hands, their olives flafh their
　　dyes,　　　　　　　　　　　　　470
And their applaufes rattle 'long the fkies.

　　Rous'd with the cries that thro' the city ftray
Quick rofe the fages, who the nation fway.
The caufe unknown, and ftruck with deep furprife,
To fee large clouds of duft obfcure the fkies, 475
Of this uproar demand the fudden caufe,
Who leads the crowd, and whence this vaft applaufe ?
But thofe, who thro' his fame the Godhead fpy,
Augment his train, and fwell the rapt'rous cry.
The ftreets, he vifits, they with purple ftrew,　480
And on the pavement Indian carpets glow.
Some roads are kindled with profufive flow'rs,
And the broad furface fwells with crimfon fhow'rs.

　　Not far he pafs'd, when lo ! another train
Salute his entry in a gladfome ftrain :　　　485
Pleas'd he receives the raptures of their hearts,
And full of wonder from the crowd departs.
　　　　　　　C 2　　　　　　　A vale

A vale subsides among umbrageous hills,
Where spreads a pool fed with perpetual rills :
The city dames for water hither came   490
The cattle here drown'd deep their thirsty flame
And sickly flocks rose healthful from the stream.
Hence after times, as fame divulges, gave
The name Bethesda to the healing wave.
At certain seasons of the circling year,   495
The morbid patients to its banks repair ;
For oft the pool in tumult seem'd to rise,
And spout its azure current to the skies.
The moving principle long latent lay,
Which youths and virgins usher'd into day :   500
They sung, a cherub, blazing on the face,
His pure robe streaming in the airy space,
On wings incumbent ting'd with golden dyes,
Shot from the summit of the starry skies,
And staining his etherial route with blaze,   505
His hands compress'd to rage the placid waves.
So the bright star, hung in the front of heav'n,
To mariners or camps a signal giv'n,
Darts from its seat, and flashing wild its fires,
The subject world with panick fear inspires.   510
And now the sickly groupe the pool surround,
Eager to catch from heav'n the bathing sound :
Each views the liquid plain with ardent eye,
And of the breeze, each drinks the softest sigh :
Panting to plunge the first into the flood   515
When in the air the waters trembling stood.
Tho' woo'd by all, to him alone, health came,
Who first div'd for it, in the troubled stream.

                        A band

A band of youths, thus in a lawn's fmooth fpace,
Collect their vigour for the rapid race;   520
Their fouls already ftart, their hearts thick beat,
And for the tedious fign they throbbing wait.
Hope crowns them all, and with delufive eyes,
Each for himfelf regards the unwon prize.

Among the fick, young Jetrus helplefs lay, 525
Whofe finews fhrunk, whofe members dy'd away :
Of ancient wealth he flourifh'd with a ftore ;
But trufting much in Med'cine's faving pow'r,
He tried each virtue of the faithlefs art,
To ftring his nerves, and motion fwift impart, 530
But feeble for the tafk, art flies and leaves
Pale-hagard want affociate with difeafe.
Thus forty years beheld his limbs to fade,
Himfelf a prey to want and void of aid,
Whom when the God had ey'd in fuch diftrefs, 535
With tender looks he pours this foft addrefs.

Ah fay, unhappy ! why this long delay
Upon the margin ? while the ftreams convey
Their balmy moifture, and their healing pow'r
To all the ills, that in their channels low'r,   .540
Hence home they vifit, mindlefs of their pains,
Strength in their limbs, and fpirits in their veins.

Weak Jetrus thus ; and while he ftrove to fpeak,
His burfting forrow trickled down his cheek.
I tarnifh not the pool's falubrious fame   545
But while I wait the motion of its ftream,

Others more active, than inactive I,
Into the roaring waters headlong flie:
For none, to bathe me, his affistance lends,
Want feldom feels the benefit of friends.   550

  To his complaint the God vouchfaf'd an ear;
And faid, arife, and to thy home repair,
Nor think thefe waters have the pow'r alone,
To brace the nerves and to fupprefs the groan.
Scarce had hefpoke, when lo! before the throng, 555
Erect ftands Jetrus, in his movement ftrong;
Throws on his back his couch, without delay,
And with quick ftrides he ftalks the rapid way.
The fhepherd thus, who in the foreft toils,
To cull of broken boughs the fcatter'd fpoils; 560
Cafts in the pile, unconfcious of the prize,
A fnake, in leaves involv'd, and numb'd with ice.
Wak'd with the flames, that crackling round him
          fpread,
Quick ftarts the fnake and lifts erect his head:
Darts his red eyes, and rowls in fpires along   565
The dome, vibrating faft his forky tongue.

  Another view prefents the temple's gate,
Beneath whofe ample arch the fervants wait
To fell oblations for the brazen fhrine
To thofe, who labour under vows divine;   570
Here bleat the flock, whofe fleece the day improves,
Here lowe the oxen, and here cooe the doves.
When the God faw the traffick in the fane,
And heard rude noife the facred place prophane,
                              Infpir'd

Infpir'd with holy rage, the Hero glows,   575
And with reproaches deals about his blows:
The whip's percuffions on their backs refound,
And drive the rabble off the holy ground.
So Boreas from his Arctick cavern flies,
Rufhing in furious blafts along the fkies,   580
Expels the low'ring clouds th'etherial plain,
And roaring arrogates the Ether's reign.
Thefe walls are hallow'd (thus the Hero cries)
And to JEHOVAH's honour facred rife,
Which you with mercenary traffick ftain,   585
And caft the God an exile from his Fane.
Tho' blood your altars bathes, and life expires,
A facrifice once granted to your fires;
Such rites the fupreme BEING pleafe no more,
And fheep now pour in vain their ritual gore.   590
Henceforth forbear his purer fight to ftain
With entrails warm of birds and cattle flain:
And now a fpotlefs facrifice prepare;
And taught new rites of faith, the old forbear.
Dare to be virtuous, in libation fhow'r   595
Your fpotlefs thoughts and pray the fupreme Pow'R;
Your myftick modes let thefe hereafter be,
Thefe be the offerings to the Deity.

   This faid, he at the altar fuppliant bows,
And pays his Sire in filent pray'r his vows.   600

   And now the priefts with deep refentment rife,
Grief in their hearts, and anger in their eyes;
                    C 4   Nor

Nor was their furious rage â recent gueſt,
Nor was their hate a ſtranger to the breaſt:
Stor'd in their minds, the ancient cauſe of ire   605
Lay deeply grav'd, and ſet their ſouls on fire.
Yet ſtill they fear'd their cruelty to wage,
For loth to rouze the mob's vindictive rage.
Inſtant they leave the temple's inmoſt ſeats,
Content to vent their wrath in murmuring threats.
                                                      610

The wolves at night thus to the fold repair,
But ſhepherds watchful o'er their fleecy care,
With vocal dogs their bloody progreſs ſtay,
And chaſe them headlong from the bleating prey.
Sudden they part, tho' wild with famine's ſting, 615
And the wide foreſts with their roaring ring.

    But while the GOD before the altar bends,
And to his SIRE his ſoul in pray'r aſcends,
About the temple rove his ſocial band,
Struck with its grandeur and the builders hand.620
Scoop'd from huge rocks a hundred columns ſpread
Their frames, high as their parent-mountains head.
Of equal number, and of equal ſize,
Columns of ſolid braſs reſplendent riſe.
In the large beams they view the cedars ſtrength, 625
And the arch'd cielings everlaſting length.
The brazen doors on creeking hinges ſound,
And the ſquar'd marble ſmoothes the painted ground.
Here into pillars ſheets of gold are roll'd
And tables ſpread their plains in burniſh'd gold. 630
                                                      Bright

Bright chariots in the temple votive rife,
Diftinct with iv'ry and with ebon dyes.
While on thefe objects the difciples gaze;
The Hero paid his tributary praife;
And coming forward filent and unfeen,   635
Thus fpoke abrupt with a dejected mien.
Already Solyma the vengeance due
To all thy deeds, hangs frowning to the view.
This pile fo large, this temple fo divine,
Shall rufh, ere long, to fragments like the pine 640
(Whofe roots the wind tearing from parent ground)
A victim tumbles to the tempeft's found.
The blood of Prophets, envoys of the Lord,
Which purpled once your facrilegious fword,
Or ting'd your rocks, their bodies thrown from
        high,   645
Againft you point the thunder of the fky.
Yet ftill to fave you from impending pain,
How oft I anxious ftrove, but ftrove in vain,
To clafp your children in my fond embrace,
As the hen, anxious for her feather'd race,   650
The little rovers to her bofom brings,
Panting the mother in her voice and wings.
Your ftate, already nodding, foon fhall feel
The civil fury, and the hoftile fteel.
From dome to dome vindictive flames fhall bound,
                                              655
And human blood run crimfon on your ground.
In vain to heav'n afcend repeated vows,
To prop your kingdom, which already bows.
                                    Jehovah

Jehovah haftes the period of your reign,
And in a foreign clime erects his fane.   660

This faid, the fculptur'd figures he difplays;
A true and mighty roll of ancient days.
Where the Creation fhifts her varied face,
With all the annals of the human race.
No human image fwells this myftick fcene   665
Nor paint belies Jehovah's awful mien :
But lines myfterious labour'd nice on ftone,
Sketch the bold draught to bards themfelves unknown.

The Sire of Heav'n here burfting from a cloud,
Seems the drear realms of darknefs to behold.   670
And whilft before him lies the chaos-ftate,
The world's creation feems to meditate.
Now from the burfting brightnefs feems to roll,
The fpacious concave of the ftarry pole;
The earth's brown orb, the ocean's azure tide, 675
And floods of light, that thro' the ether glide.
Whence Sol fhall draw effulgence from his rays,
And Heav'n her ftars fhall kindle with the blaze.

The winged myriads of the heav'nly fpace,
The firft day's labour of the Supreme grace,   680
With plaufive wings, and with melodious found,
In fwarms their parent and their guide furround.
Yet ftill with earth was mix'd heav'n's burning gleam,
And ftagnant on her flept the briny ftream,
For ev'ry matter lay confus'dly hurl'd,   685
Which gave, arraing'd, exiftence to the world.
                                      With-

Without delay, the orb of heav'n he frames,
And on it fprinkles drops of ftarry flames;
Now all things flow affume their proper face,
And Heav'n in vigour firm retains its place.   690

Earth in the mid, and delug'd now no more,
The heaving waters form a winding fhore,
On fhallows tortur'd into fury rife,
And fpout their azure current to the fkies.
As yet the fea no fhrowded veffel bore,   695
Nor in the waters-bent appeared the oar,
But Zephyrs, fporting innocently gay,
Dimpl'd the fhining furface of the fea.
And now the mountains rife in beechen pride,
And vales in long extended plains fubfide.   700
Inftant the ground with feeming virtue heaves
Her lap with flow'rs to fill, the tree with leaves.
Now fields adorn their broad expanfe with green,
Now trees embrace, to form a fylvan fcene.
Oaks wave their branches o'er a length of glade
To join the olive, and the cyprefs fhade.   706

To light this infant world, two globes of flame
Full in the concave arch of ether gleam;
To guard the world, they, leagued, alternate rife,
To drop their melting luftre from the fkies;   710
The Sun by day Olympus' round furveys,
And Earth glows lucid with his native rays.
The Moon with guardian care the night adorns
Streaming a filver palenefs from her horns.
                                        Ether

Ether at night on his black forehead wears   715
A blaze of ftars, revolving in the fpheres.

The fcaly herds in wanton gambols play,
Brufh with their fins and fwim along the fea.
The birds their bodies poize in ethers plain,
And with indignant bills a war fuftain.   720

Not diftant hence, another profpect yields
Whole herds of cattle cov'ring all the fields;
With pafture cloy'd the woolly flocks are feen
Playful to fkip along the fruitful green.
Fierce beafts feem here to lurk in caverns deep, 725
And tortoifed fnakes along the ground to creep.
The Sire of Heav'n ftands in a cloud confefs'd,
And in glad accents, thus his will exprefs'd.
" With genial love increafe and multiply,
" And give from age to age a progeny."   730

Frefh from the earth at length man naked ftands
To whom the God feems utt'ring his commands;
Gives him to fpread o'er earth his wide domain;
And life immortal, focial to his reign,
Had been his lot, had he obey'd the God,   735
Obferv'd his mandates and rever'd his nod.

Her lies a garden glitt'ring on the eyes,
With branching trees and flowers of various dyes:
An azure dragon keeps his vigils nigh
To guard the fruitage blufhing on the fky.   740

A branch-

A branching fountain in the center sheds
Its silver currents in four various beds :
And streaming widely o'er the subject plain,
Fosters the herbage, and calls forth the grain.

Here rolls the serpent on the storied wall,   745
The fraudful worker of the first man's fall,
Who heedless of the mandate and decree,
Spoils of its apples the forbidden tree.
The youth scarce to his lips the fraud had giv'n,
But aw'd with all the majesty of Heav'n,   750
Sheds fast, to lave his crime, repentant waves
And strives to wrap him and his shame in leaves.
But o'er him, rising in a fleecy cloud
The Almighty seems to speak, as thunder, loud,
Kindling with threats that may the vengeance speed,
Reponsive to the horror of the deed,   755
Which once he bore, and all his race must bear,
Who shall by birth inhale this vital air.

Mean time, his confort, who with vain desire,
First broke the mandate of the supreme Sire,   760
Seems here the thickest of the shrubs to gain,
And hide her folly in their shades in vain.
The victor serpent, flush'd with fraud, appears,
On flaming spires his wreathing body rears ;
Thrice round the tree his length depends in rings, 765
And to applaud his conquest, claps his wings.
Of his success regards with scorn the tool,
And laughs her easy faith to ridicule.

Not

Not far remote, extend the realms of night,
With darkness chequer'd and a livid light.   770
Where shades of righteous men their freedom wait,.
Debar'd, for one man's crime, their happy state.
Here Sages stand with hoary rev'rence crown'd,
Here bands of bards with sacred fillets bound :
With hands expanded and effus'd in pray'r   775
They seem to court the God at length to spare
The human kind, obnoxious to the rod
(For Adam's fault) of an offended God.
Superior by the shoulders Abraham spreads,
The wrath to bar, his garment o'er their heads. 780

Here stops the God ; and says in broken sighs,
Behold the scene, whence all my labours rise ;.
Yet still to free them from this gloomy state
I, self-devoted, all their tortures wait
Live o'er the scenes, which follow, mark'd by few,
                                              785.
That paint my future death to fancy's view.

In figur'd surges here the waters rise,
And earth beneath the foaming burden lies.
The ark secure, rides o'er the liquid space,
Charg'd with the reliques of the deluged race. 790
If any mountain's height superior stood,
Emerging from the ocean's gen'ral flood,
The bursting clouds indignant roll their ire,
And blast the summit with a flashing fire.

                                              In

In act to flay his Son, the Father ftands   795
(Unhappy made by hearing Heav'n's commands)
And now his ftrength collected in his arm,
He waves the fteel in Ifaac's blood to warm.
When lo! An angel wing'd from ether's round,
Recalls the mandate, and prevents the wound. 800
A white-fleeced ram near for a victim's fed
And plac'd for Ifaac, on the altar bled.

Stung with their brother's dream the brothers
    ftand :
Who's fold a flave, and feeks a foreign land.
To the fad fire, the youth's dire death they feign, 805
Torn by wild beafts, and barbaroufly flain :
He views the filial veft befmear'd with blood,
And his eyes bathe it with a briny flood.

Here fhines the Hero, famous for his laws,
Aided by Heav'n, and aiding Heav'n's great caufe,
              810
While he reftores from Pharoah's fpacious reign
To promis'd realms, his long exiled train.
The bite of ferpents and their pois'nous breath
Strew his pale wand'rers on the verge of death.
But quick he bids a brazen ferpent rear   815
Its fpiry volumes in the middle air ;
At it directs the fickly groupe to gaze,
As fure and whole reftorative of eafe.

A bird in figure lays her entrails bare
And with her life fhe feeds her new hatch'd care. 820
                    All

All fond of blood their mother's breaſt ſurround,
And with contending bills probe deep the wound.

Thus having traced the wonders of the ſcene:
The Hero full of thought departs the fane:
But ſcarce had touch'd the Temple's ſpacious ſtairs
                                                    825
When tumult in loud clamor wounds his ears:
Amid the crowd, behold Suſanna's led,
The youthful bride of old Manaſſes's bed.
Pale are her features, beamleſs are her eyes,
And down her back her hair diſorder'd lies.   830
Averſe, indignant, in her bloom of charms,
Her father plung'd her in the old man's arms.
But now the ſtaining of the nuptial ſtate
Dooms her unhappy to a public fate.
And here the vulgar, here the youths prepare   835
To whirl the ſtones againſt the guilty fair.
But when the prieſt ſaw Chriſt the portals grace
Inſtant he bids the execution ceaſe;
The trembling matron from the crowd withdraws,
And veils his baſe deſign in ſmooth applauſe. 840
This dame (ſays he) has broke the marriage knot
And faithleſs to her bed was baſely caught:
For ſuch a crime, it is by law decreed,
By miſſive ſtones, yet how ſevere! to bleed.
We, Soft interpreter of bards! preſume   845
To aſk your counſel of this matron's doom.

He ſpoke, and with deluſive hope is fed,
That by his force of ſpeech the Hero's led

                                    Into

Into a fnare, where all evafion's vain,
Each paffage block'd, and flight a fruitlefs pain. 850
For fhould his tender nature fpare the dame,
And wave the death, due to her lawlefs flame,
He'd foon upon himfelf the rabble draw,
And fuffer as the fcorner of their law :
Yet fhould he, for the crime, pronounce her fate, 855
He'd then incur the vulgar's barb'rous hate.
Himfelf the prieft, for fuch fuggeftions, hails,
And his breaft fwells with conqueft's flattering gales.
Thus while in fleep the Hind with fplendent fhare,
In ridges feems the cultur'd glebe to rear,   860
Huge heaps of gold difcover'd in the clay,
Vain throbs of gladnefs to his heart convey,
But fudden flits the vifion of the dream,
And of the golden ftore foon dyes the flame :
Awak'd, he rails at fortune and the fpoil,   865
Compell'd to ftick to poverty and toil.
But God fhall for himfelf ftrike out a way,
(A God no human wit can lead aftray)
At once from death the wretched wife to draw,
And keep alive the fpirit of the law.   870
Fix'd on the ground awhile, he rais'd his eyes,
And to the crowd prepar'd for flaughter cries ;
'Tis true, the ftatutes which your fires decreed,
Confign to death this woman's fordid deed.
Whoever then a finlefs life has led,
Let him firft whirl the ftone, and ftrike her dead.
And can one boaft among this num'rous train,
By wounding her, a life without a ftain ?

D

While

While thus he fpoke, his looks, feverely ftrong,
Oblique he glances thro' the waving throng,   880
In act to write; who fhould prefume to claim,
In the dame's maffacre, his fpotlefs fame?
" A mind unfhock'd by actions bafely done,
" A life crown'd with the palm by virtue won."
Before the crowd the fair ftands chill'd with fright,
                                              885
Her eyes fuffus'd with death's approaching night:
Proftrate fhe finks beneath her load of care,
Nervelefs her knees, no lefs diffolv'd in fear,
Than is the doe, which o'er a length of ground
Purfu'd and breathing the voracious found   890
Of panting dogs, fees her ftrength fmoak in air,
And her limbs captive in the trait'rous fnare;
Hem'd round with foes, no hope of freedom nigh,
All other views forfake her but to die.

    His tender fpeech among the vulgar glides, 895
And all their rage of murder foon fubfides:
Each in his mind revolves his actions paft,
There views a groupe of ills, and ftands aghaft.
Among fo great a train no man fteps forth
By rectitude of life to prove his worth;   900
But each, as confcious of fome moral ftain,
By ftealth lets fall his ftone and leaves the fane.
And now the porch unchock'd with riot-cries,
Off her bound hands the God the cord unties,
Difmiffes her with words, that veil her fhame. 905
Depart, let virtue cleanfe thy tarnifh'd fame!

                                        Then

Then his Difciples thus addreffing, faid,
This race, how hard ! how obftinately bred !
Undar'd leave nothing, judge in each debate,
And always wrong, grow bolder by defeat.   910
Ev'n me, who violate their feftive days,
To give them health, and chafe away difeafe;
Tender to thofe, who weep their finful ftains,
Their guilt to pardon, and avert their pains:
Ev'n me, who give to fpread the genial feaft,   915
And the foft gufhing of the vine to tafte,
Setting afide the lotion of the ftream,
And gorge on meats for which they blot your fame;
Ev'n me they feek by artful fraud to flay,
And roufe all Rome to chafe me as her prey ;   920
Glad, fhould I own it lawlefs, that their tribes
The money tax fhould pay, which Rome prefcribes,
Nor can my deeds above the reach of art,
The leaft conviction to their breafts impart ;
Blind to the force, by which my acts afpire,   925
They dare oppofe the counfels of my Sire,
Their rites I break not, nor their laws repeal ;
For maxims, more fublime, beneath the veil
Of their dark ceremonies, latent lye,
Than what are offered to the naked eye.   930
Why is Swine's flefh (an inftance to rehearfe)
Amid their various food, forbid a place ?
For minds, refin'd with thoughts fupremely good,
Can catch contagion from no mortal food :
The mind's diftemper is her bafe defire,   935
Yet as the briftly kind delight in mire,

D 2   As

As in this beaſt an innate lewdneſs roves,
She lives a type of Venus' obſcene loves.
Beſide, by gentler diſcipline to draw
Their ſtubborn minds, to hear celeſtial law;   940
To fix, whom no religion long could hold,
By bloody ceremonies, in one fold;
The ſupreme BEING bad the tribes prepare
To call, for death, ſome of their bleating care;
The guiltleſs heifer on their ſhrine to wound, 945
And purple, with her harmleſs blood, the ground.
Theſe rites, to them, if not ſuffus'd with gloom,
Shone types of the religion then to come.

   This ſaid, already the declivous ſkies
O'ercaſt with ſhade, the trait'rous town he flies. 950
And willing now, before his inſtant fate,
To pray his Sire, and ſecret vows repeat.
Unnoticed leaves his friends in Tabor's plains,
And the mount crown'd with lofty cedars gains.
None of the train he order'd to attend,   955
But Peter, James and John, a faithful friend,
Who meditating ſtand, and to the ſkies
Extend their ſupine hands and piercing eyes.
And now the Son, in flam'd with heav'nly fire,
In extaſy addreſſes thus his Sire.   960

   O father? ſee, tho' innocent I dye,
And meet the pangs of fate without one ſigh:
Since ſuch your will, and ſuch is your decree.
And ſince mankind is ever dear to me:

                         Yet,

Yet, thefe, who left their friends and native foil, 965
The follow'rs of my fortune and my toil,
Indulge propitious; and avert the harm,
Aim'd at their virtue by a lurking arm,
I dread not human hate, nor do they fear;
For impious men fhall wound them ev'ry where, 970
Nor fhall my anger or furprize run high,
To fee them tortur'd, or to fee them dye;
To fee you, father, to compleat their woe,
In duft to fpurn them, and commence their foe.
No; let your light'ning, if it is your will,   975
Flafh fierce around them, or your thunder kill,
If fuch the toils, that men to heav'n elate
And bring back nature, to her priftine ftate;
At leaft deny not to my pray'r this grace,
Let not of hell's domains the cruel race,   780
(Whofe hate to human mortals never dyes)
Deftroy my focial pupils with furprize;
Seduce them from their lore with wicked arts,
And pour the love of earth into their hearts;
Nor in the praife of vice let their tongues roll, 985
And ftrive to blot my Image from the foul.
Soon, too foon, fhall thefe infidious foes
(In whofe unfated breafts revenge ftill glows)
Revolve deceits, o'er baleful projects low'r,
And wear ftrange forms to fpread abroad their pow'r;
To feize the harmlefs, whom they cannot blame,
And with polluted breath their breafts inflame.
But fruftrate, SIRE, their meditated care,
May their curs'd fchemes evaporate in air,
And bid them conquer'd, to betray forbear. 995

And when my mortal days shall set in death,
Give some to rise to teach the sons of earth,
In the firm path of righteousness to move,
And glow transported with religion's love.
Will not paternal fondness lend an ear   1000
Propitious to his Son's most ardent pray'r?

   Your Sire's true Image, and pow'r of his skies,
Your fears remove (the heav'nly King replies)
The frauds shall ne'er annoy your chosen train,
Which hell now meditates thro' its domain.   1005
Let Satan grim a hundred forms assume,
Spread wide his snares, and cover thick with gloom;
My presence shall the treachery disclose,
The frauds detect, and dissipate the foes.
Yet one shall fall a prey, thro' whose dark soul 1010
Base plots, already, in disorder roll:
Now he, unhappy, weary of the pain,
(The sad reward attendant on your train)
Repents, indignant, of the toils he bore.
Sooth'd with the sweets, which life had given before.
                                        1015
But prior to the world 'twas our decree,
This wretch should fill an Apostolic see.
Not mindless of the bards, who sung his fall,
A warning great to those, you deign to call.
The rest, the snares shall flie by culture free, 1020
And hold life lightly for the love of thee.
Death shall not fright them with his dreadful mien,
But find them tranquil when he rules the scene:
                                Watchful

Watchful of life, and proud of death's embrace,
From their heart's gore fhall rife a num'rous race :
                                                    1025
Yet after the long paffion of their fates,
Triumphant they fhall fill heav'ns vacant feats.
Proceed then glorious, and compleat, my Son,
The mighty labour, which you have begun.
From your religion, fee, what crowds fhall fpring ;
                                                    1030
Unfhaken how their breafts efpoufe their King ?
Ev'n thofe, who now relunctantly obey,
Of fpeech unpolifh'd, fhall without delay
Inhale the breathing of the fpirit-gueft,
And feel conceptions new diftend the breaft ; 1035
In all the pomp of language drefs your law,
And into virtue raptur'd nations awe.
This race extinct, another fhall arife,
And fpread your name bright kindling to the fkies ;
Your ftandard fix on the remoteft fand,   1040
Where the waves check the further growth of land.
To you fhall victor kings, in humble pray'r,
Their arms and crowns fubject, and altars rear,
Majeftick Rome, whofe womb with empires heaves,
Who rules, along th'Appenine Tibur's waves; 1045
Vaft crowds, the faireft of the cities, fee,
Her fafces gives and the world's reins to thee :
Thefe with her temple's fhall religion ftand,
And cenfers blazing in the Pontiff's hand :
There, fhall a Prieft to Kings his law ordain,   1050
And teach the world to praife you in a ftrain.

                    D 4   Yet

Yet should, by lapse of time, the human race,
Their morals with the stain of crimes disgrace,
Should they, by chance, degenerate from their Sires,
And studious tread the walk which vice inspires;
I will by toils and sad affection try   1055
To make them fond of virtue, which they flie,
By ills reform'd all mortals mount the sky.
Oft shall the city ravag'd by the foe,
Her superb structures in wide ruin strew,
The more oppress'd she feels the hostile dread,
The loftier shall she raise her tow'ry head;
Her walls shall rise, into destruction hurl'd,
Nor shall she cease till mistress of the world.
Our GODHEAD there shall dwell, such is our grace;
He said, and lock'd him in a fond embrace.   1065

But on a sudden mingling glories rise,
The thunder rolls and light'nings wrap the skies,
The Sire omnipotent expands a cloud,
Bedrop'd with lustre dazzling to behold.
All space glows bright: now Christ, rapt in a wind,
                                             1070
On high is borne, and in the cloud enshrin'd.
The God, the true resemblance of his Sire,
Like the pure essence of ethereal fire,
Bursts through his visage; while his frame exhales
A fragrant sweetness on the balmy gales.   1075
Nor less effulg'd his beauty on the sight,
(The Ether bathing with unusual light)
Than when the matin sun, bright font of day,
The heav'ns o'erflows with his irriguous ray,

                                             The

The feas reflect his Image in the waves,   1080
And with his gold, groves tinge their faffron leaves.
His wond'ring friends the Hero radiant ey'd,
Two bards attending, one on either fide;
The one, on flaming chariot rais'd fublime,
Gliding along the heav'ns aerial clime.   1085
The other, leader of an exil'd band,
Once led the Jewifh flaves from Egypt's land.
To civilize the tribes prefcrib'd a law,
And fram'd new rites, to worfhip God with awe.
The heav'ns feem now to fpread their portals wide,
    1090
And pour their glory in a radiant tide :
Then from a cloud on fire with golden ftains;
His Son within his arms Jehovah ftrains ;
And failing on the Zephir's fcented wings,
A liquid voice this facred meafure fings ;   1095
" Behold my fon, behold my joy fupreme,
" Hear him ye nations and revere his name !"
The voice here ceafed : in heav'n the winged throng
Unite their gladnefs in a choral fong.
At length the Hero drops his heav'nly air,   1100
Moves to his friend, fepulchr'd deep in fear,
Wakes them diffolv'd in wonder of the fcene,
And lives among them in his mortal mien.

End of the Firft Book.

ARGUMENT of the Second Book.

Alarm'd at the honours paid to Chrift, and inspir'd by Demons with malice againft him, the Priefts and Leaders of the city repair by night to the Temple, to deliberate how to oppofe and deftroy the Lord. Mean time Satan affuming the garb and mien of Joras, endeavours to withdraw Judas from Chrift's party, and betray him to his foes. Nicodemus, one of the Fathers of the Council, harangues in favour of Chrift, for which he is banifhed. Then Caiphas rifes and animates the people againft the Redeemer.—The tribes are enumerated, who come to Jerufalem at this time, to attend and participate of the Paschal Feaft. Chrift alfo comes with the fame intent, and after having perform'd the rites of the feafon, he inftitutes the Lord's fupper, wafhes his Difciple's feet, and foretells the treafon of Judas, and the denial of Peter. Retiring to mount Olivet, he is bath'd in a bloody fweat; and here Judas betrays him, and delivers him to a ruffian-band, who conduct him to Caiphas, in whofe houfe Peter denies his Mafter. In the morning he is brought to Pilate, who confines him as a prifoner in his palace, to fave him from the infults of the rabble.

THE

THE

CHRISTIAD.

BOOK II.

BUT blind with fear, and anxious for the ftate,
The Sages and the Flamens fleeplefs wafte
The live-long night; their heart-corroding care
Forbids their eyes the balm of reft to fhare.
For on their minds, in lafting colours fhone   5
The Hero's entry in the joyful town:
The feftive honours, paid by youthful choirs;
The growing rev'rence, which his name acquires;
The climes, which fame o'erfhadows with her wings,
And where the wonders of his actions fings.   10
What can they do? each hour, more clear the lays
Unfold, once fung by bards in ancient days:
" A King, fhou'd come, who boafts in heav'n his
      birth,
" And dwells a man, among the fons of earth;"
At whofe approach, the Temple's facred wall,   15
And proud Judea's regal ftate fhou'd fall;
Her altars broke, the Temple fhou'd deplore,
Her rites extinct, and off'rings brought no more.
With fuch thoughts gloomy, and with fear o'ercome,
Each lurks, obfcurely fad, in his clos'd dome.   20

The

The Bees, thus wont to range the fields in show'rs,
And sip the country, kindled wide with flow'rs;
When winter's rage, Ether's offus'd plains
With mists distends, and wat'ry Orion reigns:
A tedious leasure pass, deep plung'd in hives,   25
Hum their concern and sluggish waste their lives.

The time when sleep bedews the limbs with rest,
And soft oblivion lulls the tortur'd breast:
Ghastly to view, black forms from hell's deep shade
Emerge, and in dread troops the town invade.   30
Some the high tow'rs with sooty wings imbrown;
And some the temple's airy summit crown:
Whole troops thro' streets and domes their presence.
        wing,
And from the roofs in cluster'd Myriads cling.
In Spring, the Birds thus, o'er a length of sea,   35
To fair Italia bend their airy way;
Perch on some island, which repose first brings,
Fill the wide shore, and rest their weary wings.
Secret, they drop a poison in the breast,
Then breath a vip'rous spirit in the guest:
Hence hate engenders, furies headlong roll,   40
And to all vices, mold the fashion'd soul.
Some stalk abroad, belied in human form,
With various fame ⚹ the raging town alarm,
The houses fill, and of a direful kind,
Bid dreams start up, and haunt the drowsy mind: 45
Some to the mansions of the nobles go,
And summon all their force to hurt the foe;

                                    Spread

Spread true and falſe reports with fraudful ſkill
And their ſtun'd minds with drear ideas fill :　50
That Chriſt ſtands threat'ning on the holy place,
And that in fire the ſhrines and temples blaze.
Others in prieſtly robes the fathers call,
To meet in council in the temple's wall ;
While the fell tyrant of th' infernal ſtate,
Diſcloſes broad the brazen ſounding gate.
Tho' ſcatter'd in the town, each leader's dome,
Yet they, thro' night's obſcure, ſpontaneous roam,
From various parts purſue their gloomy way,
And to the Temple ruſh without delay.　60
Shou'd ſleepleſs fame, thus, in the night ariſe,
And ſing the city enter'd by ſurprize,
Within the walls the foe their armies pour,
Burn down the houſes, and invade the tow'r ;
Soon ſwells the mob ; the road with tumult glows ;
　　　　　　　　　　　　　　　　　65
Nor know the throng, from what the tumult roſe :
Terrifick furies from their eye-balls gleam,
And from the domes the tapers faintly beam.
Rage leads the rout ; while torches pour a ray,
To ſhew the ghaſtly horrors of diſmay :　70
Still ſecret rolls the ſprings whence flows the fray,
Their minds to rage, their breaſts to hate a prey.

　　Mean while, twelve ſprites are order'd to eſſay,
To draw Chriſt's twelve diſciples from his ſway ;
But theſe, (forewarn'd, by his preſcient care,　75
Of the falſe project, and deſtroying ſnare :)
　　　　　　　　　　　　　　　　Their

Their minds maintain, by error's fcheme unaw'd,
'And their breafts bar'd to all the wiles of fraud ;
The foes affume an hundred fhapes in vain,
O'er the difciples' captive minds to reign.   80
Yet one devoted to the bonds, they wave,
Ifcariot Judas finks into their flave.
This peft and fcandal of the chofen band,
Once rang'd with them, to act the God's command;
His fortune left, his friends, and native foil,   85
To fhare his exile, and his travelling toil ;
Ready from ev'ry vein his blood to draw,
To promulgate the fupreme Sovereign's law.
But foon grown weary of his holy care,
His enterprize feem'd hard, his toil fevere,   90
And raging, that no fruits his toil attend,
In filence waftes whole days, to put an end
To the fubmiffion, which the ftatutes charge,
And then indulge his priftine life at large ;
Impatient of fatigue, and loth to bear   95
The joylefs lot of poverty fevere,
To drop his province, he low'rs now in fchemes,
Now flight delights, now other projects frames.
Thus wreck'd with cares, and tott'ring now in
      thought,
Him the black leader of the cohort fought,   100
With no lefs joy ; than when the lion fpies,
(His jaws with hunger dry, and wild his eyes)
Not far a deer, along the mountains fide,
Seeking the pafture, where the vales fubfide.

                   Now

Now clad in Gallilean Joras' air,   105
(By blood was Joras to falfe Judas dear)
He thus accofts him as he fleeplefs lay ;
Ah! fay, unhappy, why you nightly ftray
The mountains drear, why in loud tempefts chill
And wafte your manhood at a mafter's will,   110
Who (how great's the frenzy, which your mind ex-
          cites)
Dares boldly to fruftrate our holy rites :
Whom none attend, but outcafts of the land,
A female mob, and femiviral band.
Our nobles with concordant anger rife,   115
Devoting him to death a facrifice :
He, foon, for all his holy rage fhall pay,
And all his boafted courage fume away ;
Then his feign'd glory of rewards fhall fade,
And his thick clouds of cunning drop no aid : 220
While his fine arts expiring round him lye.
Rife then, and from th' impending carnage flie.

    This faid, his borrow'd figure melts in air,
Transfixing Judas' breaft with rage and fear :
Hence in his mind infernal thoughts prefide,   125
And his pulfe beats convulfive with its tide ;
Now he revolves, the labours which he bore,
And of his dangers paft the frightful ftore ;
With fin's polluted love now frantick glows,
·Fix'd to betray the Sov'reign to his foes.
Ah Wretch ! deaf to the Godhead's moving gale,
His prefence nor your eyes nor ears inhale !
                                    Yet

Yet view yourself, how chang'd, befet with woe;
How high, your eminence! your fall, how low!
What error in vile fchemes your mind employs; 135
And feel your heart, corrupt with worldly joys.
The lot you forfeit, future men fhall prize,
When thoufand fec'lar funs fhall gild the fkies.
The wifh, you cherifh, and the hope, you feed;
The joy, which fparkles, of your future deed, 140
Into diforder foon fhall hurl your mind,
And fleeting vanifh like a guft of wind.
While time permits, then, caft thefe pefts away,
Which deep corroding on your vitals prey.

And now the Priefts and Fathers of the ftate,145
Retir'd to the Temple's inmoft feat:
When Caiphas prime prieft (around whofe head
Their myftic rites the facred fillets fpread)
Afcends the throne in blazing colours dreft:
According to their rank, fat down the reft.   150
Unbodied ghofts, impervious to the eye,
On ardent wings around the Senate fly,
Breathe horrid fury through the panting foul,
And in confufion bid the paffion's roll.
Some voices were, that Chrift fhould fuffer death,155
Either by publick force, or fraudful ftealth:
Others for fanction call'd, the youth to flay,
Whom lately Chrift had rais'd, to vifit day,
From the dark grave; of which the great renown
Soon for him cull'd the rev'rence of the town. 160
Yet ftill they fear'd the mob fhould Chrift fuftain,
Won by his merit, or his gentle mien.

                                        Hence

Here Nicodemus took his ancient place,
Not the laft noble of the noble race:
Who folely free from the infernal peft   165
Which gnaw'd infectious ev'ry other breaft;
Yet loth alone the Senate to oppofe,
Tho' better maxims in his bofom rofe;
Still once like them, contemning Heav'n's decree,
He ftrove on Chrift to vent his enmity: 170
But when he found his works a God declare,
Like one, call'd forth from night to breathe the air,
His vows in fecret to the Godhead pays,
Fearful by public homage to difpleafe.
But now Chrift's blood and life are in debate,   175
And ev'ry fpeech is pregnant with his fate;
Deep pain'd to hear the innocent condemn'd,
He drop'd the mafk, and fpoke the public friend.
Fathers, the caufe of the debate, this night,
Lies not obfcure, for want of proper light: 180
To ferve my country then, I will difclofe
The real truth, fhould torments 'round me clofe:
You muft all fee, his actions greater rife
Than a mere man's, fupported by the fkies:
That, by his deeds, he proves himfelf to be,   185
(If truth can win us) God's own progeny;
The very God, by bards in former days,
(Big with the Godhead, which infpir'd their lays)
So oft foretold, who fhould for man expire,
And reconcile him to his mighty Sire.   190
So far, we, guided by the Prophets, fay;
Malice can't find a weaknefs in this plea.

E

On

On numbers, whose dull eyes suffus'd with night,
He spread the lucid sparks of visual light:
On some, whose ears were from their birth-day bound,

195

He gave to drink, and pour'd the charms of sound;
The nerveless limbs, o'erspread with livid stains,
The bodies, languid with relentless pains;
To these, he gave the lustiness of strength;
To those, the smiles of unexpected health.   200
Three has he rais'd (the wonders fame has spread)
To breathe the skies, once number'd with the dead:
The late rais'd Laz'rus was the people's theme,
And thro' the city, still vibrates his name;
Weak then the mind is, and obscure the heart, 205
That would such virtue try to draw from art:
Suchwonders flow not from mechanic laws;
Behold a God! a God alone's the cause.
As oft as he pronounc'd an heav'nly strain,
So oft with cunning fraught our words prov'd vain:

210

Combin'd, he should in death our fury feel,
Our stones we pointed, and we edged our steel;
Wrapt in a cloud, he sudden mounts the sky,
And hosts of guardian spirits round him fly:
So shines the God; who can his vows refuse? 215
Tho' met for ill, let's rise for public use;
Approach whom Heav'n had sent, to save by Grace,
Our faults confess, and suppliant sue for peace.

While thus he speaks, and warm rehears'd the same,
He adds a fresher violence to their flame,   220

Strikes

Strikes out intenſer furies in the ſoul,
And tides of anger thro' their ſenſes roll.
At length the rage, which inward boiling lay,
Obſcuring reaſon's intellectual ray,
Suffuſing on the mind a heavy cloud,   225
Againſt him burſts, in exclamations loud.
Thus in a brazen tube a ball glows red,   .
And burns the fiercer, as with ſulphur fed;
Confin'd too much, it rolls on ev'ry ſide,
And finds no flight but through a flaming tide: 230
At laſt the ſulphur melts into a flame,
And the wing'd ball flies in a ſmoaky ſteam
With ſuch a crack, as if ḣeav'n's axis broke;
The domes and turrets tumble at its ſtroke;
Its flight the ball with death and carnage ſtrows, 235
And opes an ample paſſage through the foes.
So on him they with furious anger frown,
Expell'd their temple, and exil'd the town.

    Then Caiphas, while rage was mute confin'd,
Aroſe, and ſpoke the dictates of his mind: ·   240
By artful wiles allur'd, no doubt (he ſaid)
This Nicodemus to the foe has fled;
Who often ſuffer'd in his country's cauſe,
And dar'd maintain the ſanction of her laws:
Who late in all thé pomp of language roſe,   245
To ſtop the rapid progreſs of our foes.
But ſuch's the magic of the hoſtile tongue,
That, they, who hear, are by the ſound undone:
                    E 2   Shall

Shall we believe him come from heav'n's high choir
To fave, who impious boafts our God his Sire : 250
Who in the havock of our law delights,
And toils to fix a new parade of rites :
Whofe advent, he afferts, fhall fatal be
To this great Temple, which, by God's decree,
Our anceftors had built, with fo much toil,   255
And decorated with barbarian fpoil ?
What's the religion which nov'lty can frame ?
Can morals pure from fuch religion ftream ?
Still he, left any crime fhould lye untried,
The guilty joins, and deals his pardons wide : 260
To their bafe doors his fteps impure conveys,
And fcorns our antient rite of feftal days.
As he deferves, the vile feducer treat,
Hafte, fpread your fnares, and drag him to his fate.
Extinguifh, citizens, his growing fire,   265
Left flames victorious to your domes afpire,
Wind round your columns in a lambent train,
And o'er the airy fummit blazing reign;
Elfe fhall he gain the city with his arts,   270
And with fedition warp the people's hearts :
Elfe foon the country round fhall be the prize,
Of his falfe wonders, and prodigious lies :
Religion elfe, which many ages fway'd,
Shall into nothing, with her altars, fade :   275
I fear that Rome, the infult to repay,
The priv'lege we enjoy, fhall take away ;
By her dejected, foon compell'd to roam
Far from our country and our native home.

                                    Let

Let ONE die then for all, and expiate
The sins of many, and secure from fate :   280
Such be the gen'ral voice, and thus shall we
The homage pay due to his Deity.

   This said, the Fathers own'd the penal choice,
And each approv'd it with a furious voice.
But on the means while roll'd the deep debate,285
In secret to allure him to his fate :
Amaz'd, they see, before them Judas stand
Withdrawn unnotic'd from the chosen band :
Aw'd they receive him looking fiercely great,
And 'mid their Nobles offer him a seat ;   290
Ardent demand of his approach the cause,
And then to hear, in throbbing silence pause.

   Then Judas, throwing round his glaring eyes,
Fathers, I know, you dread the rage (thus cries)
Of our Galilean, who spurns your laws,   295
And is of your sage council now the cause :
But, tell the price, and I'll assume the pain,
(Which now employs your tortur'd thoughts in vain)
To give him to your rage an easy prey,
Before the setting of this new-born day.   300

   Twice fifteen silver coins, with joyful speed,
They count, a huge reward for such a deed !
Gladly attend his egress from the fane ;
He seeks the mountain, and rejoins the train.

                    E 3   Religious

Kept facred in the town, and on the plains, 305
A folemn feaft about this feafon reigns:
Sev'n funs their holy joy and leifure fee,
According to Religion's old decree:
Sev'n funs behold their feftive tables fpread,
(But yet forbid the ufe of leaven'd bread)   310
With the fheep's offspring, and with hafty cakes,
And all the herbal pomp of rural feafts.
This day, with joy memorial, they relate,
Their ancient Sires had left th'Egyptian ftate;
Had pafs'd fecure, thro' the fea's blufhing tide, 315
Enrich'd with many fpoils, and Heav'n their guide.
To view the regal town, vaft numbers rife
From ev'ry part, and fhare the facrifice:
Nor in confufion they the highway trod,
But each tribe march'd beneath their Leader's nod.
                                         320
Tho' 'mong the Ifra'lites, their blood's the fame,
The fame their laws, and from one ftock they came,
The nation ftill into twelve tribes divide,
And fpread o'er Paleftine their numbers wide:
A nation in the caufe of freedom bold,   325
Their towns in numbers ftrong, and rich in gold:
But at this time, their country foil expell'd,
Were diftant far, and Cafpia's mountains held.
Amid the tribes fcarce one with freedom reigns;
For tho' the Benjamites poffefs their plains;   330
Tho' the great offspring of fam'd Judah's race,
In wealth and arms fupport the higheft place;
Still both, fubdued by Rome's victorious bands,
Enlarge her empire by their conquer'd lands;
                                    Their

Their arms and fceptre render as her prize ;   335
Their laws preferving and their facrifice:
Now weeps the land, where lofty turrets rofe;
And peopled cities dreadful to their foes,
Are now in afhes laid by hoftile rage,
Or noding by the mould'ring hand of age.   340
Jehovah thus againft them flafh'd his ire,
Nor faw, without revenge, his Son expire.
But fhall I fee the land inglorious lye,
Without a fong, to foothe their mifery';
Behold the nation and her name forgot,   345
Unknown to after ages ev'n in thought?
The verfe is due, as Chrift his infant-cries
Amid them rais'd, and walk'd beneath their fkies.

Wherefore ye Myriads of the cryftal round,
Who o'er th'Olympic azure lightly bound ;   350
Who often gliding thro' the fields of air,
Our country vifit, and our tables fhare ;
Defcend propitious, and vouchfafe to guide
My fteps, that wander o'er the country wide:
Let's bring to light the ancient names that fade 355
Beneath the horrors of oblivion's fhade ;
Bid fame preferve alive their wither'd bow'rs,
Their towns demolifh'd, and their nodding tow'rs.
Then foaring with you on a rapid wing,
This earth I'll leave, and fcenes immortal fing : 360
With you thro' pathlefs ether fhall I fly,
And tread the lucid pavement of the fky.
Thron'd in my chariot, I fhall pour a fong,
To chafe the clouds, and charm the ftarry throng ;

Thro' walks untrod by mortals, largely breathe, 365
And pluck'd from Ether's brow, bear back a wreath.
But firſt, before this glorious height we gain,
Let's tell the numbers thronging to the fane.

Before this time, ſuch throngs ne'er uſed to wait,
On theſe great rites, nor crowd the temple's gate ;
                                                    370
Nor ſacrifice alone ſuch numbers drew,
 But a fond impulſe urg'd them Chriſt to view.
Great Judah's offspring firſt the temple grace,
For ancient monarchs an illuſtrious race !
This tribe, above the reſt, ſuperior ſtood,   375
In arms and men, as ruler of the wood ;
The lion fierce his fellow-beaſts exceeds
In energy of ſtrength and valiant deeds.
Crowds pour from Saba, and from Gaza's ſhore,
Engada's left with her vindemial ſtore.   380
The towns Andulis, Lyde, Raphan low,
Selis, Jamnia, where fierce tempeſts blow ;
Hippa, Aſcalon, with Azotus' tow'rs,
Acharon, Sachon, and where Joppa low'rs
With waves tempeſtuous rolling to her bay,   385
And with her rocks rough-riſing o'er the ſea ;
Are all deſerted by their num'rous train,
Marching in holy ſquadrons to the fane.

Next with Damaſcus' ſons glows warm the way,
Where (ſo fame reports) of prolific clay,   390
                                             The

The firſt man form'd, and in exiſtence new,
With frame erect, the vernal Zephyrs drew.
Sad ſits Emaus, deſerted by her crowds;
And ſilence blank the front of Nepſe clouds:
Anthedon bord'ring on th'Egyptian reign,   395
And Bethlem, Chriſt's birth-place, attend their train.
Galgala with Beſſura ſadly low'rs,
And Marathon ſtands ſad with Erme's tow'rs.
As mute in all her houſes Sigor's grown,
As the unhappy woman chang'd to ſtone;   400
Who, turning back to view Gomorrah glow,
Stands ſtiff in ſalt, a monument of woe.
The neighb'ring villas ſend away their band,
Where burns Aſphaltus o'er a length of land;
Spouts tow'ring to the ſkies a lambent flame,   405
And the air charges with a ſulphureous ſteam.
Here corn once ſmil'd and roſes early born,
Now ſleeps the pool, and ragged grows the thorn:
This fatal change by monſtrous love was wrought,
For by the angels' youth and beauty caught,   410
The natives thought by force to make them ſtay,
And to devote them to their luſt a prey;
Slaves they might be, had they not wing'd their flight,
And with their plumage gain'd the fields of light:
But in loud thunder flam'd the ſupreme SIRE,   415
And delug'd all their plains in floods of fire:
With aſhes ſqualid, barren lye their ſeats,
Fruitleſs their lawns, and pathleſs their retreats.
The trees here crown'd with flow'ry bloſſoms reign,
By ſwains deſir'd, and by the virgin train;   420
                                             But

But when the fouth pours out its' floods of air,
And the ripe buds in fruitage difappear ;
Apples with fhaggy rinds the branches ftore,
The fwains defire, ar.d virgins long no more :
Yet found and folid fwell they on the eye,   425
But touch'd burft ufelefs, and in afhes lye :
Ev'n the ripe fheaves fwept o'er by blafting gales,
Drop on their ftalks and the whole harveft fails.

.The tribe, who follow, Simeon's lineage boaft,
And dwell in Saro, and Moloda's coaft ;   430
Enjoy the crops which Sicelegis yields,
And the fat moifture of Sipabota's fields. .
All whom the brow of Afanes confines,
And Atharis' afcent bedew'd with wines :
Whom Remmon feeds, and Ain's cultur'd hills ;435
Where fair Idume with its towns diftills
Her frankincenfe, and where the plains around
Breathe the fweet gales, that fkim Arabia's ground.
The race of Ifachar with ardour loud,
The temple enter, and the altar crowd ;   440
Content with meals fpread thin by nature's hand,
And with the circle of their narrow land.
Next come, whom the Hermonian mountains feed,
Of bees the nurs'ry, and the neighing fteed :
And who the floping fide of Tabor tread,   445
And breathe where Carmel points his rocky head.
Here in a fiery chariot thron'd on high,
The Prophet rofe, and reach'd the purer fky.
Now Senfena void of her children ftands,
And on the road Hennad pours forth her bands; 450
                                                        While

While noble Affra all her fons unlocks,
Once thirfty cities, built fublime on rocks ;
Senus with Rebotes their train refign,
And Remetes infpers'd with fruit and wine.

The tribe of Dan flow move the town along, 455
And fadly feek the temple with the throng;
Thus when ftern Winter fharpens Autumn's breeze,
And threats to fhake the verdure of the trees,
The fnake begins his flight to meditate,
And glide with filent lapfe to his retreat.   460
No hifs betrays him, while he foft retires,
Nor o'er the rocks erects his tail in fpires.
They feem in pain, fad with the Prophets fong,
That one fhould monftrous rife among their throng,
Who fhould the character of Chrift profane,   465
And mark with crimes and blood his impious reign:
This terror of mankind fhall then arrive,
When man fhall be to ev'ry crime alive ;
When fhortly after, the laft fire fhall prey,
On nature's frame, and melt it quite away.   470
But God's true offspring, to confirm his reign,
Shall rife vindictive with an heav'nly train,
Tofs the vain boafter in a whirlwind round,
And plunge him deep into the yawning ground.

To thefe fucceed a troop in graces young,   475
From the illuftrious blood of Afher fprung :
Each taught by cuftom, a wheat'n chaplet wears,
And on their temples nod the bearded ears,
                                    Thefe

These Balagus and Horma ftrew with grain,
And Aphega's high domes thofe entertain ;   480
A part Robœa fends and Ama's fields,
Nor Aziba in fwarms, nor Laban yields.

Next come with gifts. Zabulon's feftive hoft,
Who dwell befide fair Pontus' fea-girt coaft ;
Thefe fet the fhore on fire with myrtle light,   485
And fheets of flame ftream on the face of night.
A part proceed from Jeptha's rural feat,
And crowds from Jedaba's high ftructures hafte.
Then Cana came, which wond'ring faw the ftream,
It's nature change, and with wine's blufhes flame.
                                                490
Their natal Naz'reth fome with joy recite,
And lofty Sembros handed fome to light :
Naim her thoufands pours, where once from death
The youth arofe, and breath'd a vital breath :
Dotha with Natole in numbers ftrong,   495
And high Cathetia mourn their wand'ring throng.

But who can tell Naphthali's num'rous tribe,
Their crowds of cities and their tow'rs defcribe ?
Which on the rugged hills of cedar rife,
Or holy Lebanus tip'd with the fkies :   500
Who in great Naphthali and Nafon dwell,
Blefs'd with the love of truth and fpeaking well.
Who live upon the banks of Jordan's courfe,
His ftreams frefh bubbling from a double fource.
All Galilee of fight infatiate comes,   505
And all Samaria guardlefs leaves her domes :
                                Jehovah's

Jehovah's offspring often here delay'd,
And oft his Godhead by his works difplay'd ;
Affeda with Caperna found their fame,
And the old town which Greeks Sebafte name. 510
Crowds Bethel leave, and Beffa's fublime tow'rs,
And wher: Genefara her waters pours.

The race of Levi mix with ev'ry band,
Nor are confin'd to any tract of land,
But by the Legiflator giv'n to ftray,   .   515
Among the people, and their victims flay,
To load their altars with the bloody fpoil,
And call down plenty on their cultur'd foil.

Manaffes not content with the domain,
Which o'er the river's bank enjoy his train,   520
Reigns wide, where Nepheca expanded lyes,
And Berfa ringing with the hunter's cries ;
For him fpreads Tenachos her lowing fields,
To him her favage beafts fierce Dora yields:
The town of Magedos her bands refigns,   525
And all the fparkling treafures of her mines :
Jebla for him imbrowns his front with woods,
And for him Taphua rolls her filver floods ;
Where lafting fpring her balmy dew diftills,
And meadows live refrefh'd with gurgling rills. 530
Then they, who dwell beyond clear Jordan's flood,
Their veins vibrating with Manaffes blood,
Succeed ; the toilfome dreffers of the plain,
The lib'ral fowers of the fruitful grain.

God's

God's offspring also the parade increase,   535
Conjoin'd with hoary Reuben's num'rous race.
(Reuben once famous for the warrior's rage,
And of his father's sons the first in age)
As once, they wish'd their country were the same,
Beyond the river's far translucent stream,   540
(Fields once, by men of monstrous stature, trod,
And trembling under their tyrannic nod)
So now their tribes combin'd in one appear,
The same their entry, and the same their pray'r.
To them belong, who dress Argobia's land,   545
And they, who dwell beside Besania's strand :
Or whom, thy shade, O Galadine, imbrowns,
Or live in Ogg's twice thirty conquer'd towns ;
Or whom Galatia in her towns contains
Jabis, Sebama, built on level plains :   550
Balme, Romatha, Selca, and Nabe,
Esdren with half demolish'd Cariathe ;
These names unknown are now supplied with new,
Tho' on fame's plumage, once they distant flew.
His train Arimene sends with cedars crown'd,   555
Their brows with leaves, with arms their shoulders
        sound,
Whom Gaulis, Rabath, Bosoris contain :
Who till with oxen rich Balthaltis plain,
On whom high Arnon pours his waters down,
And whom Abilla's meads with herbage crown.560
Nor shall you mow unsung green Elcale's turf,
Aserot, Esebon with huge rocks rough,

                        Nor

Nor you, who make Efonia's fields your care,
And Cade's wilds, fhall want of fame your fhare.
Whom Phafga's bounds inclofe, approach the band,
                                             565
With all the town fpread thin, o'er Hermus' land.
Abaris comes next, from whofe lofty fide   ·
The fhepherds Jordan faw his ftreams divide,
On either bank; in air erect his wave,
And a dry channel for the Ifr'lites leave,   570
When to the promis'd land they bent their courfe,
Calling his headlong tide back to its fource.

    Laft come the Benjamites who ftudious toil
The neighb'ring villas fruitful in their foil,
Where fair Jerufalem, Queen of the land,   575
Jarephila and Luza's turrets ftand :
And Bethany, who faw her King, in death
Four days compreft, inhale his vital breath :
Samar and Sarcla, the number fwell,
And who in Gabaoth crown'd with maftic dwell,
                                             580
To the wild rage of favage beafts a prey,   ′
For which her youth advance in rough array,
Drefs'd in the fhaggy wolves' victorious fpoils,
Torn by the hounds or captives in the toils :
Her lufty fons rife with the pearly dawn,   585
Break thro' the wood, or pour along the lawn ;
And when the evening veils the heav'ns blue fpace,
They eafe their fhoulders and divide the chafe,
                                             And

And fcatter'd gladful o'er their native fields,
Revel in feafts, on what their labour yields :   590
They join the tribe who breathe in Mafpha's town,
And Hemen's rocky hills which threat'ning frown ;
Whom Recen and Berathis tow'rs contain,
And Shyla's ho ly with her humble fane.
Nor Avin, Amafa refufe their throng,   595
Nor Sela, nor expanded Helephon.
Crowds flow from Rhama pierced with Rachel's
    cries,
Myriads from Jericho and Gabeon rife,
Whofe natives faw, 'tis fung, the fun ftand ftill,
(Submiffive to their Leader's mighty will)   600
And ling'ring long, forgetful of his way,
Slow from their hemifphere withdraw the day.
Among this band, fuperior to the reft,
A youth appears in crimfon beauty dreft,
From venerable Saul he draws his name,   605
And with the fage's blood his veins rich ftream :
In language potent and in action bold,
Him hoary bards unanimous foretold.
But while bewilder'd in dark error's maze,
Againft the truth what furies fhall he raife !   610
But when the God fhall glide into his breaft,
Repel the darknefs and remain his gueft,
Then fhall the youth with an illumin'd mind,
Ardent diffufe his lectures on mankind,
Waft through the world religion on his breath,615
And deeply tinge her beauty with his death.

                                        The

The town now full of Ifrael's twice fix tribes,
To pay the homage which the time prefcribes,
And confecrate the days with feftive praife,
To his difciples Chrift thus gently fays.   620
Soon will the light begin to ftreak the Eaft,
When ev'ry houfe fhall brighten with a feaft :
Among you who fhall to the town firft tend,
In fearch of fome rich one, the poor man's friend ;
Who may, before my fate, with us delight   625
To fhare the banquet, and the annual rite ?
Nor long your fearch : you'll fee a boy return
From the clear fountain with a brimful urn ;
Obferve his motions, keep him ftill in view,
And to the houfe he tends, his fteps purfue :   630
Afk, in my name, the mafter to afford
A chapel facred to the feftive board.
A fpacious hall, on fire with liquid gold,
And hung with tapeftry, he'll foon unfold ;
There on the tables fpread the facred meat,   635
There my companions' and my prefence wait.

He faid ; Peter and John the word obey,
And to the city bend without delay ;
Along the city they uncertain roam ;
But quickly fpy a boy returning home,   640
With a full urn from a neigb'ring fource :
Soon after him, they bend their haft'ning courfe,
Thro' various windings, clofe his footfteps trace,
And with him enter to his manfion-place.

F   Hither,

Hither, illuſtrious for his ancient race,　645
And for his ſeven ſons of manly grace,
Simon repair'd, join'd by his filial train,
When for the town he left the verdant plain.
Beyond the honours, which the city yields,
His joy was ſtill to breathe his native fields;　650
To lye at large beneath his wood-land ſhades;
To ſee the waters purling thro' his meads;
To view his farm productive as his vows,
Dreſs'd by the labour of an hundred ploughs.
Tho' old, he pour'd the verſe, and touch'd the
　　　ſtring,　655
Beſide a river or a flow'ry ſpring;
And vers'd in all blue Ether's various ways,
Into hereafter rapt, he told in lays
The ſigns, which might the huſbandman inform
Of heat approaching, or the chilling ſtorm:　660
Provide againſt the blazing Sun's deſigns,
And all the labours, which the Moon divines.
He gain'd the town, religious in parade,
To paſs the days by cuſtom ſolemn made:
And while the rites, the ſervants' care require, 665
He wakes the inſpiration of the lyre:
The cords beneath his fingers ſoftly thrill,
Or ſwell harmonious to his ivory quill,
And in bold ſounds reſponſive to the wires
He ſings the actions of his glorious Sires:　670
But chiefly from the origin he draws
Of all theſe banquets and their rites the cauſe;

And

But as his numbers gently glide along
Peter arrives and interrupts the fong:
We have a King, fays he, called Chrift by name,675
To none inferior in a pious fame,
Who bade us come, and afk an humble feat,
Sacred to rites and decent for a feaft.

When Simon heard, new joys dilate his breaft,
And all his doors flie open to his gueft.   680
Without delay, he orders to illume,
With wood Arabian, ev'ry ample room;
Then in the mid, he fhews a vaulted hall,
Where pictur'd tapeftry informs the wall;
Where the floor blufhes with luxurious dyes,   685
And ivory beds on filver bed-fteads rife;
Of gold each difh is fram'd, and ev'ry vafe;
And thro' the manfion gold and filver blaze.
Then thus he fpoke; let him our manfion fhare:
Before this time his name has reach'd our ear, 690
Yet tho' his virtue on fame's plumage flies,
His voice ne'er blefs'd my ears, nor mien my eyes:
But here his coming and his prefence wait,
I'll order fome to guide him to this feat:
And I could wifh, he'd fix his dwelling here, 695
And all th'indulgence of this palace fhare;
Then might I boaft the honour to my race,
And they point out with joy the facred place.
But let the verfe, by your approach untold,
The juft applaufes of our Sires unfold,   700

While

While earth with night's foft dew-drops humid lies,
And darknefs fheds her fable from the fkies.

He faid ; his voice accordant to the ftrings,
From the foft concert rapture melting brings ;
Thro' all his ftrains fuch vivid colours bloom,   705
As paint can boaft, or texture of the loom.
For lo! his numbers lead from Pharaoh's reign
Thro' various realms the banifh'd Hebrew-train :
Wave high in air the wandering Leader's wand,
Obedient to whofe touch the billows ftand ;   710
Their rigid waters roll on either fide,
And in the midft the tribes attend their guide ;
From moifture free his daring footfteps tread,
And without failing pafs thro' Ocean's bed,
Behind them Egypt fends her fons in fwarms,   715
Elate in chariots and illumed with arms :
The further fhore obtained, they view the foe,
And feek the woods, that on the margin grow.
Again their Hero waves his wand around,
And with its holy point light wounds the ground :
                                  720

Sudden the waters lofe their rigid force,
Diffolve and fwallow up the trodden courfe.
The foe, furrounded with the rapid tide,
Sees fwift deftruction on each billow ride ;
Before the fight, the bodies of men drown'd   725
Float for a while, then feek the fea's profound.
Horfes with arms, chariots in eddies toft,
In circles reel and fink for ever loft.

                           The

The fupreme Being next becomes his theme,
The great Creator of the world's huge frame :   730
Who touched with pity, for the hungry bands,
Wandering diftrefs'd along a wafte of fands,
From the deep concave of his azure tow'rs,
A heav'nly banquet to the wretched pours.
Like feather'd fnow the food feems in his fong 735
To lapfe from Heav'n to earth amid the throng,
Which fpread at large along the level fields,
Enjoy the Manna, which Heav'n bounteous yields.
Again, the Hero fends to Heav'n his eyes,
And to a rock's huge height his wand applies : 740
The rock relents, as confcious of the blow,
And floods of water from its bofom flow ;
Struck with the novel font, each thirfty tribe,
Scoop the frefh waves, and breathlefs draughts im-
          bibe.
To Him, the Lyrift next his numbers pours,   745
Who firft had rear'd Jerus'lem's fpiry tow'rs ;
Paid the firft offerings of the cultur'd feed,
And bade the new invented vine to bleed ;
Who rais'd the pomp of altars in the glade,
Built of frefh turf beneath a wild afh-fhade.   750

While all drank deep the mufick of the lyre
Tho' confcious of the Hebrews' mortal ire,
Still Chrift the mountain's airy brow defcends,
And to the city's hateful portals tends :
And now the fun fhot down the azure plain,   755
When he had gain'd the palace with his train ;

Where

Where all things sparkle with a regal taste,
And the board glows odorous with the feast.
Amid the guests, with well diffembled face,
Breathing feign'd love, Judas affumes his place. 760
And now the Hero takes into his hand
The pureft bread and breaks it 'mong his band.
The wine then blending with the recent ftream,
He confecrates it to the Pow'r fupreme.
And as he dealt the holy cakes, he faid,   765
My Body's real Image is this bread:
Then cried, diftributing the purple flood,
This cup's the real Image of my Blood,
Which to my Sire I'll pour a victim flain,
To wafh away mankind's infectious ftain: 770
When you fhall drain this cup or tafte this meat,
The feries of my death commemorate.
Such honours to my torments fhall be paid,
And their fad memory fhall never fade.

He ceas'd to utter more : and from that day, 775
Mankind, fubmiffive to the mandate, pay
The holy homage : and inftead of beafts,
By ancients flain for facrifical feafts,
On altars confecrate, with rites divine,
The bread myfterious and the facred wine.   780
By the prieft's words the God defcends the fkies
And veil'd beneath th'Euchariftic form lies :
God's body hence is offer'd with his gore,
And men the victim religioufly adore.

Hunger

Hunger appeas'd, the Hero lays afide   785
His ample robe, and ftudious to provide
The implements of lotion, he firft difplays
The towels white; next, fills a caldron's fpace
With floods of water which vehement afpire
Above the margin by the fubject fire;   790
Then fcoops the frigid ftreams, which foon affuage
The turgid eddies of the boiling rage.
Peter, with his companions in amaze,
Exhorts the Hero from the deed to ceafe:
But he, defirous to his train to fhew   795
The glory of fubmiffion, bending low,
Wafhes their feet, and with the towels dries;
Then pours this fad addrefs in heavy fighs.

The night, which I foretold, now mantles earth,
And the day haftes to fummon me to death.   800
I'll leave you, friends, and in my death fulfill
The rigid orders of my Father's will:
There's mid you one, believe what I relate,
Who, fraudful, fhall betray me to my fate:
The traytor's breaft the furies now inflame,   805
And his mind labours with the murd'rous fcheme.
Can love like mine, be crown'd with fuch bafe fpoils?
Is treafon the reward of all my toils?—
But let the wretch this fatal truth imbibe,
He fhall not long enjoy his bloody bribe;   810
Soon fhall he wifh he ne'er had drank the day,
Or with his foot-fteps mark'd life's flow'ry way.
For you, who would my low example try,
In due fubmiffion with each other vie;

F 4   And

And while obedience o'er your minds preside,   815
Look down superior on the pomp of pride,
Nor shall the crew of hell desist this hour
A trembling panic in your breasts to pour;
The courage, vow'd so often, dare to shew;
Now bid your ardor flash against your foe: 820
With watchful care provide against their pest;
One night at least forbid your eye-lids rest.

Amaz'd the Hero's prophecy to hear,
One genial sigh betrays their common fear;
And while, the wretch to know, they feel distress,
                                            825
Devoutly Peter offers this address,

Thou, brightest splendor of the blue serene;
Can human breasts such baseness entertain?
But, where's the man, who dares the crime essay?
For, tho' old age has clad my head with grey, 830
With manly vigour still my blood is warm,
With lusty sinews still is brac'd my arm,
To take the vengeance to the treason due;
He said; and from the sheath his weapon drew.

Tho' with sure signs, the traytor was reveal'd;
                                            835
The Hero still their minds with deep night seal'd,
Nor would divulge him till his acts betray:
But thus replied to Peter's suppliant plea.
This night supreme, I shall alone remain,
Relinquish'd, shun'd by all my faithless train. 840

5   Ev'n

Ev'n you, who now in pomp of language rife,
Your verbofe courage fwelling to the fkies ;
Beneath this roof provoking ftorms to blow,
And fafely rufhing on the diftant foe :
When you fhall fee me 'mid the hoftile train,   845
Inglorious fhackl'd with the fervile chain ;
·Then fhall you lurk beneath a lying tongue,
And with a trembling flight the danger fhun :
And when, bedrop'd with dew, the fable night
Shall o'er the world obtain her middle height,   850
Thrice, me, your Lord, you fhall deny, afraid
To ftand the queftions of an armlefs maid.

Touch'd with the fpeech, more zealous Peter glows,
And boafts a courage fearlefs of the foes.
Me to proclaim, faid he, a coward, fpare,   855
'Till from your foe I bafe recede thro' fear.
Let others place their fafety in their flight,
I fhall be always prefent to your fight ;
Your fmiling fortune or difafters fhare,
Nor force compel me to forfake your care.   860

The rites perform'd Chrift rifes from the feaft,
And from the town retires with eager hafte :
With darknefs fhrouded, feeks the lonefome plain,
And climbs the Olive mountain with his train ;
There bids them the noclurnal vigil keep ;   865
But their eyes clofe, beneath the weight of fleep ;
They ftrew their limbs along the rocky way,
Spent with the labours of the bufy day.

But

But lulling reft the mournful Hero flies,
Who feeming thoughtlefs of his natal fkies,'   870
To fancy gives his forrowing mind to gloom
With the fad picture of his future doom.
His nature fhudders at the ghaftly view,
Which, as a man, he from his mother drew,
For tho' the ills that fhake the human heart,   875
He feels terrifick in his mortal part,
Still his foul ftands fuperior to the woes,
And with unconquer'd zeal his virtue glows,
And now before his Sire he proftrate falls,
And on him oft, with hands erect thus calls.   880
Muft I, O Father, undergo this fate,
And others' faults feverely expiate ?
Snatch me from death ; foften your hard decree,
And fhift this ftore of forrow far from me !
Yet if your mind to no new change will yield;   885
And to fubdue your wrath, your Son muft bleed ;
I ftand a victim for the public good,
That man may draw luftration from my blood.
He faid : to more complaints fupprefs'd the way,
And to reflection gave his heart a prey :   890
And lo ! his frame is purpled with his gore,
The bloody fweat frefh bubbling from each pore.
Struck with the fight, a feather'd Angel flies,
Charg'd with a ftore of comforts, from the fkies,
To foothe his cares, his fpirits to renew,
And from his body wipe the bloody dew,   895

Mean

Mean time the chief of traytors, Judas goes,
And from the mountain calls the lurking foes;
Who ready at their Leader's fignal rife,
To feize at once, and lead in chains, their prize,
                                            900
Their arms fhed wide the panting lunar beam,
Shrill found their fhields, and harfh their weapons
        fcream;
They cleave the wood, and taper to a point,
And with an unctuous juice the fticks anoint:
They move in long proceffion with the light,   905
The greafy flames wide ftreaming on the night.
The din of weapons and the ruffian cries
Shake the firm mountain and bid echo rife.
The Lord advancing pour'd thefe accents bold,
Stop here your march : me, whom you feek, behold.
                                            910
But why thefe arms, thefe burning torches, why;
In the full town, amid your Peers, have I
Announc'd my Supreme Father's great decree;
And none, though armlefs, prefum'd to harm me.
Why now do weapons glitter on the night ?   915
But if my orient glory burns fo bright,
That only death your envy can appeafe;
Let flow my blamelefs blood, and envy ceafe:
But fure my friends may go, from vengeance free;
They only act, what I alone decree.   920
He fpoke : and twice himfelf their prey confefs'd;
And falling twice, ftrange fight ! the ground they
        prefs'd :

                                    Dafh'd

Dafh'd to the ground, the maffy armour rung,
And a denfe darknefs on their eye-lids hung :
They rife : but ftare quite loft in their defign, 925
As one, who lay diffolv'd in fleep and wine.
But Judas foon, who fpurn'd the balm of reft,
By fignals chas'd oblivion from their breaft :
For veiling treafon under friendfhip's fmile,
He fawn'd and kifs'd his Lord with graceful guile.

930

Tho' in the deed he knew himfelf betray'd,
Yet the Lord whifp'ring to the traytor, faid :
Are kiffes then the fruit of all my love,
And can rewards to fuch a crime you move ?
For other ends, than golden trafh to gain, 935
I have receiv'd you votarift of my train.

Scarce had he fpoke; when on him rufh'd the
    band,
And rolling in denfe orbs around him ftand.
As when fome ftately ftag or foaming boar,
Fierce with fork'd tufks, caught in a trammel roar;

940

A mob of fhepherds gather round the fnare,
And their fharp fpears againft the favage rear.
So the fierce youths the captive Hero feize,
And burnifh'd arms around him armlefs blaze.
Some bind his hands ; fome wreath his neck with
    cord ; 945
Some lead him this, and fome another road.

Malchus

Malchus a rage fuperior yet can boaft;
(Malchus, a bond-man from Idume's coaft)
Who help'd no friend, no foe in war withftood;
In limbs no ftrength, no valour in his blood :   950
That Caiphas (for Malchus was his flave)
Might range him in the number of the brave,
Affur'd, no danger could from infult flow,
He bafely treats the felf-devoted foe.
And tho' he bellows out with tongue fevere,   955
Still fafety, fcarce, fecures his heart from fear.
Fir'd with the outrage Peter could not bear;
But with his fword cut off the coward's ear.
The God, regarding the inglorious wound,
Rais'd the diffected member from the ground,   960
Applied with healing finger to its place,
And of the wound effac'd the niceft trace :
With gentle touch he footh'd away the pain
And purg'd the ear from duft and fanguine ftain,
Then reprimanding Peter, who had glow'd   965
To crop the growth of violence with his fword,
Commands him ftraight his hoftile arms to hide,
And not in 'fteel, which Heav'n forbids, confide.
Had not his ardor, timely been fupprefs'd,
He'd foon had lodg'd it in the boafter's breaft. 970
On other weapons, the Redeemer faid,
On other valour we relie for aid :
My Sire fupreme (if he had deign'd to fave,
Or fnatch me from the difappointed grave;
Or pardon man, by his own mercy won,   975
Without the blood-atonement of his Son.)

                                        Could

Could bid a thoufand guards around me flie,
And by their arms this band before me die.
Say, know you not the Militia and Pow'rs
The battles fought and fame of heav'n's bright
        tow'rs ?   980
Now urge my Sire's commands, which heave thefe
        fighs ;
For mortal force and weapons I defpife.

Tho' thus reprov'd, his paffion fcarce fubfides:
So when a hunter thro' a city rides ;
If in the ftreets, chance offers to his hound   985
A ftag bred docile to his owner's found ;
With rapid jaws the hound the ftag purfues,
And fcarce the hunter's threat his rage fubdues.
And now the Lord, felf-conquer'd and refign'd,
O fight indignant ! all infult unkind !   990
Tho' weak of frame, they chide him of delay ;
And often falling, urge him on the way.
Thou, King of Hofts, this treat behold, and rife ;
Is hell not blended with the falling fkies ?—
When fhall your hand the rattling thunder roll ?995
Can nature now reft cloudlefs in each pole ?—
All fair proportion loft, let ruin hurl'd,
Deftroy the beauteous fabrick of this world.
Why fleeps your hand ? let heav'n diffolve in gloom,
And hiffing earth with three-fork'd thunder fume.
                                                          1000
Tho' fmitten with the love of human race ;
Tho' glory burns in your heav'n's blue fpace ;
                                                   Wher=

Where fpirits, dreft in plumage, form the choir,
And pour the fong of rapture you infpire;
Tho' here an age of gold fhall foon arife,   1005
Which on Religion's wings fhall mount the fkies;
With thefe lov'd objeƈts be not ftill fo won,
As to behold your fole begotten Son
With groupes of ills befieg'd without redrefs,
Infulted, poor, and finking with diftrefs.   1010
His friends all pallid to the woods are fled,
As at the rufhing of a boar, half-dead;
Their flight obferving fwift purfue the foes
One, feized and lapfing, leaves behind his cloaths,
And up an arduous mountain panting glows. 1015
Along deep thickets foft another fteals,
And in a concave-rock himfelf conceals.
The devious grove glows fervent with their courfe,
And with their fhouts the unfhorn hills turn hoarfe.

   Arriv'd they enter at the high Prieft's gates, 1020
Where peers and citizens affume their feats.
All with ftern looks the Captive-Hero eye,
And their fierce threats inform him, he fhall die.
Then Caiphas, fuperior to the reft,
The full affembly with his thoughts addrefs'd, 1025
Patriots! at length, fuccefs has crown'd our cares,
A chain infrangible now the pris'ner wears.
But o'er in mind, what ftill remains, let's run,
Wifdom ought crown, what glowing zeal begun.
The day draws near, when glory's liquid rays 1630
Shall on us fhed a purple flood of blaze.

                      Awful

Awful attend, and folemnly prepare,
My fentiments religioufly to hear.
You know, our laws forbid, feverely great,
To breathe on man the dreadful words of fate: 1035
To Rome alone is giv'n that awful breath,
Which either pardons or pronounces death :
'Tis our's to trace a crime, that's big with fate,
And on the Roman with the procefs wait :
'Tis his to hear, and nerve the dreadful blow, 1040
That numbers with the dead the friendlefs foe.

He fpoke, and turning to the Captive, fays,
I charge you by the God whom heav'n obeys,
To drop deceitful fiction from your heart,
And cloudlefs as the fun, your thoughts impart :
                                               1045
Left led by error, darkfome we decline
Your God-head to confefs by rites divine.
Attend ; and fimply anfwer, are you he,
The omnipotent God's true Progeny ;
A God yourfelf, whom ancient bards foretold, 1050
Should, gliding foft from heav'n, the world behold ?
He finifh'd, the Captive armlefs and weak,
With eyes half-lifted, thus began to fpeak :

He, whom you fay, am I ; drop then the veil,
Which would the malice of your words conceal :
                                               1055
I own my God-head ; and without delay,
Heav'n to my reign fhall ope a lucid way.
                                        Soon,

Soon, in the ſtarry dome, my Sire ſupreme
Shall twine around me with a Father's flame.
Me, viſiting the earth, you ſhall behold   1060
Cloath'd with the drap'ry of a blazing cloud ;
Celeſtials without number in my train,
Bruſhing with golden wings th'etherial plain.

He ſaid : when by the rites the High-Prieſt tore
The robe which flowing down his back he wore.
                                                   1065
Glows not the proof with light, he thus exclaims,
Behold, his crime before us he proclaims ?
Do not our laws condemn to bitter death
The man, who dares aſſert from God his birth ?
Haſte, drag him to the Roman Conſul's gate ; 1070
Inſtant obey : and give him up to fate.

Peter, mean time, ſtruck with the penſive caſe,
At diſtance ſighing, eyes his Lord's diſgrace.
Approaching now the Temple's ſacred wall,
Where roſe in pride the Flamen's ſpacious hall :
                                                   1075
Loneſome he ſat, beſide an open door,
With ſorrow heavy and in ſpirit poor.
A female ſlave, the Pontif's portreſs, eyes
Th'unhappy man, and inſtantly thus cries ;
Say, ſhare you not the Captive's crimes and flight,
                                                   1080
Why roam you elſe, when all repoſe, by night ?
                        G   Peter

Peter unmann'd chills with a ghaftly fear
At the flave's fpeech, (to life fuch love we bear!)
He ftands confus'd, in ftorms of horror toft,
Or what to act, or how to flie quite loft.   1085
Compos'd in fleep, fo when a virgin-child,
Left by the mother in a defert wild,
(The mother anxious homeward to repair,
With fetting day, forgets her filial care)
Awakes, and cafting round her tearful eyes, 1090
Nor mother dear, nor fond companion fpies:
The way unknown, fhe views the black'ning night,
The defert drear, and dies away with fright.
So he confus'd and impotent with fear,
With abject mind, abjur'd a friend fo dear, 1095
For whom, while o'er him reafon held her lore,
He would have ardent fpilt his vital gore.
He feeks concealment in the hoftile place,
And madly mixes with the fervile race;
But foon fufpected of the Captive's train,   1100
The more they urge, the more he ftrives to feign.
Thrice they upbraid him with his Mafter's name;
And thrice his Mafter's country was their theme:
His mind thrice ftartled at the rifing lye;
But thrice his words, at length, his friend deny.1105
Sudden the crefted bird with matin-hymns
The full departure of the midnight fings,
Wont from his vocal breaft to pour the fhrills,
That bid Aurora mount the eaftern hills:
The lays prophetick, which the Hero fung, 1110
Gufh'd on his fpirits and intenfely ftung.

Corrofive

Corrosive grief pervading faft his frame,
And fell remorse ringing his coward shame,
He steals unseen and thro' the city strays,
Pallid with vigils and the moon's cold rays. 1115
With fighs he views the basenefs of the fin,
Tearing the filver honours of his chin.
'Tis fung by fame, that at each night's return,
He ufed, thro' life, the perjur'd hour to mourn.
Aurora often liften'd to his pains,   1120
When she difclos'd to view th'ethereal plains :
And Vesper often ey'd his breaft to heave,
With grief luxurious in a lonesome cave.
Of sorrow fond, and to preclude relief,
He tells the strains of his deferted Chief :   1125
And fancy always paints his daftard-shame,
When a maid's tongue congeal'd with fear his
          frame.

    As yet Aurora, with returning day,
Streak'd not with blaze Olympus' concave way ;
When Chrift was led, his hands with fetters bound,
          1130
To Pilate's palace 'mid a ruffian found.
Who, when thron'd high on his judicial feat,
The maze of crimes purfu'd and iffu'd fate.
Pilate, whofe veins stream'd rich with Roman gore,
Judea fway'd beneath Tiberius' lore :   1135
Whom thus the band addrefs'd with furious breath;
Behold a culprit, give him inftant death.

Potent in fraud fufpend him high in air,
And the fhame let him of the gibbet fhare.
The waves of people overflow the gate   1140
And the hoarfe walls their fanguine cries repeat.

Pontius the Captive youth with ardor ey'd,
(For fcarce youth's bloffem in his form had dy'd)
Infatiate view'd his frame of graceful fize,
T'unwonted beauties of his face and eyes.   1145
Then ftood confirm'd, he had deriv'd his birth,
Either from Gods above, or Kings on earth.
And now his breaft with foft indulgence flows,
And melts with pity at the Captive's woes;
Silent he ftudies to avert his pains,   1150
And break afunder his inglorious chains:
And thus accofts him: fay, unhappy, tell,
With what black crimes your fad difafters fwell?
Whence fudden rife thefe ftorms that round you
        blow;
What ills thus plunge you in a fea of woe?   1155
Whence is your birth, what blood contains your
        vein:
What fceptre waits your hand, or realm your reign?

To his demand, Chrift fhortly thus replied;
Nor crime to this tribunal was my guide:
Nor, in dread fhape, arifes to my thought,   1160
The leaft commiffion of a venial fault:
Unlefs it is a fault, that I obey
My Sire, who o'er Olympus fpreads his fway:
                                        Nor

Nor am I anxious for a mortal throne;
Tho' of a regal race, myself I own.   1165

He ceafed : Pilate again begins to trace
The wond'rous beauties of his noble face :
His wretched cafe, with various fpeech to try;
But, mers'd, in woe, the Lord deign'd no reply.
Pontius, at length, the rabble's rage to fall,
Confines him pris'ner, in his inmoft hall.   1171

End of the Second Book.

G 3

ARGUMENT of the Third Book.

The rumour of Chrift's imprifonment having reached the town of Nazareth, Jofeph, to know the truth, comes without delay to Jerufalem where he accidentally meets John pale and penfive from the difafters of his Mafter. They both repair to Pilate, who defires Jofeph to inform him of the parentage and birth of Chrift the prifoner. Jofeph to be clear in his narrative gives a curfory account of the Hebrew nation down to the birth of the Virgin Mary. She arrived at the age of woman-hood, an Angel orders her parents to choofe for her a fpoufe among their own tribe ; which being convened for that purpofe, Jofeph is felected for her hufband, who, finding her pregnant, refolves to divorce her, but is foon convinced of her fidelity by the appearance of an Angel, relating to him the manner of her conception, and the greatnefs of the fruit of her womb. Thus fatisfied, he and his Virgin-bride pay a vifit of three months to her coufin Elifabeth, wife to Zacharias the Prieft, and mother of John the Baptift. Cæfar (Auguftus) regiftering his fubjects, Mary repaired with her fpoufe to Bethlehem to be enrolled, and is delivered of the child Jefus in a ftable. The Shepherds falute him with hymns, the Eaftern Kings with gifts. Then he relates her purification with Simeon's prophecy concerning the child : their flight into Egypt, to fhun the maffacre of Herod ; their return after Herod's death : and concludes with a defcription of finding Chrift in the Temple, difputing with the Doctors, and of his changing water into wine.   T H E

THE
CHRISTIAD.

BOOK III.

PLUM'D Fame, now thro' the vicine towns
      had ſtray'd,
And ſung the Hero, by his train betray'd.
But, as obſcure, the rumour ſtill appears,
Nor yet had eccho'd in his Mother's ears.
Yet her preſaging mind was rack'd with pain,   5
Chill'd always with the Prophet's awful ſtrain :
To free the faithful from their Captive-ſtate,
Her Son ſhould feel the agonies of fate.

But when Joſephus (to whoſe ſpouſal care,
The Mother was conſign'd, by heav'ns blue ſphere)
                    10
The tidings heard, he, from fair Naz'reth's vales,
To Solyma, with aged foot-ſteps, ſteals.
His entrance is ſaluted with dread cries,
Which wound, thro' night, the twilight of the
      ſkies :
Swarming along the walls the people low'r,   15
And thro' the town in dreadful tumults pour.

Lo!

Lo! faithful to his Hero, John appears;
Pallid, and juft elaps'd the Cohorts fpears;
Mers'd in the dangers, which his Lord attend,
With pain difcerns the prefence of his friend.   20

To whom the Sage : ftop, whither do you hafte?
What colour paints the vifage of our ftate?
Where can Jehovah-born without you be;
Or in the town, whence roars this mutiny?—
Alas! the pangs, which prophecies impart,   25
Wound not, in vain, the troubled Mother's heart:

The youth his pain with mute embraces tells,
With grief that trickles, and the figh that fwells;
Then briefly thus : alas! our hope is dead,
And all our fafety is for ever fled: 30
Our Chief, feiz'd bafely, in a prifon lies;
The Tribunes of the town againft him rife;
Fervent, confpire to rivet faft his chains,
And glow to quench their envy in his veins.
His very train, diffolv'd with ghaftly fear,   35
Forfake his perfon, and daftard difappear.—
But where's the Mother, fay?—has fable fame
Announc'd the tidings to the wretched Dame?
If fhe was here, perhaps the parent-grief
Might Pontius melt, to give her fon relief.   40
Suppliants for peace before him let us go,
And the dire envy of the people fhew.

Thus having faid, join'd by his hoary friend,
They both to Pilate's palace penfive tend.

So

So a poor peafant, when the hand of war   45
The country fpoil'd, and drove his cattle far,
In queft of them, a tedious journey goes,
His eldeft fon, companion of his woes ;
Thro'-various unknown fields, they bend their way,
To fee, if herds like their's, by chance fhould ftray:
                                                         50
Stopping, they roll, in vain, their weepful eyes,
And fill the devious valleys with their cries.
And now arrived at Pontius Pilate's gate,
Of Monarchs once the venerable feat;
While Syria was with regal power bleft,   · · 55
But now by Syria's Roman-chief poffeft :
Confufion glowing thro' all ranks they fee ;   :
Before the hall, the Rabbins difagree :
The Priefts, receding from the Rector's door,
Againft him bellow, and their hatred pour.   60

    Flufh'd with the fcene, they foftly foothe their
        care;   ,
And hope her influence fheds on their affair.
Then thus fpeaks John ; difmifs your fear, my
        friend ;
Hope dawns ; now, for thy Son, the Chief attend:
But veil the birth, which from the fkies he draws ;65
And for your prefence, plead a Father's caufe.

    Admitted now, both on the Rector wait ;
Who with his Council held in a high debate
                                             About

About the Captive's caufe; when, lo! he fees
A hoary Sage bend low, and clafp his knees.   70

Thou beft of Romans, thus Jofephus cries,
To tame proud Syria, ftation'd by the fkies.
To curb the nation's hate, your pow'r engage,
Which reafon guides not, and whofe ftrength is rage.
His Sire am I, 'gainft whom their Chiefs confpire,
                                        .   (75
And on him fhed, in fictious crimes, their ire:
Before you brought, as bafeft of the bafe,
To feel a fanguine undeferv'd difgrace.
But virtue only is his mighty ill,
And deeds, that bleffings on the world diftill: 80
The peals of praife their blafting envy claim,
And all the honours paid his tow'ring fame.

Anguifh, in copious ftreams of tears, bedew'd
The hoary vifage, while the fuppliant fued.
Pontius, with foothing words, and placid brows, 85
Confoles them both, and hears the old man's vows:
Gives him to reft, on a foft couch reclin'd,
And thus relieves the tortures of his mind.
How welcome is your prefence at this hour!
You'll not, perhaps, lament its want of pow'r. 90
Say then, (who better than a Father can?)
A fhort relation of the Captive-man.
Fear not your thoughts with liberty to fpeak;
To guard you harmlefs, I my honour ftake.

                                        For

For I atteſt the ſtars of yon blue ſphere,　　95
How much your Son employs my tender care :
What ſchemes I form'd to ſave him from his foes;
To calm this nation's rage, that madly glows.
Detail, (for oft his fame has reach'd my ears)
His race, his fortune, and the blood he ſhares: 100
His mother's progeny, and your own rehearſe ;
For my mind colours him of no low race.
His mien how ſtately, and his frame how fine !
And from his viſage flows an air divine :
What awful beams of honour dart his eyes ;　　105
And when he moves, the Monarch ſeems to riſe.
Then in his breaſt I felt the Godhead ſwell ;
For on his tongue, more charms than mortal dwell.
That's he's a God, his actions loudly ſay ;
And nothing of an earthly birth betray.　　110
Then ſatisfy ; for he averts my pray'r,
And deigns no anſwer to my friendſhip's care .
His mind regardleſs of the air he draws ;
And of the aid, I proffer to his cauſe.

The Sage, theſe accents utter'd, doubtful ſtands,
　　　　　　　　　　　　　　　　[115
To ſpeak evaſive of the Chief's demands ;
Or, void of fraud, ingenuouſly proclaim
The birth celeſtial, and the Father's name.
When John, advancing, in ſoft whiſpers ſaid ;
Offspring of Kings, fam'd for the virgin's bed; 120
Whence this blank pauſe, or why this long delay ?
The truth expand, and lay aſide diſmay :
　　　　　　　　　　　　　　　Safety

Safety reigns here ; with fortitude confide.
He said, the Sage embolden'd thus reply'd.

Rector of Syria, I will now unveil   125
The mystic annals of a mighty tale.
But to indulge your wish, I'll simply trace
First the fam'd lineage of our Hebrew race.
Know then, tho' poverty my hands confine
To fabric-tools, I boast a regal line ;   130
A line, illustrious in the roll of fame,
And to of Orbs advanc'd celestial flame.
Of many nations the primeval Sire,
(A theme, you heard, oft eccho'd in our choir)
Abraham, guardian of the Hebrew line,   135
Who first enacted laws and rites divine ;
Engender'd Isaac, who, to manhood bred,
Enhanc'd with Jacob his connubial bed.
Jacob with twice six Peers prolific shone,
Whom founders of our twice six Tribes we own : 140
Above his brothers, Judas held a place
For pious actions and a num'rous race,
Enjoy'd this realm, which to his portion came,
And stil'd the land Judea from his name.
But to descend into the mid of things,   145
Hence David sprung, the sire of Israel-kings.
From him, as from our origin, our line,
With blood sublim'd thro' fourteen Monarchs shine.
But your young Pris'ner claims a nobler birth ;
Tho' mortal-born, he treads this mortal-earth; 150
Olympus still he calls his natal place,
And from the Parent-god, a birth may trace :
                                        That

That God, his Father, whom the earth obey,
The purple ether, and the shrouded sea.
A maid, unconscious of a man's embrace,   155
Brought forth the child, beneath the solar space :
Who, tho' a mother, (Bards once sung the strains)
The rosy graces of a maid retains.
For God descending fill'd her with his breath,
And the creative SPIRIT gave the birth.   160
Hence, tho' esteem'd his Sire by vulgar fame,
I'm Guardian only of the holy Dame :
To soothe the pungent troubles of her breast,
And bear the labours, that might wound her rest.
But in male-honour dubious to confide,   165
And fearful to defame her virgin-pride ;
She deign'd to hear my Hymeneal vows,
And make, with rites, unworthy me her spouse.

This maid, the fairest of the Hebrew-fair,
(With my whole course of love to fill your ear) 170
Is call'd Maria, in Naz'reth was bred,
And the sole fruitage of her parents bed.
To win her heart, a hundred suitors strove ;
But of fair chastity smitt'n with the love,
The joys of Hymen, she, averse, declin'd   175
And in the fane her virgin vows enshrin'd.
Her mother, Anna, venerable dame,
Full of hereafter, and the Prophet's theme,
That from her virgin daughter soon shou'd spring,
Egregious for his deeds, a future King ;   180
Who shou'd his sway o'er many nations hold :
So Heav'n decreed, and so the Bards foretold.

                                        Often

Often a voice, defcending from the fkies,
(While fleep its influence fhow'r'd on her eyes)
Bad her the Nobles of her Tribe convene,   185
And for her daughter chufe one of the train.
But tho' to woman-hood arrived the maid,
Still no regard was to the vifion paid.
At laft, in the full azure of the day,
The voice was, to the parents, heard to fay : 190
" To bind in Hymen's bands your daughter hafte ;
" Nor for a diftant Son, your moments wafte ;"
But of your blood, by ufe, a fpoufe provide ;
Break off delays ; and crown your maid a bride.

Thro' the fmall town flies foon the fwift report;
                                        [195
And foon conven'd, the kindred youth refort.
The virgin's manfion ecchoes with the band,
Each flufh'd with hope to gain the virgin's hand.
Ev'n I, led by proximity of blood,
Amid the crowd of rival fuitors ftood ;   200
That I might hail the fortune of my friend,
Who fhou'd the virgin's nuptial bed afcend.
For, far from me, advanc'd in hoary age,
With fprightly bands a rival to engage :
Who equal all in manly beauty fhone,   205
And whofe fair flow'r of youth was then new-blown.
Tho' all gaz'd, trembling, the decifive fkies,
Each bofom heav'd to clafp the virgin-prize.
While flutter'd hope, and events roll'd in clouds,
We rufh'd into Joachim's hall in crowds,   210
                                    Where

Where rofe an altar, awful for its age,
And where he us'd the Godhead to affuage :
Built by our race, and facred by their fears,
Was held in rev'rence for three hundred years :
Before this altar proftrate we implor'd   215
The hoft Angelick and the Angel's Lord ;
Placid to mark, by fome fure fignal giv'n,
The hufband he defign'd, from his high heav'n.
In the mid ftood tearful the beauteous fair,
With eyes dejected and diforder'd hair :   220
A blufh fuffus'd her face with crimfon glows,
Like the pale lilly blended with the rofe.
As when the new-born moon defcending, laves   .
Her virgin-vifage in broad ocean's waves :
With guardian ftars afcending, bright adorns 225
Olympus' azure, with her flender horns.
So ftood the Virgin 'mid the circling train,
Her God invoking in a plaintive ftrain,
And much attefting God's wing'd-tow'ring choir,
She yielded— how adverfe to her defire !   230
Her Sire kifs'd off her fear, and dried her eyes,
And taught her foon the mandate of the fkies.
Her mother, Anna, rev'rend for her age,
Full of the God, heav'd with an holy rage,
Rav'd through the palace, wond'rous to be feen, 235
And her fhrill fhouts roll'd through the ftarry plain ;
Approaching me, unworthy of fuch grace,
She fix'd her eyes, and liv'd upon my face.
Seizing my hand, for you alone, fhe cries,
The Maid is deftin'd by the ftarry fkies.   240

All

All ftood amaz'd, yet none among the band,
Envy'd my honour of the Virgin's hand.
But I, ftill confcious of my hoary head,
My prefence wail'd, and fhun'd the nuptial bed.
The faithful youths againft my coynefs rife,   245
And prefs me to receive the offer'd prize.
I yield perfuaded, and lamenting lead,
To rites connubial, the lamenting Maid. .

Now, night her hoft of ftars on ether brings,
The world fuffufing with her fable wings :   250
We, fecret, enter both the nuptial door ;
Sad wept the bride, and lav'd with tears the floor.
So in the fpring when mounts the plantal juice,
And in the trees its fecund foul infufe :
The flender vine's luxurious branches feel   255
The pruning virtue of the peafant's fteel ;
Should 'gainft the root, the hook imprudent found,
The mother-vine ftreams blamelefs by the wound.
Tho' willing not to crop the Virgin's pride,
To foothe her grief with fofteft words I tried.   260
When drawing from her breath the long-breath'd
         fighs,
In accents fweetly plaintive, thus fhe cries :
Within me dwells fome virtue of the fkies,
And pure Relïgion prompts me to defpife
The nuptial-bed, and chaftity purfue,   265
With love perpetual, to her merit due.
For, tho' the Prophets my refolves oppofe ;
With other mandates, tho' my Mother glows ;

                                          Still

Still I poffefs an order, which defeats
My Mother's raptures, and the Prophet's threats.
                                            270

Wherefore fhall Jordan fooner feek his fource,
And the wild ftars defift their vagrant courfe,
Than I fhall light the nuptial torch, to fume
My virgin-mind, ftain'd with its groffer gloom.
She faid : her forrow, fwelling into tears,   275
In large round drops her gen'rous cheeks befmears :
A creeping horror fudden feiz'd my frame ;
Trembled my knees, night veil'd my vifual beam ;
Thrice I attempted to announce my pain, .
And thrice my tongue effay'd the tafk in vain. 280
And lo ! a voice, defcending from the fkies,
In awful and majeftick accents cries :
" The joys connubial to indulge forbear,
" But guard your fpoufal vows with holy care."
I rofe and wildly gazing on my bride,   285
At length, with painful paufes, thus replied.
Say, Virgin. candid fay, 'gainft Heav'n's command,
Why have I ftretch'd to you a bridegroom's hand ?
Who has (the nuptial joys I never fought)
On my pure conduct fuch difafters brought ? 290
A better fate breath'd in my Father's ftrain,
At once a bard, and flamen of the Fane :
" Or you, he fung, no Hymeneals wait ;
" Or honour fhall attend your bridal ftate."
Now fince the fkies have tied our fpoufal band,295
But with dread figns the fpoufal joys withftand ;

To my refolve a due attention give,
As now, with Virgin honour always live :
Nor shall I dare the facred union break,
Nor with volatile steps your dome forfake :   300
But gaze upon you, with a parent's eye ;
And you, with filial love, on me rely.
'Tis my department, now, to bear your cares ;
So wills your ardor, and my riper years.
Pleas'd with the plan, the wedded Virgin rofe, 305
And in a lonefome chamber fought repofe.
Untold, I'll pafs my fufferings thro' that night ;
The fleeplefs horror, and my imag'd fright.

Now darknefs fled before the blufh of day,
And Sol extinguifh'd fhadows in his ray.   310
My couch I leave, with fofteft filence tread,
And vifit, fmoothly flow, the virgin-bed.
Scarce had the portal on the hinges roll'd,
When on my eyes flafh'd lights of beamy gold ;
Which veft the walls, and to the roof afpire,   315
And radiant feem to fet the room on fire.
Entranc'd and luftred with a melting beam,
On the foft bed reclin'd the Virgin-Dame.
Nor deign'd to anfwer my repeated prayers,
Nor feem'd diftreft or melted with my cares ;   320
But like Aurora, blufhing in the eaft,
With hands and eyes erect, fhe Heav'n addrefs'd.
What better change improv'd her beauteous form!
Her eyes how bright ! with grace her looks how
        warm !

                                    The

The artift thus to grace fome temple's fhrine, 325
And call forth rev'rence to his fine defign ;
A maple falls, of it a ftatue forms,
And bids it breathe with all the chiffel's charms :
With graces ftor'd and polifh'd to behold,
It's beauties he fublimes with blazing gold.   330
Gufhing with floods of radiance, fo a cloud
Around the raptur'd Maid a luftre roll'd.
A crown of ftars feem'd on her head to beam,
And veft her temples with a lambent flame.
With pureft light replete, a filver moon   335
Beneath the Virgin's feet ferenely fhone.
Such wond'rous fcenes my mind with horror fill'd,
And while I fpoke, my breaft with fear was chill'd.
O, from this maze of wonders, fet me free,
Almighty Sire! they own your Deity :   340
Your hand in all thefe prodigies I find ;
Then placid breathe your Spirit on my mind,
That I, no longer in fufpence, may fee,
How to purfue, and act your juft decree.

I ceafed to pray : at length the beauteous Dame
[345
Woke from her trance, as from a broken dream.
Her fighs heave fadly, and her eyes befmear
Her fnow-like bofom with a burfting tear.
Aw'd I approach, and bending low, demand,
By the new union of our bridal band ;   350
And by that Veftal love, whofe flames refine,
And all her zeal to chaftity confine ;

Fearlefs

Fearlefs to ope the fcene of this affair,
And make me focial in her anxious care.

Bright, as the rofe, furcharg'd with matin dew,
                                                    355
Her eyes, about the floor, a luftre threw ;
Then ftarting from her paufe, fhe thus reply'd :
My joy, from thee, no longer fhall I hide :
Attend— but where fhall I commence the tale,
Or who'll believe the wonders I'll reveal ?   360
But I conjure you, by thefe gladfome tears
To guard in filence, what fhall reach your ears ;
Nor let it roll abroad, a vulgar theme,
'Till Heav'n configns it to the trump of Fame.
What time, Aurora man to labour wakes,   365
And new-born day the earth with luftre ftreaks ;
The ftrange events, in Prophets' fongs foretold,
Pour'd on my mind, and o'er my fenfes roll'd :
But chief the fong, it's conftant influence fhed,
(And to my mind the God, the picture led)j   370
Which hymn'd the Virgin, of a regal race,
Who fhould bring forth, without a man's embrace
(Strange to relate) the Rector of the fkies,
Whofe birth fhould on a golden world arife.
I thought her blefs'd, on whom, the Supreme Pow'r
                                                    375
Should, fmiling, fuch illuftrious honour fhow'r,
And tacit in my mind, began to hymn
The future Mother of our heav'nly King ;

                                        Prepar'd

Prepar'd with gifts the Infant-god to praife,
If in our city born, or in our days.   380
Dark in events, whilft I revolv'd this theme ;
Before my eyes expands a fheet of flame ;
Soft gales of air in cloudlefs brightnefs glide,
And (wond'rous to relate) the fkies divide :
Whence Heav'n's bleft hoft, incumbent on the wing,
                                              [385
The poles mount joyful and applaud their King.
Thro' portals barr'd and walls with marble lin'd,
The ftars effulg'd, and all Olympus fhin'd.
When lo ! a Boy, defcends at God's command,
Heav'n in his fmiles, a lilly in his hand ;   390
Sparkling the chamber with his rofy wings,
To me this falutation raptur'd fings.
O, Thou more happy, than the happieft fair ;
Than other mothers, Heav'n's more pleafing care !
Olympus' King, to dwell with you, prepares, 395
Collects his God-head, and forfakes the fpheres.

' Thefe words fcarce heard |(the maid continu'd)
       fhed,
On my admiring frame, a chilling dread :
But, he to foothe me with a pledge divine,
Inftant replied, O maid, your fear refign ;   400
By you the God, above your fex, more won,
Is pleas'd to make you mother of his Son :
A Son, you then fhall bear, who fam'd fhall be,
And ages own him God's own progeny.
Him born a Saviour to the faithful train,   405
You fhall call Jefus, in your native ftrain ;
             H 3   A name,

A name, already hell begins to fear,
And from its center draws an iron tear.
His foaring fame, and wond'rous acts, shall rise
Above the natives of this earth and skies.   410
The skies ordain, he shall the pow'r embrace,
And mount the throne of his illustrious race.
Nor time nor limits shall confine his reign,
.And everlasting shall his sway remain.

He said: my fear receding by degrees,   415
I spoke: my reason starts at your decrees:
For, I, resolv'd, the virgin-blush to guard,
Have, always, free from man, my heart preferv'd.

Finish'd my speech, the Angel his resum'd:
With great Jehovah's breath divine perfum'd, 420
Without man's commerce pregnant you shall be,
And in due time bring forth your progeny:
A God all nations shall your offspring call,
And Son to him, who rules this world's great ball.
Of this strange truth, to make all doubt subside, 425
Eliza, know, to you by blood allied,
Who sterile pin'd, when purpl'd with youth's glow,
Now ag'd despairs to feel a mother's throe:
Yet the sixth moon with lustre circles earth,
Since she swell'd pregnant with a future birth. 430
So great's his pow'r, on whose commands I flie,
The King and author of the starry sky.

This

This having faid, he wings the ether blue;
Whom thus with eyes and language I purfue :
Say, winged beauty of the azure plains,   435
I gladly yield to what your King ordains.
Flying to earth, mean time, a crimfon cloud
Involves my body in a fheet of gold
Fretted with ftars of varied luftre, glows
The ample concave, and with rays o'erflows.   440
Fair Iris emulates fuch chequer'd dyes,
(Her pictur'd veft winding oblong the fkies)
When adverfe Sol his melting radiance pours,
Full on her bow diftent with rainy fhow'rs.
Soon as the Sire fupreme breath'd on this cloud 445
From the bright ftars burfts forth a fpirit loud :
Its fpreading progrefs darts a length of ray,
And golden flafhes vibrate on the day.
Wrapt in the whirl-wind, all my limbs inhale
The potent virtue of the facred GALE :   450
Th' ethereal vigour, thrilling thro' my frame,
Diffolves my heart, with an impaffion'd flame.
By nature's inftinct fo the fecund earth
Conceives, and pours to day her various birth,
When Ether to her parent-lap-repairs,   455
And Zephyr fans her with his genial airs.
This fcene concluded, bright Olympus' throng
Clap their glad wings, and burft in varied fong :
Hoarfe thunders o'er blue ether's fummit roll,
And op'ning fkies flafh fire from pole to pole. 460

While thus the maid the wond'rous tale purfu'd,
The fmiling tears her rofeat cheeks bedew'd.

H 4   Of

Of little faith, yet full of pray'r I stand,
The stars addressing with a supine hand:
(For so incred'lous was my stupid mind)   465
Such prodigies to credit I declin'd;
Persuaded well, that youths, with studious care,
Weave the fine fraud, frail virgins to ensnare:
That maids of easy faith, ah, too soon won!
Imbibe man's pois'nous words and are undone. 470
And now I meditate, oh direful shame!
My virgin-wife for ever to disclaim;
When on my sleep an angel-form arose,
The same in looks, the same his sky-spun cloths,
Which to my bride his starry visit paid,   475
And bore the message, which I now display'd.
Naked his rosy shoulders stand confest;
Save from the left depends a golden vest,
Which three-folds clasps compos'd of fusile gold
The floating plaits about his loins infold.   480
His girdle blushing with a purple dye
Thick setts of golden studs around him tye.
His waist's fine down, which scarce the eye-ball sees,
Steals, mounting, on the sight by slow degrees,
Scaling his shoulders, more luxurious springs, 485
Then starts at once into a shade of wings.
A diamond-chaplet round his calves he wears;
Thence, to the knees undrest, the Form appears:
His beauteous looks, his mien's sweet-breathing
        grace
Proclaim the boy of no terrestrial race;   490
But some fair offspring of Olympus high;
Nurs'd in the region of the starry sky.

Nor

Nor was his tunic of lefs wond'rous art;
With jewels fpotted, fhines the upper part;
The low'r borders meander'd twice with gold, 495
Within their orbs, a texture tale infold;
Three pictur'd boys walk, harmlefs, thro' a blaze,
And hymn, with looks erect, Jehovah's praife.
Circling the furnace roof, fierce glows the fire,
And head-long, from the youths, the flames retire.
[500
While I in filence gaz'd, Heav'n's beauteous gueft,
To me, with fear congeal'd, thefe words addrefs'd.
Offspring of Kings, what crime o'ercafts your foul;
Can you, thefe figns, that fpeak the God, controul?
Sufpect no fraud to drop from her pure tongue;
[505
Truth tunes the ftrain, the facred virgin fung:
She has conceiv'd, ftranger to human aid;
By God's eternal SPIRIT pregnant made.
When God breath'd on her from his lucid dome;
The Godhead fled from Ether to her womb.   510
Boldly affent: For on our azure plains,
Pleas'd with our homage, truth eternal reigns.
Your Prophets, once, thefe miracles foretold,
Their lays obfcurely vefted with a cloud:
This maid is figur'd by the cryftal gate,   515
That binds eternal, Ether's deep retreat;
When human traces never print the road,
Frequented folely by the fupreme God,
Whofe ingrefs and regrefs ne'er violate,
With motion's noife, the portal's dormant ftate. 520

To

To you this maid he yields, who rules the fky,
But bound by Hymen, Hymen's freedom flie :
Let her thro' life, your fage protection fhare,
Tho' fafe beneath God's tutelary care.

He faid, and winging ether, fades a way,   52
But glancing thro' the cloud ftrews realms of day.
A fudden love my breafts pervading, fills
With foothing rapture, and exftatic thrills.
As iron drops its rigour in the fire,
So melts my ftubborn foul with love's defire :   530
Owning my mad'ning folly, I arife,
And call down meek-ey'd Mercy from the fkies.
Now reafon to my mind reftoring light,
The SUPREME's deep decrees expand more bright,
Which he infus'd into the Prophets' breaft,   535
The truth in fhades of ancient phrafes dreft.
This virgin is the bufh, which he, (whofe head
Sharp-pointed rays of ftreaming glory fhed)
Beheld, aftonifh'd, on the mountain's brow,
Burning with crackling flames at diftance glow. 540
Thro' harmlefs fires twinkl'd the untouch'd leaves
For ever verdant 'mid the lambent blaze.
She is the fleece, (unlefs the Bards are vain)
Which kept its drynefs 'mid a flood of rain :
Impervious to the fhow'rs, on whofe broad tide,
                                            [545
Earth's humid furface, lucent feem'd to glide.
Before fuch thoughts my night of error flies,
Our fcene moves faith to own fuch prodigies.

                                Spread

Spread thro' the towns of Galilee, now Fame,
Sings, wond'rous to tell, a venerable Dame, 550
Who lives as recluse, on a mountain's height,
And hoary bends, beneath old age's weight,
How with first offspring pregnant swells her womb,
Defam'd as sterile, in her youthful bloom.
The winged Nuncio of the tow'ring skies 555
Foretold this event, thus the virgin cries ;
Eliza is her name, the same our line,
And on her pregnancy, twice three moons shine.
Pleas'd with the thought, we rise without delay,
And to our Kindred-dame direct our way : 560
Thro' arduous mountains, and fatiguing pain,
The Flamen Zachariah's house we gain.
Scarce we, arriv'd, had touch'd the mansion-gate,
When nodding comes the Dame, strange to relate,
With fond embrace hangs on her welcome guest,
[565
And in the act, God rushes to her breast :
A sudden heat suffuses thro' her frame,
And this the language of the hoary Dame.

Above all other Parents, Parent blest !
Blest is the burden of your ut'rine Guest ! 570
Whence these unwonted heav'nly graces show'r,
Why on my silver head so smiles this hour,
Which gives me to behold with ardent eyes,
And speak to her, selected by the skies,
'Mid many, parent of the supreme Lord, 575
Gracing my mansion, of her own accord ?

At

At your approach, with rapture throb'd my breaſt,
And my womb's Babe his joy with bounds expreſs'd.
Hail, ſacred Mother, to the ſkies moſt dear;
For faith conſpicuous and to truth ſincere;   580
Who with glad faith held what the Angel ſaid,
Unconſcious of ⁂ being the Mother-maid.
Hear, Ether's Queen, and touch'd with human
          cares,
Smoothe life's misfortunes by your potent pray'rs.

She ſaid: with bluſhes, as the roſe, replete, 585
And mildly humble in an high eſtate,
The holy Maid, bedew'd with crimſon rays,
Rais'd to the ſtarry King her ſong of praiſe;
Who eyed her, gracious, from Olympus' throne,
Poor, loneſome, humble, and to praiſe unknown.
                                        [590
Then of hereafter full, ſhe ſung the Fame,
So often preſag'd, that ſhould crown her name.

To you, too tedious, would appear the tale,
Should I the portents and the ſigns reveal,
That on the trembling world diſtill'd a fear,   595
Soon as the mighty Infant breath'd this air:
The Caſpian kingdom heard the bards with dread,
And Nile's rich waves roll'd to their ſecret head.
Egypt receiv'd the oracle with frowns,
And eaſtern realms were ſhock'd thro' all their towns.
                                        [600
                                          If

If fame is true, your own Aufonian plains
Refounded horrid with the Prophets' ftrains :
That foon a King fhould drink the blaze of day,
And o'er the fubject world extend his fway,
Strong in his own, and Father's virtue rife,   605
And all his people tranflate to the fkies.

Firm'd by thefe figns, fpontaneous I obey
My pregnant Spoufe, and God-like rev'rence pay.
When the plum'd youth (the fame I often ey'd
Vifit, by day, the chamber of my Bride)   610
Her pregnant ferv'd, defcending ether's pole,
Charg'd with rich food and nectar's facred bowl.
Oft have I panted for the natal day,
But oft my hope was dafh'd with dull delay :
Thefe wifhes I revolv'd within my breaft.   615
O may the Babe celeftial ftand confefs'd
Before my death ; fince evident appear
The portents which befel the beauteous fair.

Crop then without delay your purple flow'rs,
Your lucent lillies fhed in copious fhow'rs,   620
To God new-born your balmy prefents bring,
And awfully approach your Infant-king,
And could I wifh to my old age more days,
It would be, Infant, on your deeds to gaze;
Then fear expell'd, peace on the world fhall rife,625
And you, a God, reign in your native fkies.
Truth, join'd with piety, this earth fhall tread,
And nodding now, Religion raife her head.
                                        Juftice

Juſtice the ſcenes of life at large will range,
And earth ſurpriz'd admire its better change;   630
Into the ſcythe the ſavage ſword be roll'd,
And nature brighten with an age of gold;
To ſoothe delay, my fancy pour'd ſuch hues,
And hope was nouriſh'd with ſuch diſtant views.

Cæſar (Auguſtus ſtiled) who that time reign'd,
                                              [635
To regiſter his ſubjeƈt world ordain'd.
My ſteps to Bethlehem's ancient walls inſiſt,
To have our names rang'd in the civil liſt.
The Virgin following leaves her manſion-ſeat,
The town of Naz'reth gave the ſafe retreat.   640
To Bethlehem come, with houſes thinly ſpread,
What time the ſkies, wrap'd in night's ſhadow,
        fled:
A loneſome houſe the city's walls ſucceeds,
The roof imbrown'd with turf and marſhy reeds:
Apt for the peaſant, whom noƈturnal gloom   645
In town detains far from his ruſtic home.
We ſeek this cot to weary travellers free,
Led on by chance, or rather God's decree,
Who not content his only Son ſhould groan,
And feel thro' life misfortunes not his own,   650
But in a ſtable will'd, he ſhould be born,
With want diſtreſs'd and of relief forlorn.
The aſs I feed, whoſe help made ſhort our road,
And whoſe fatigue made light our houſhold load.

                                     Next

Next whom, her ftraw-ftrew'd bed the Virgin prefs'd,
[656
The houfe too throng'd, to number her a gueft.
An ox fheds, on her left, his tepid breath,
Whom a poor plowman work'd to till his earth,
Cutting with crooked plough the fide-laid clay,
Nor ceas'd the toil, till ceafed the live-long day. 660
He cultures with fuch pains his rented field,
Himfelf from famine and his babes to fhield.

Now midnight from her fummit had declined,
When fleep (on a bare ftone my head reclin'd)
Receding foftly from my waking frame,   665
Op'd on the ambient gloom my vifual beam,
A flood of radiance thro' the ftable flows,
And the brown ftraw with golden tincture glows.
I rife; and lo! an Infant naked lies,
Bedew'd with rays, and ether's richeft dyes; 670
Whom on her poor ftraw-couch the mother maid
Brought forth, exempt from anguifh and of aid.
The Afs and Ox on either fide admire,
Forget their food, and with their heads afpire.
The Mother felf with brightnefs glad appears, 675
Her knees bend low, her eyes diffolve in tears;
With hands directed to the fuffus'd fkies,
Her new-born babe of drap'ry bare fhe eyes,
Like to the ftars appears the Virgin's form,
Their luftre pallid with a gufhing ftorm,   680
When the dark ether roaring Boreas fhrouds,
Expanding wide the rain-diftended clouds.
                                        Sheep's

Sheep's-fkins I ftrew for cloths of purple dye,
And forks invers'd a cradle's place fupply;
More ufeful things and want the night withold, 685
The birth demanding fcenes fuperb with gold.

Nor yet night's gloom had chas'd the blazing day,
When thronging fhepherds urge their rapid way;
The door with flow'rs and varied chaplet glows,
And the wild pipe with ruftic numbers flows.   690
With down-caft eyes they feek the facred ftall,
And prone to earth before the Godhead fall.
Struck with amaze I queftion'd how cou'd fame,
Along the fields, the birth fo foon proclaim.
When one thus quickly anfwers my demand; 695
Shepherds are we, and graze the woody land;
Our ufual vigils we nocturnal keep,
To guard from beafts of prey our folded fheep.
What time the world was wrap'd in mid-night
          fhade,
Around our heads a gufhing luftre play'd,   700
And as we tott'ring ftood unnerv'd with fear
This voice was wafted from the void of air:
Mortals, fear not, glad tidings I difplay,
In your confines a God is born this day,
Who fhall reftore (as prophecies relate)   705
Mankind from darknefs to his priftine ftate.
In yonder town, you may behold him laid
His place a ftable, and of ftraw his bed.
The voice our guide, our eyes we throw around,
And view the town flow rifing from the ground, 710
                                        An

An heav'nly band, with wings of various dyes,
On clouds incumbent float along the fkies ;
And when they rang'd the fkies in thrice three
        throngs,
And thrice they harped fweet their feftive fongs,
In a full chorus, fwift the poles they wing,   715
And ether's plains with their applaufes ring.
This faid : amaz'd, they gaze the Infant's face,
And his bright charms with eyes and fouls embrace.
Such floods of beams gufh from the Infant's frame,
That overflow the ftable with a flame.   720
So when the rofe unfolds her crimfon leaves,
The fun burns brighter with her new-born blaze
Or when the vernal day burfts from the eaft,
Of melting light it fheds a rofeat wafte.

Tho' we the Godhead in the Babe confefs'd 725
And without food and aid a God is bleft;
Yet, as an offspring of a mortal Dame,
He breath'd the mortal in a mortal frame ;
Inhal'd the moifture of his mother's breaft,
And fhe his Infant-limbs with drap'ry dreft :   730
More, to fulfil the rites our law prefcribes,
He bore the circumcifion of our tribes ;
We call him JESUS, mindful of the name,
An angel bore, wing'd by the Sire fupreme.
To mark his priefthood and his regal race,   735
The nations name him CHRIST in Grecian phrafe,
And tho' no male embrace his mother ftain'd ;
Beneath her roof, fhe forty funs remain'd.
        I   The

The royal Maid to her luftration haftes,
And with her Infant tends to Salem's gates ;   740
We bring a pair of turtles to be flain
(Our rites fo order) in the facred Fane.
The prieft by cuftom at the altar waits,
His fnowy robe defcends in flowing plaits,
A mitre of two horns his temples fhrouds   745
And the watch'd fire meanders high in clouds.
A crown of children round the altar ftood,
And from a chalice pour'd the heifer's blood,
Which to the God fupreme the Flamen flew,
To ftop the vengeance to the people due.   750
With hands the fages of the nation prefs'd
The heifer's front, with holy fillets drefs'd.
Their fingers, blufhing with the victim flain,
The priefts the altar lightly thrice diftain :
The altar's flames imbibe a deeper hue,   755
And ruddy drops the feven lamps bedew.
Sprinkled with blood flafhes the ample veil,
Whofe ambient folds myfterious rites conceal.
Finifh'd the rites, the prieft prepares to tafte,
Join'd with his fons, the facrifical feaft.   760
And now proceeds the Virgin humbly mild ;
Her right hand holds the birds, the left her child :
Shall I rehearfe, what figns the heav'nly King
Struck out, that fpoke the Child his true offspring ?
How chill'd the prieft, when he the Infant gaz'd,
                                                765
And what new light about the altar blaz'd ?

                                                He

He aw'd thrice heap'd with frankincenfe the flames,
And thrice the fire above the veffel ftreams:
Yet ftill according to his country's laws
From the flain birds the vital gore he draws,   770
Scatters the plumes and o'er the entrails ftrays,
His face converted to the eaftern blaze;
Then breaks the wings, and on the fubject fire
The crackling entrails into fume expire:
From the burn'd victim grateful vapours rife,   775
And Panchean odours fcent the balmy fkies.

Another fcene infpir'd the breaft with fears;
And awe feiz'd Simeon bent with hoary years,
Than whom, no man among the city's crowd,
With fairer homage, to ftrict juftice bow'd: 780
Th'Almighty SPIRIT of the bending fky
Into hereafter granted him to pry,
And faid, he fhould not ceafe to drink the day,
'Till he the promis'd Saviour fhould furvey.
For worn with age, he would confign to death,   785
Life's painful labours, and his panting breath;
But the fond hope, to view the fource of life,
Gave him to live, and fecond nature's ftrife,
With holy inftinct now diftends his breaft,
And feels, that God now dwells the temple's gueft.
                                                   790

So, when his mafter's fteps attends a hound,
His fenfe of fmelling o'er a length of ground.
A hare detects: with ears erect he ftands,
And fnuffs the gales that brufh the fcented lands.
                    I 2   Then

Then ftarting from the path, he devious ftrays, 795
And traces with his eyes the hare's wild maze.
Along this path, and now o'er that he flies,
And the wide meadows vibrate with his cries.
So, in the fane, exults the rev'rend fage,
And clafps the Infant, with an holy rage :   800
With liquid eyes, big with the pearly tears,
He in thefe words his joyful fenfe declares.

Jehovah-born, almighty Infant, hail,
The fplendid author of this world's great weal !
Thou com'ft to wafh away the people's ftains, 805
With the rich fluid of thy precious veins,
And to their manes ope a liquid way
To the bright realms of eternal day :
Welcome to earth ; now to your words comply,
Father Supreme ! 'tis granted me to die,   810
Now from this body's clofe confinement free,
In peace difmifs me from life's mifery,
Since on me ftreams the Gentiles' light divine,
And the new glory of the Hebrew-line !
Now to the Dame this fond addrefs he pays : 815
Who can thy mien affume or fing thy praife ?
To thee what thanks can pour the fickly earth,
Who brought falvation by this happy birth ?
Yet ftill this fruitage of ethereal love
To many Hebrews fhall deftructive prove.   820
The time approaches, when your heart fhall feel,
Oh fad and joylefs time ! the dolorous fteel :

When

When you, unhappy, fhall be join'd to woe,
And Jordan's troubled wave retorted flow,
Then late and heavy fhall arife the day,   825
And meafure with fick looks its pallid way :
The earth herfelf fhall joy to leave her pole ;
And thro' the void, her weight rejecting roll.
This faid, as mers'd in fudden fleep and tir'd,
He clos'd his eyes, and fmiling foft expir'd.   830
All ftare aghaft ; but from amazement free,
We ftand ferene vers'd in the fkies decree :
Yet painful we revolve the fage's word,
That to the mother points the naked fword :
Anxious to know to whom the child fhould be 835
The fatal origin of mifery.
But time too foon the dubious truth reveals
The prefent fcene the menac'd woes details :
Unlefs for us fome deeper wounds remain,
And ills are pointing with acuter pain.   840

About that time, three Kings forfook their ftate,
And hither bent their fteps from extreme eaft.
And to the Infant ample prefents bore,
Myrrh, breathing frankincenfe, and golden ore :
The fphere revolving thro' its ftarry figns,   845
Proclaim'd a Monarch born in our confines ;
Whofe fceptre fhould the fkies and earth obey,
And whom to fee they march'd a tedious way.
A ftar hung in the fkies, a faithful guide,
Illum'd their paffage with a blazing tide.   850

I 3

So,

So, when our Sires abandon'd Egypt's toil,
And fought, thro' dreary wilds, the promis'd foil;
A fiery globe preceded them by night,
And on them gufh'd a liquid wafte of light.
The town obtain'd, they bent, without delay,   855
To Tetrarch-Herod's gate their glowing way:
Their meffage told, thinking, as he was King,
The royal Babe to be his own offspring.
Struck with amaze, with chilling fear unman'd,
Left this ftrange royal heir fhould feize the land,
Herod difpatch'd a nuncio in hafte,   861
To bid the bards the royal prefence wait;
Of the new-born Infant the time, the place,
He curious afk'd, his country, and his race.
Beth'lem, they cried, the birth by fame fhould boaft,
                                              865
Whofe crown and deeds fhould fway the ftarry hoft.
Now more confounded in the maze of cares,
He ftrove to fmoothe his brows and veil his fears;
And to difmifs the eaftern Kings with grace,
He thus reply'd with well diffembled face.   870

Monarchs, the caufe which hither urg'd your way
Has always on us ftream'd hope's fmiling ray.
No dearer object than this child can rife,
Whom prophets promis'd, infpir'd by the fkies.
The city Beth'lem borders on this place,   875
Of ftructure old, and peopled by our race.
Thither, to feek the royal Babe, contend,
And when confefs'd, to us a nuncio fend,

                    5   That

That to the Child our homage we may pay,
And in our gifts our regal fenfe difplay;   880
Such joyful words dropt from the Tyrants tongue,
While round his heart a dreary envy clung:
Mad, that Heav'n's Monarch, whom the ftars obey,
Sould dwell on earth and bear a regal fway.

The ftar beheld, the Eafterns feek the town, 885
Of Ifraelites environ'd with a crown.
Now on the roof the ftar's long travels ceafe,
And all the cot ftreams dimpling with a blaze.
So, when the death of kings, or wars dread rage,
Fierce comets from the wrathful fkies prefage;
    890
Behind them, flows a length of livid beams,
Which on the frighted globe with horror gleams.
Of pomp exempt, and ftor'd with want's parade,
Into the low-roof'd cot the Monarchs lead,
Who rob'd in textur'd gold and crimfon veft, 895
Proftrate on earth the Infant-God confefs'd.
While next the Dame thus bow'd the royal band,
Each pour'd his treafures with a lib'ral hand.
Before the door, in long proceffion, wait
A courtier train, who fwell the pomp of ftate: 900
While fteeds with coverings glowing to behold,
Paw the rent earth, and champ the polifh'd gold.

Their homage paid, exulting they purfue -
The ftar, its progrefs ftain'd with blazing hue.
        I 4   Advis'd

Advis'd to flie the regal city's gate,   905
Far on the right they roam from Herod's feat;
Who, furious with the fraud, an army calls,
And secret sends to Bethlem's hated walls,
To seize by night when all creation rests,
And slay the babes that suck their mothers breasts;
                                                      910
That in the infant-crowd the royal heir
Might fall a victim, and the carnage share.
But o'er my sleep, hover'd a voice by night,
To shun the bloody scene and haste my flight.
The Dame and child convey, (the voice exclaims)
                                                      915
And seek the Nile which parts in fourteen streams;
There dwell, (nor is that land remote from thee)
Nor thence remove, until recall'd by me:
For Tetrach-Herod with ambition wild,
Now meditates the slaughter of the child.   920
I rise, and to the Dame the speech reveal:
Her limbs grow languid, and her visage pale;
Runs here and there while haste retards her flight
And scarce can trust the shadow of the night.
There she, unhappy, felt the sword of woe   925
And all the pain that can from torments flow.

We go and soon depart the trait'rous town,
And plunge in devious paths with horror brown.
Thro' palmy woods and old Elusa tend,
And high Idume's panting brow ascend.   930
                                               Mapsa

Mapfa receives us famous for her oil
Which parts the Afian from the Libyan foil ;
We enter now great Pharaoh's large domain,
On whofe fpread fields defcends no foft'ring rain ;
Whofe natives found the ether's vivid force,   935
The ftars, the lunar orb, and folar courfe.
Along ftrange floods we glide, ftrange mountains
        fcale,
And near to towns with turrets pointed fail.
Anthedon's banks we trace, whofe gentle waves
Smoothly reflect Papyrus' fhrubby leaves.   940
We ftart with horror at each whifp'ring air,
Fearful and anxious for our infant-care.
The groves bend to the child their boughs of bays,
And zephyrs figh with balmy breath his praife ;
The rocks and mountains, to exprefs their love, 945
Their craggy brows with feftive lightnefs move.
A vocal fignal of their joy to raife,
The floods fatigue their ftreams in varied maze ;
With gentle lapfe they tinkle down their bed,
Now over rocks their roaring water fpread.   950
To caft a deeper azure on the ftream
The rocks with moffy vefture verdant gleam.
Chiefly the birds, who dwell the banks along,
Inrich the ambient gales with liquid fong :
Of fuch foft notes pleas'd with the theme and caufe,
                                                 [955
With founding wings they lengthen their applaufe ;
Rejoicing at her God's approach, the earth
Expands her lap, and pours a verdant birth.

                                        The

The herbs wide shed abroad their rich perfume
And nods Amaracus its shady gloom.   960
The Nile, whose head retires with secret pride,
Proclaims God's presence with exulting tide ;
Riding on waves, he spouts sublime in air
His secret springs, and all his sands appear ;
Where channels meet, or ways confront to ways 965
Unknown to chuse, lost in the doubtful maze :
A winged Beauty, from his bright abode,
With sword and shield, illumes the proper road ;
Lest, straying, into devious paths we run,
Into the murd'rous hands, we toil to shun.   970
His flaming back blush'd with cerulean dyes,
The same his form, who left his native skies,
Forbad the divorce, that I once design'd,
And chas'd the jealous darkness of my mind.
Our journey, others in the air pursue,   975
The child protecting from nocturnal dew :
Above his head, they cluster into rings,
And form a canopy with out-spread wings.
Thro' perplex'd travels bold we coast the shore,
Whose vicine fields with cymbals wildly roar.   980
Tho now the Babe inhales a foreign air,
We yet to Egypt's farthest part repair ;
Fearful we dread, where safety largely reigns,
And think no place too far, from Herod's plains.
Displeas'd we flie Hermopolis' proud seats,   985
And Thebes seems dang'rous with her hundred
            gates.
Our travels Memphis to a period brings,
Illustrious for the tombs of Egypt's Kings :
                        A friend

A friend receives us in his cottage-feat,
Indeed, an humble, but a fafe retreat.   990
Along the coafts, where Nile expands his ftream,
In fadly-folemn dirge, fings mournful fame,
That Bethlehem's town deplores her babe-offspring,
(Slain by the mandate of Paleftine's King)
Who innocent in vain, with tender cries,   995
Ceafe with their lives to breathe the luftred fkies.
Preffing her child, the mother-maid turns pale,
Her mind ftruck with the image of the tale;
For fancy brings the bloody fcene to view ;
The tears, the flaughter from the nation drew : 1000
The matron's fhrieks, that pierce the pitying air,
While thro' the town, they roam'd in wild defpair :
The earth, with vital purple, that abounds;
And houfes, ftreaming with infantile wounds.
So when a ftorm o'er heedlefs fhepherds reigns, 1005
Low'rs on the woods and fweeps along the plains;
Struck with the rattling tempeft, expire the lambs,
And the fame fate attends their bleating dams.
So infant-carnage on the pavement ftrew'd,
The forum ftain'd and chok'd the ghaftly road. 1010
Hence fadly true appears the Prophet's ftrain,
Of many fhou'd the infant prove the bane :
The flaught'ring day gleams yet in fancy's eye,
And from the childlefs mothers draws the figh.
Nor long, the author of the barb'rous deed,   1015
Surviv'd the children he ordain'd to bleed ;
For foon his limbs with foul corrofion feiz'd,
He died unpity'd, as he liv'd unprais'd.

                                                Soft

Soft o'er my fleep again the image glides
And bids me leave Nile's monfter-bearing tides. 1021
Back to their country, mindful of the way,
The mother and her infant I convey.
You may defire to know his tender cares ;
Or did his wifdom far excell his years .
Or did he, rip'ning into rofy bloom,   1025
In infant fports, his infant days confume ?
But fhou'd I, to the wonders fketch'd, engage
To draw the portrait of his buding age,
Unequal to the tafk my voice wou'd fail   -
And fhrouding night the day from Ether fteal.
How oft' did we, unnerv'd with chilling fear 1030
Words, more than mortal, from the infant hear :
In ftaring horror loft, how oft have view'd
His tender frame, with facred fire bedew'd :
While from his hair drop'd fparks of liquid blaze
                                                  1035
And to fublime his mien, Heav'n fhower'd its rays.
When to his Sire he pour'd his private pray'r,
How glow'd his words, how blaz'd his raptur'd air !
His tender mother, as fhe plied the loom,
Oft faw celeftials foft invade the room ;   1040
To foothe the child, appear in human forms,
Improve with ftudious labour all his charms
In wild rotations revel on the wing,
And fhade him with the product of the fpring.
Yet fweetly mild he yielded to our fway,   1045
And all our words was ready to obey.

                                        Till

Till rip'ning time his vigour fhou'd improve,
To fpread his Father's glory and his love.

No figns divulg'd him to the public ear,
Till he of life attain'd the twice fixth year.   1050
His virtue then impatient to fubfide,
Spreads o'er Judea's town a radiant tide.
Religious to our tribes fhines out a day,
Therefore to this great town I bend my way ;
The royal maid departs her fweet abode,   1055
Her child attends, companion of her road.
The homage paid, our travels we repeat,
Fond of retiring to our humble feat ;
Our wearied fteps the folar beams illume,
And o'er the fkies night cafts a pitchy gloom, 1060
Before the abfence of the child we fpy,
Who filent fled his mother's guardian eye.
'Mid friends we trace the fugitive with pain,
And the road's vocal, with his name, in vain.
From the fad mother gufhes faft the tear,   1065
And down her iv'ry neck wild flows her hair :
The confus'd locks her neck's pure whitenefs grace,
And tears fublime the beauties of her face.
Thus foft Amaracus in its Veftal urn
Whom rains deform, and raging tempefts fpurn,
                                             1070
Hangs down its flow'ry head, but foon regains
Its tow'ring pride and frefh with odours reigns.
With me reluctant, the fad mother ftrays
And thro' the town, we fought the boy three days ;
                                             The

The fourth day fhines, at laft in fervent pray'r 1075
Our hopes we fix, and to the Fane repair,
The portal trod, when we the child furvey,
(Of all his future pow'r the firft effay)
Rehearfing fervent, 'mid the prieftly throng,
Of each infpir'd Bard the raptur'd fong.   1080
Afking the page's obfcure fenfe, in vain ;
And fheding luftre on each myftic ftrain.
The vaulted temple with applaufes rung,
To hear fuch language from an infant's tongue,
By art untaught, without experience fage,   1085
A man in wifdom, and a child in age.
Nor lefs enchanting was his youthful frame ;
To view him, crowds, of fight infatiate, came ;
His rofy looks exhal'd an heav'nly air
Mild beam'd his eyes, and golden flow'd his hair ;
                                              1090
His budding childhood had fuch pleafing pow'r
Nor yet unfolded blufh'd his youthful flow'r.
Frefh drops of light gufh'd from his rolling eyes,
Bright as a ftar new rifing in the fkies;
Caught, with his beauty nature fmil'd ferene, 1095
For breathing loves refulted from his mien.
Thus fhines Narciffus fweet, above the flow'rs,
Which an uncultur'd field promifcuous pours,
When thro' his op'ning foliage he difplays
His purple head, and fhines with crimfon blaze. 1100
So beams an em'rald, azure to behold,
Inchas'd with filver, or in burnifh'd gold.

                                        From

From this firſt ſcene ſparks of envy roſe,
And for the boy ſtruck out a train of woes;
For malice ſeiz'd the Sages' hearts that hour, 1105
Who rag'd to view, and fear'd his growing pow'r.
Hence now the wrath, that thro' the town proceeds,
And hence the flames, that urge to bloody deeds.
Of omens full, the youth I oft implor'd,
Frugal of life, to fly the hoſtile ſword; 1110
But mountain tow'rs lye veil'd as ſoon by light,
And blazing ſummits burn obſcur'd by night,
As virtue can, forgetful of a name,
Evade the plauſive voice of plumy fame.

Of all his actions, none more rous'd their rage,
Then when ſix luſtres had matur'd his age. 1116
The ſtream obedient to his pow'r divine,
Deep bluſh'd, transfigur'd into roſy wine.
About that time a friend, by blood allied,
In holy marriage gave his virgin-child; 1120
With us the youth was call'd, a welcome gueſt,
To ſhare at once and grace the nuptial feaſt.
While round the genial board the Nobles lay,
And with the feaſt indulg'd the bridal day,
The menial train in wild confuſion roam, 1125
And whiſp'ring murmurs eccho thro' the dome:
That the broad caſks an empty ſpace confine,
Void of the cauſe of mirth, the gen'rous wine.
Touch'd with the fortune of the wedded fair,
My ſpouſe implor'd her ſon the wants to hear. 1130

He

He feem'd difturb'd, but foon inclin'd to aid,
Won by his mother's vows, the bridal maid.
The train he orders fix large urns to fill,
With water flowing from a gurgling rill.
Soon as the ftream was offer'd to his view,   1135
Into a blufh it chang'd its pallid hue.
Bewilder'd with the change, our eyes we roll,
And quaff for water pure the purple bowl.

Lo! of his infancy a flight portrait,
And of his Deity the firft effay,   1140
Nor is there caufe his other deeds to name ;
By them this country is extoll'd by fame.
But, if you wifh to hear a fuller ftate,
He can the beft (regarding John) relate,
Who prefent view'd each glorious wonder blaze,
A true attendant on his Mafter's ways.   1146
While a lefs glorious, but a pleafing care,
My fteps confin'd to wait my wedded fair.

Jofephus tir'd, in filence feeks a feat.
Your Hero's tales, thus Pontius cries, complete :
                                                 1150
What's his Religion ; for if truth I hear ;
The Syrian tribes one God alone revere :
Eternal, fpringing from no human caufe ;
Nor houfhold Gods find altars by their laws.
Th' unfinifh'd feries of your God detail,   1555
And all his portents, known to you, unveil.

                                                 Weak

Weak for the tafk, the Sage's ftrength retires,
And you, his fubftitute, his wifh requires.
Thus Pontius faid : while o'er the crowded train
Silence expands its mute and folemn reign : 1560

End of the Third Book.

K

ARGUMENT to the Fourth Book.

John the Evangelift attempts, at the inftance of Pilate, to give an idea of the nature of God, the eternal birth of Chrift, the proceffion of the Holy Ghost from the Father and the Son; the Trinity of the Persons, and the Unity of the God-head. He then defcends to the creation of the Angels, the rebellion of fome of them, and the formation of Man. Next follows an account of the Impatience of the Souls of the Righteous for the coming of the Redeemer to deliver them from their prifon. The birth, preaching, and baptifm of John the Baptift. He clofes his narrative with that part of Chrift's life, which fpeaks him a God, wherein, among many other miracles, he recites the refufcitation of Lazarus, the Widow's fon, and Ruler's daughter; the calling and chufing of the Apoftles and Difciples, together with the feeding of the multitude in the Defert, and Chrift's fafting and being tempted in the Wildernefs.

THE

THE

CHRISTIAD.

BOOK IV.

TO none inferior in a beauteous face,
  Where youthful revels ev'ry rofy grace,
The youth declines the tafk with decent pains,
Feigns an excufe, and filent ftill remains.
Launching at length from this terreftrial fpace,   5
The man abforpt in wonders' cluft'ring maze;
His foul wings ether, and afcends fublime,
Where hofts celeftial tread the ftarry clime;
There quaffs the finer air, the liquid blaze,
And on the God with am'rous eyes delays.   10
The queen of birds from humble earth thus fprings,
And winding ether foars on plaufive wings,
Conceals her airy paffage in the clouds,
And darting on, the neigb'ring fun beholds;
Undazzled dares on his bright fource to gaze,   15
And with a ftedfaft eye inhale his rays.
Mean while his filence all the crowd admir'd,
And mov'd him if in death or fleep retir'd:
The rapture fled, he thus the Chief addrefs'd,
While a long figh rofe heavy from his breaft.   20

       In

In the beginning the Almighty Sire,
Nature's fole fource, held o'er all an empire,
Struck out no ftars, the ether to adorn ;
Produc'd no world as yet, nor was time born :
The azure plains no ftreaming lights o'erflow'd, 25
Whatever then exiftence had, was God.
Where'er he dwelt, himfelf was his own fpace,
And what contain'd him, was his own embrace.
He had an only Son, no Goddefs born,
Nor new from mortal womb inhal'd the morn, 30
But in his Sire's eternal mind conceiv'd,
Th'eternal Son a wond'rous birth receiv'd ;
No human limbs his facred form confin'd,
But pure and fpiritual as his Sire's mind.
The WORD in the paternal breaft conceal'd,   35
To the foft air no voice had yet reveal'd.
The WORD almighty from commencement free,
And whofe celeftial reign no end fhall fee ;
From whom the fea and fkies receiv'd their birth,
And who from nothing call'd the verdant earth. 40
The Sire is God, fo is his only Son ;
Two Gods to hold them, yet with caution fhun,
As the fame Godhead in them common flows,
So the two Perfons but one God compofe.
The LOVE, proceeding from the Sire and Heir, 45
We name the SPIRIT, and as God revere.
The FATHER, SON, and GHOST, as God we own ;
Three diftinct PERSONS, and the Godhead ONE.
This Holy Ghoft fans Ether, Earth and Seas,
And all things flourifh by his facred BREEZE.   50
                                         What

What may furprize, the God whom we behold,
Tho' made a man, and human limbs infold,
Now rules Olympus with his Father-God;
Arranging all things with his Godhead's nod;
Unbounded in the narrow wilds of fpace,   55
And prefent totally in ev'ry place.
For God diffus'd fills all creation's plan,
Too fine for touch to feel, or eye to fcan.
So the rich luftre that on the world ftreams,
From the Sun gufhes in full floods of beams: 60
Nor without Phebus glows the fcatter'd blaze,
Nor Phebus reigns without his crown of rays.

What mov'd the God fuch labours to fuftain,
And roam, to death expos'd, from pain to pain;
From its firft caufe I will the theme purfue,   65
And ope the latent profpect to your view.
The heav'nly orbs and earth which you behold
The Lord had fcarce into exiftence roll'd;
The Father made, won with eternal love,
The Spirits, who in his bright regions move;   70
The feather'd train, with the unbodied ghofts,
The fwift celeftials, and the thrice three hofts,
To cull the pleafures, and at large to fhare,
Which he enjoy'd, and his coeval heir.
Some burft at once into a grateful praife,   75
And to their Author God inton'd the lays.
But luft of rule (who unreveng'd could bear?)
The greater number fwell'd with regal care,

Urg'd

Urg'd them to grafp the throne with dazzl'd mind,
Their wifhes impotent, their fury blind.   80
But full of wrath, God bids his cohorts rife,
And hurl the crowd inglorious from the fkies ;
Baffl'd their fcheme, they lie in caves deprefs'd,
O'er which eternal night and horror reft.

    Hence man's creation ; to whofe ample fway 85
Jehovah gave the earth and azure fea.
The brute creation bends to his domain,
The tribes that glide with fins along the main;
The feather'd crowd, that wing the airy fpace,
And all the dreary mountains favage race ;   90.
To him and to his line the feats are given
Which once the angel-rebels held in Heav'n.
He faw all nature blooming for his ufe,
Solely prohibited one tree's produce;
But foon enamour'd of the fruitful boughs,   95
And too uxorious toward a preffing fpoufe,
(Herfelf the Serpent's prey) in a fad hour,
He broke the mandate of the fupreme Pow'r.
The fruit prophan'd no fooner by his tafte,
Than He, who pours the ftorm thro' Ether's wafte,
                                                 100
Thro' redd'ning clouds bids claps of thunder break,
And wrathful feems his vengeance to awake,
Which Adam bore, and all his race fhall bear,
That drink the luftre of the folar fphere.
Soon barriers ftop'd the paffage to the fky,   105
And horrid rofe an impious progeny.

                              A group

A group of crimes defil'd the virgin-earth ;
Then fraud and daring luft emerg'd to birth,
Hence to hard toil was human kind betray'd,
Hence fprung fad care, and death his gate difplay'd.
                                                    110
Difeafes ghaftly ftalk'd with pining grief,
Bafe want and famine hopelefs of relief.
Was man obedient, he had felt no care,
But breath'd thro' many years this vital air.
Then man unfkill'd and thoughtlefs rang'd the fields,
                                                    115
Untutor'd in the good, that order yields.
Howe'er they mov'd their God by victims flain,
From ftorms to fhield their flocks, and bladed grain.
Two thoufand years their ftate unvary'd ey'd :
At length God gave his vengeance to fubfide. 120
For in Olympus tho' they found no place,
Yet ftill to civilize the wand'ring race,
The fupreme pow'r refin'd them by advice,
Struck out new laws and modes of facrifice.
Our tribes he form'd ; the knife to mark them glow'd
                                                    125
With blood, that from the circumcifion flow'd,
Then with the future truth the bards diftent
On the rejoicing world their numbers fpent ;
The time was rolling, when the forbidd'n fky
Should to the pious wide fpontaneous fly.   130

    Beneath earth's circle, in a dark retreat,
The pious ghofts, mean while, devoutly wait
                    K 4   The

The purple dawn of the redeeming days,
Once the fond fubject of prophetick lays.
With hands uprear'd, they beg the fupreme Sire135
To put a period to his burning ire,
Nor, for the devious fault of one, deface
From the expanded earth the human race.
Spare, Almighty! fpare, (was the gen'ral cry)
Give us at length to claim the promis'd fky,   140
From whofe bland light, thefe regions long detain;
Nor have you on us life beftow'd in vain.
But if fome trace of former faults remains,
Unlock your fprings, and lave benign the ftains.
Oh what celeftial fhall Heav'n's moifture pour, 145
And kind refrefh us with the holy fhow'r?
Drop dew ye orbs, that wind the blue ferene;
Aid us ye clouds, diftent with facred rain.
Come chiefly you, whom ages wifh'd to fee,
To whom with awe hell bends the trembling knee.
                                                        150

Jehovah born; bright as the dew defcend;
And hither fwift from ftarry ether tend;
Break down the gates, that block the facred way,
And, cloth'd with pow'r, glide from eternal day.
Such was the invocation of their ftrains;   155
To which, the potent Sire touch'd with their pains,
And full the Angel—damage to repair,
From high Olympus bent a fav'rite ear.
Tho' at his nod Heav'n's gate might open wide,
Or fome wing'd minftrel from Olympus glide, 160
Free the fad captives from the gloomy plains,
And waft their fouls to'ether's ftarry fanes;
                                                        His

His Godhead still to print on human kind,
And with a glorious act, their love to bind,
He sent his Son from his ethereal throne,   165
Made man, for man's transgression to atone:
But unconfess'd on earth, lest he should stand,
Or be expell'd an exile from the land,
Himself proclaiming God's own Progeny,
Forbidd'n by the statutes of the country,   170
He sent a Bard his advent to proclaim,
A native of these regions, John by name,
Whom to Zacharias Eliza bore,
Sterile her womb, her head with old age hoar.
He lab'ring with a Prophet's sacred throws   175
To the glad world the God incarnate shews.
In infancy he from the world retir'd,
With love of woods, and brooks, and mountains fir'd:
His mansion are deep caves with horrors rude,
Uncultur'd shrubs bear fruitage for his food;   180
Or hollow trunks their honey wild distill,
And for his cup clear rolls the lucid rill.
Religious to the sight his frame appears,
Rough vested with a camel's shaggy hairs.
Yet tho' a solitaire he pours his strains   185
To mountains, sandy shores and desert plains;
But woodland shades can't quench fair virtue's beam,
The vicine towns soon catch the Hermit's fame;
On him, as wafted from the skies, they gaze,
(The theme divine of Sibyl's raptur'd lays)   190
Who should, from shades o'ercast with dreary night,
Translate the human world to fields of light.

                                        And

And now full crowds invade his wild retreat,
His race demanding and bufinefs of his ftate :
Was he the ONE, who from the fkies fhould glide
                                                    195
To fuccour wretched man at once, and guide ?
He cry'd, beneath his fylvan bow'r reclin'd,
Hear and rejoice, you race of human kind ;
Long have you ftray'd imbrown'd with night's dark
        hue ;
The light now dawns, you wifh'd fo oft to view ;200
But fpare to view me as the promis'd flame,
(For undeferving honours I difclaim.)
As Lucifer precedes, with flender ray,
The matin fun, and faint announces day :
So I foretel your flood of radiance fhines,   205
And God himfelf fhall vifit your confines ;
The God fhall on your mortal plains be feen,
Confefs'd a mortal in his frame and mien :
At his approach your feftal joy difplay,
With blufhing carpets ftrew his facred way ;   210
Your verdant fields with flow'ry chaplets drefs,
And in your holy pomp the God confefs.
Righteous, mean while, and moral be your fame,
And let me lave your follies in the ftream.
With the celeftial Spirit, he will clean   215
Guilt's firft contagion, and each finful ftain :
Then the whole world with wonder fhall behold
Itfelf tranfigur'd to an age of gold.

                                        Thefe

Thefe words pronounc'd, the neighb'ring towns
    defcend,
Where Jordan's ftreams along the vallies bend ; 220
The fkies imperial they for peace addrefs,
And all their faults fpontaneoufly confefs.
With hollow palm the Baptift fcoops the waves,
And with the ftream their naked bodies laves.
The God in private mixes with the band,   225
And for luftration feeks fair Jordan's ftrand ;
That he might (vefted with a mortal frame)
The rites perform, that man's attention claim.
That after ages need not blufh to fhare
The folemn duties, which employ'd his care. 230
Soon as the Lord had 'mid the water fhone,
The Baptift's vifual orbs the Godhead own,
And while his hands are rear'd to Ether's beams,
His fuppliant knees comprefs the wond'ring ftreams.
Abforp'd with rev'rence he declines to fhed 235
The luftral moifture on his facred head :
But paffive foon to the divine command,
He laves his body with a trembling hand :
With luftre purpled, Jordan's ftreams appear,
And peals of thunders rend th'ambient air :   240
Lo ! from the fkies a Dove directs his flight,
His wings with gold, his back with filver bright,
Sloping his blazing courfe, his plumage fpreads,
And breathes his holy influence on their heads.
The Father's lays along Olympus run,   245
Impaffion'd with the love he bears his Son.
                                            Mean

Mean while a youthful band of Heav'n's bright
    sphere,
On wings incumbent press the crowded air :
Are charg'd with drapery of a snowy hue,
In act their Sovereign's mandate to pursue ;   250
Quickly to dry his darling Son's moist frame,   .
And tresses, droping with the sacred stream.

The God when he had shar'd the holy rite,
Forsakes the tumid flood, and steals from sight.
At whose recess the Baptist pours this strain,   255
To all the banks throng'd with a num'rous train :
The God is come, he dwells on earth, behold ;
By all desir'd and oft by me foretold,
Mild as a lamb, on incens'd altars slain,
Who by his blood shall wash each human stain ;260
A willing victim to his Father fall ;
Then own your God, and on your Master call.

The Bard no longer haunts the wilds and groves ;
But now from town to town incessant roves ;
Distilling on the ear in raptur'd strains ;   265
The promis'd God treads earth, the Godhead reigns !
But few believ'd till God, himself proclaim'd
By deeds, above the reach of mortals, fam'd.
For thirty years the Lord himself conceal'd
His deeds obscure, his Godhead unreveal'd :
But first he calls twelve friends among his train
To share his fortune and laborious pain.   270
Nor think he fix'd on them of lineage great,
Or taught by nature, or by art deceit :

                              His

His choice were men, whofe veins roll'd vulgar gore,

275

Of manners fimple, and in fortune poor.
Among us five from fmall Bethefda came,
Employ'd to lure the fifhes from the ftream
With guileful hook; or launch into the main,
Where fcaly fhoals enrich the wat'ry plain.   280
When he defir'd, we fhould attend his lore,
I was my nets repairing on the fhore.
My brother James obferv'd with watchful eye,
Lafhing the fhore with panting life, the fry.
Andrew and Peter near us plough'd the ftream; 285
Brothers, the fame their thought and art the fame.
Philip likewife, by blood to me ally'd
Left at the call his nets and briny tide:
Thomas and Thaddeus next increas'd the train,
And Simon fprung from Galilean Cane,   290
With the like art, whofe breaft was wont to glow,
Fond of the flood and to the fifh a foe.
For Alpheus James by blood to Simon dear,
Before this time had join'd the focial care.
Behold a lift of an inglorious race,   295
Names harfh to hearing and of accent bafe !
Nor we alone appear of horrid mien;
Three alfo at the fummons join'd the train.
Matthew, who glories in no better line ;
Whofe hoary treffes next to Peter's fhine,   300
The lift Bartholomew and Judas fill,
Judas, the horrid inftrument of ill.

Scarce

Scarce can I count the wonders which my eyes
Gaz'd on, or ears imbib'd with deep furprize,
In a fhort fpace, for only three years roll'd,   305
Since he embrac'd me in his chofen fold.
Who fhall this ocean of his deeds effay ?—
I will, however, your inftance to obey,
Tho' hard the tafk, exhibit to your view,
And draw, from crowds of progenies, a few. 310
To tell his actions therefore I'll forbear,
Wrought in the vicine towns,which reach'd your ear.
For all this coaft with foaring fame proceeds,
Illuftrious with the glory of his deeds.
Has not Bethania's vales with palms embrac'd, 315
Her ruler lately ey'd from death releas'd ?
On whofe remains, in darkfome tomb outfpread,
The fun four days his mourning influence fhed.
What numbers has he call'd from death's drear gate,
How many fnatch'd from all-devouring fate ? 320
Equal's the tafk, to tell, when Boreas roars,
The waves that frothe, the fands that ftrew the
        fhores,
As to rehearfe the throngs, with languid breath,
Who morbid fought him, and return'd with health.
What groups of blind, of deaf-born men, what
        fwarms,   325
Whofe ears ne'er drunk, nor lips drop'd vocal
        charms !
The lame to feek him bend their limping way ;
And carriers thofe of movelefs limbs convey :
                                        With

With ulcerous bodies fome polluted glow,
And putrid juices from their members flow.   330
Thofe guileful draughts in their fwoll'n frames inftil,
Whofe thirft nor ftreams can quench, nor human
      fkill;
While thefe their limbs, with trembling palfy weak,
Beneath the burthen of their bodies fhake.
In fome the fever rages thro' their veins;   335
Some lie, their members torn with unknown pains.
In others while difturbing furies rife,
The mind deftroy, and redden in the eyes.
The fad difeafes fhun his holy fight,
Or from his touch wing fwift their baleful flight.
                                340

The patient hence exalts his healthful head,
And bounds rejoicing from his fickly bed.
And hence his walks contain a morbid train,
The road, the forum, and the facred Fane.
The dead felt not his power, 'till Sidon's land 345
Gave him to lofty Naim with his band.

   A range of lights in long proceffion flames,
And thro' the town a dewy fadnefs ftreams.
Now on his bier the mournful caufe appears,
A beauteous youth dead in his bloom of years, 350
The ghaftly white fpread o'er his pallid face,
Blots out the crimfon of each youthful grace.
So prefs'd by oxen coming from the plains,
The Hyacinth refigns his purple ftains.
                                    Or

Or thus the rose, crop'd by some virgin, lies 355
'Mong shaggy thorns obscure, decays, and dies.
The wretched mother, with her sorrow wild,
Roams thro' the city, and laments her child.
Sanguine with mangl'd cheeks her hands appear,
And down her back dishevell'd flows her hair. 360
Touch'd with her mien, and wounded by her cries,
The matrons swarm, and fill with shrieks the skies.
The men deplore by soft compassion led
The childless mother and her widow'd bed.
When the God saw the corse with paleness fade,
                                                    365
And the soft down the youthful features shade;
He bids the tears to cease, the pomp to stand,
And moving soothes the body with his hand.
Life moves the corse : and wond'rous to the eyes,
Amid the crowd the youth is seen to rise ;   370
Forsakes his bier and with a soft embrace,
His parent clasps, and bids her sorrow cease.

A few moons after, he from death's drear shade
To blooming life restores a beauteous maid;
All vital heat and breath forsook the fair,   375
And flying vanish'd into common air.
Jairus the Virgin's sire the wonder ey'd,
Jairus rich, facund, and the people's pride.
Touch'd with a friend's distress he bids the stream
To wine transvers'd assume a rosy flame.   380
The sun begun to shoot his western rays,
When on a mountain plac'd, the Lord surveys

                                                    Of

Of males and females a promiscuous knot,
Themselves forgeting, and their cares forgot ;
Who of his person fond, forsake their home,   385
And with him rush into the desert's gloom.
With tender pity mov'd he here delays ;
For on their fasts three suns had spent their blaze ;
No corn stood near, nor towns to purchase meat ;
Nor was the fruitage then matur'd by heat.   390
By chance a boy is found, who five loaves bore,
And too small fishes, his nutricious store,
Which his fond mother, to support his ways,
Involv'd in balmy grass and myrtle leaves.
But what were these to feed a num'rous train ?—395
And now his friends sad with despair complain ;
His little senate he to soothe them forms,
And into hope, their fears thus mildly charms.
Tho' in the subject vale vast numbers stray,
None shall retire unsatisfy'd this day.   400
Then to the ground without delay he falls
And on his Sire supreme thus rev'rend calls :
Hail mighty Parent ! by whose suns and rains
All things with food the fecund earth sustains ;
If once, in wilds, you fed the Hebrew race,   405
By sheding banquets from the heav'nly space ;
If to no seed creation owes its birth,
And once were nothing ether, seas, and earth ;
Propitious hear, dire famine chase away,
Nor let so many thousands be her prey.   410
He ceas'd to pray ; and on the grassy plain,
Outspreads, with hunger keen, the num'rous train,

L.   Then

Then placid cuts the loaves with niceſt care,
And ſtrictly deals to each his ſcanty ſhare.
Five thouſand men for food then preſs'd the green;
                                                    415
When lo ! (heard with ſurprize, with wonder ſeen)
The little portions in their hands embrac'd,
Augment and ſwell into a gen'rous feaſt.
The gnawing rage of hunger now ſedate,
With copious liquids and mirac'lous meat;   420
Of ample ſize twelve baſkets ſcarce contain
The copious ſcraps that of the feaſt remain.

    Another wonder lately was diſplay'd ;
A tree diffuſes wide a leafy ſhade :
Beneath it oft the weary traveller ſtood   425
And drain'd the fruitage of their ſparkling flood.
Imbrown'd with duſt our Hero paſs'd that way,
And ſought to quench his thirſt, the blooming
          ſpray
In vain: The tree with barren branches waves,
And ſpends its juices in luxurious leaves.   43●
His diſappointment flaſhes on the boughs,
And the tree feels the terror of his vows.
Inſtant I ſaw the tree and branches die,
And the leaves circling in a whirlwind flie.

    Nor to his pow'r leſs ſubject are the ſeas ;   435
The waves, or ſwell, or reſt, as he decrees:
I ſaw fierce Boreas on the billows wild,
Subdue his rage, and at his word breathe mild.
                                        Scarce

Scarce has bright Cynthia thrice her circle roll'd,
Since on the fea a midnight tempeft growl'd : 440
Smooth flow'd the waves, in whifpers blow'd the
        wind,
When firft with nets we fought the fcaly kind.
But foon the waves our fhatter'd bark o'erflow'd,
And death on each contending billow rode.
When lo ! our Chief, whom on the diftant fhore
                                445
We left attentive to the furges roar ;
Comes treading light the furface of the main,
Secure amid the wa'try hurricane.
Our eyes at the approaching figure fade,
Doubtful to judge it folid or a fhade.   450
So fwiftly without oars he fkim'd the main
Till he confefs'd himfelf in this foft ftrain :
Whence flow your fears, and why your hope fub-
        fide ?
Hence in my words hereafter ne'er diffide.
He ceas'd, and mounts the bark, the finking prey,
                                455
To the devouring fury of the fea ;
Forbids by nod the raging ftorm to blow,
And free from threats, the furges gently flow.
The ftorm thus hufh'd,with fwifteft oars we glide,
Safely to fhore, along the dimpling tide.   460

The harbour gain'd, an event foon befell,
Wond'rous to view and ftranger ftill to tell ;
                    L 2   The

The Magiſtrates, on our arrival, ſtood
On the green margin of the briny flood,
Claiming, by cuſtom due, the yearly fee,   465
Impos'd on each by ancient Kings decree.
While they delay'd his placid ſpeech to hear,
Chriſt whiſp'ring drop'd theſe words in Peter's ear.
Haſte hence and caſt the line into the ſeas,
And the firſt fiſh the fraudful hook ſhall ſeize,
                                        470
Diſſect; the victim ſoon ſhall drop to view
What ſhall abſolve the debt to Cæſar due.
The Sage obeys: the prize now beats the ſhore
Within whoſe jaws ſparkles the tribute ore.

A riſing horror always writhes my mien,   475
As often as my mind lives o'er this ſcene:
Culling of late ſome fiſh caſt by the flood,
A man of furious mind beſide me ſtood.
His eye-balls, thrown about with wildneſs, gleam'd,
And from his mouth a frothing moiſture ſtream'd:
                                        480
If fame ſings true, a lawleſs Hymen led
His guilty parents to the genial bed.
There joys to taſte forbidden by our rite,
What time the land to mourn the tribes invite,
But they enjoy'd not long their foul delight;   485
The crime commenc'd and ended in one night:
For 'mid his joys the baſe adulterer dies,
And into air his wicked ſpirit flies,
                                When

When urg'd her throes, from ether fhot a flame, ·
And lambent round, confum'd the lab'ring Dame,
                                                490
And was not fnatch'd from her cut womb the birth,
Both had, at once, refign'd their lives in death.
Their brother's orphan child the fifter nurs'd,
Who with the pain due to his parents curs'd, 494
His eyes with light, nor ears with founds were fill'd;
Nor human accents from his lips diftill'd ;
But when arriv'd to youth's vermilion age,
He foam'd with madnefs and infernal rage.
An hundred pefts from Erebus' dark fhade,
On his weak mind an hundred furies prey'd. 500
Thro' his deep throat (who can the tear refrain ?)
They pour their fhouts, and wake their howling pain,
And when chance freed him from his guardian's
            hands,
His irons broken. and his knotted bands,
All fhun'd the fhocking and the foaming fight, 505
And ghaftly fought their roofs with headlong flight.
Thro' devious mazes now he joy'd to roam,
Forgetful of his friends and native home.
Chofe, focial with the brutes, the fylvan gloom,
Lodg'd in fome rocky cave, or mould'ring tomb.
                                                510
Thus poor he rang'd the wilds with haggard eyes,
And with his naked body brav'd the fkies.
This wretched man, his hands faft bound with
            chains,
His friends and kindred led, by cogent means,

Before the Lord; that touch'd with his diftrefs,

515

He might perhaps his mifery redrefs.
But fcorning aid he ftrove his bands to tear;
While his fierce cries afcend the ftarry fphere;
The warrior bull, with cords to altars led,
Thus toffes thro' the town his roaring head. 520
His dewlaps white with foaming rage appear,
And with his horns he wounds the yeilding air.

A fervile crowd with fticks around him glow,
And his back ecchoes with each frequent blow.
While to their gates the vulgar bend their flight,

525

And fafe at diftance view the dang'rous fight:
So rag'd the youth, at length his friends with pain,
Before the God the captive wretch conftrain.
His holy aid they lowly bending fue
To calm his fpirit and his rage fubdue. 530
The pious Chief, with hands rear'd to the fkies,
Invokes his Father to his enterprize:
When lo! a prodigy both ftrange and foul;
Dogs feem to bark and rav'nous wolves to howl.
The furious wretch fuch bellowing clamours pours

535

Loud, as from mountains rufh the headlong fhow'rs.
Should Lake-Velinus burft by chance his bed,
And o'er the vales his ftagnant waters fpread,

Towns

Towns float in waves, an ocean drowns the plains,
And Rome o'erwhelm'd, turns pallid for her fanes.

540

Now cracks are heard as when the fupreme King
His thunder rolls and ether's temples ring.
The noife now emulates the ocean's rage;
Now feigns the clafh, when hoftile fpears engage:
Now rattling chains feem now the ear to wound,

545

And earth and heav'n return the direful found.
While the God chides the horrid fiends delay:
Within the wretch they trembling fue to ftay.
Why, God's true Son, you bid us to retire,
From this man's body fubject to our ire ?   550
Grant us at leaft to invade this briftl'd band;
(A herd of fwine then graz'd befide the ftrand.)
Nor plunge us into gulfs with fhades imbrown'd,
Nor into nether earth's opaque profound.
He nods confent: lo! by the furies feiz'd   555
The fwine rove wild with madd'ning pangs difeas'd,
So rages keenly fharp each inward gueft,
The herd ftray furious and enjoy no reft;
Then headlong plunge into the azure plain,
And in the waves extinguifh life and pain.   560
The youth, mean time, his captive arms unbound,
His weary'd limbs diffufes on the ground,
Biting the earth with proftrate vifage lies,
And as expiring draws the painful fighs.
To whom God's offspring tends, and with his
        hands   565
His eyes difclofes, and his ears expands :

L 4 .   His

His eyes drink light, lo! from his tongue words
    glide,
And in his heart the frequent throbs fubfide.
With Chrift's applaufe, crowds wound the bright
    abode ;
Jehovah born confefs him, and a God.   570

    What can't his pow'r perform ? at his command
We chafe difeafes from the morbid band ;
Sicknefs retires foon from our prefent aid,
And many difappoint death's gloomy fhade;
Nor ftudious art we boaft nor mortal care   575
From painful beds the languid group to rear,
But bid fair health invade the rofy frame,
By calling thrice upon our Mafter's name.
Among the hoft that fought us to be heal'd.
On one alone our invocation fail'd :   580
The more we ftrove to chafe the hellifh gueft,
The fiercer pangs he rous'd within the breaft :
When God affiftance brought, by goodnefs mov'd,
Our little faith in him he difapprov'd ;
Would you from bodies caft fuch fiends ? he cries,
    585

From food abftain and fupplicate the fkies.
Nor fhall this pow'r on you alone be fhed,
But ev'ry one who fhall my glory fpread,
(If his faith ftaggers with no dubious air)
Each wond'rous action may fecurely dare. ·   590
Mountains will change their place at his command,
And headlong rivers with attention ftand.
                            Go

Go then refolv'd in ftable faith confide
And the bright feed of radiant truth fpread wide.
Sprinkle the night-fepulchr'd earth with rays, 595
And be mankind's and offus'd nature's blaze.

Thus having fpoke, feventy men he chofe,
To fhare our labours and to feel our woes.
Yet his heart throb'd with fighing grief replete,
So few the actors and the tafk fo great.   600
The peafant fo, who with affiduous toil,
And hundred ploughs tills his paternal foil:
When the ripe wheat nods yellow to the plain,
And barns wide wait to hide the copious grain,
With fadnefs views his fmall domeftic band, 605
And roams for aid o'er all the vicine land.

How oft men's thoughts and latent cares he told,
Which God alone could poffibly behold.
Our dubious minds, our vain and tacit fears,
He angry echoed in our wond'ring ears.   610
When his foes glow'd with direful vengeance blind,
And dread deftruction labour'd in their mind,
He oft difplay'd their fchemes with ire replete,
And all the fruftrate rancour of their hate.

Nor is the woman's cure unknown to fame, 615
Who twice fix years pin'd with a fanguine ftream.
Exhaufted now with her difeafe's pain,
She fought by touching Chrift her health to gain;
                                                While

While round him youths and rushing people stream,
She mov'd behind and touch'd his robe's extreme.
                                            620

Lo! at her touch her old distemper flies.
And to retire unseen she vainly tries ;
But God soon felt the trembling flying fair,
And with soft counsel fill'd her list'ning ear.
Nor is the time long laps'd, since I have seen 625
The Lord burst either from his mortal mien,
Or bathe his body in such radiant blaze,
As floods the Sun, when he darts down his rays.

These wond'rous acts resulting from his nod,
And others, which I saw, acclaim the God.   630
His mortal nature yet he ne'er forgot,
And willing bore the woes of human lot,
Our model to pursue : for oft at feasts
He mixes chearful with the chosen guests :
In council when the citizens convene,   635
He's often pleas'd to join the civil train :
And when the nation 'gainst him furious rise,
He, as a man, their hate and temple flies,
The caverns seeks, while impotently loud,
The foes assault, shap'd like his frame, a cloud. 640
But when John's recent murder fame had told,
Scarce yet has Sol his annual measure roll'd ;
With whose lop'd head the King distain'd the floor,
His brother's ravish'd spouse urg'd to restore.
The Lord, I mark'd, impatient to recede,   645
From town and crowds sought quick the wood's
        deep shade.
                                            Nor

Nor hell's grim King, bafe foe of human kind,
From right who labours to divert the mind,
Abftain'd his double nature to annoy,
The God to fcorn or manhood to deftroy.   650
Our Chief once fled his friends and waiting band,
And gain'd the fummit of a fhady land.
Twice twenty funs fat on him without food ;
Twice twenty nights their ftarry courfe renew'd.
The Prince of darknefs thought the prefent hour 655
Moft apt his baleful vengeance then to pour.
Firft to his aid he call'd a numerous hoft
From the fad borders of the infernal coaft ;
But when he found his malice vainly fhed,
He fhock'd the horrors of his beaftly head.   660
His hopes of hurting now in words confide,
And from his lips thefe artful accents glide.
I own thy birth divine, thyfelf a God ;
And all things are obedient to thy nod,
Why fuffer famine o'er thy limbs to fpread ? 665
But fudden change thefe ambient rocks to bread.
The God perceives the fraud, and thus replies,
Nor on fole bread my mortal frame relies,
But on my Father, whofe repeated ftrains
Chafe food's defire, and hunger's gnawing pains. 670
He faid ; tho' conquer'd in his firft effay
The foe defifts not, and renews the fray ;
Infults on infults ardently repeats,
And, tho' repell'd, thrice urges his deceits;
With luft of rule now ftrives his mind to fire, 675
And quench with love of praife his pure defire.

                                        So

So when the winds along the ocean roar,
The threat'ning waves lash thick the foaming shore.
But on the rocks when their vain rage they shed,
They glide confounded to their azure bed.   680
To stop the frauds foreseen, the God forbears,
And gives the foe to forge his fruitless snares.
To lead him passive to the Temple's spire
And to rough rocks whose brows in air retire.
Just when the foe with hope delusive smiles,   685
And thinks to reap the harvest of his wiles,
Our Chief begins his Godhead to display,
And drags the lurking mischief into day.
The horse, thus free from his coercive reins,
Ranges at large the broad expanded plains,   690
Joys the pursuing menials to elude,
Now near them moves, now crops the verdant food.
But when they hope the captive steed to seize,
He neighs, high starts and scours the grassy space.
With schemes defeated and with anger fir'd,   695
The foe stalk'd fierce, and from the God retir'd.
Sent from his Sire a thousand Angels wing
The skies, and to their God refreshment bring.

Would you the origin of their hatred know,
Whence the people 'gainst the prisoner glow,   700
They best can tell ; for sure his life's not stain'd
With the foul acts, of which he is arraign'd.
For, of mankind, than he, they must confess,
None better is, more easy of addrefs :

                                              To

To'all his foft indulgence he extends,   705
Beneficent to foes, as well as friends.
Some blame him fuffering thofe, who him annoy,
When, by his nod, he might his foes deftroy.
Along the coafts of Sidon once he ftray'd
A weary trav'ller, in the midnight fhade,   710
Defir'd beneath their roofs his limbs to reft,
But the barbarians heard not his requeft.
We penfive call'd the SUPREME from his feat,
Quick to revenge his SON's inhuman treat.
On the bafe people dart celeftial fire,   715
And caufe their walls in vengeful flames expire.
With indignation at our vows he glow'd,
And for the wicked town with pity flow'd.

Tho' confcious of his foes, he deign'd refort
Their domes, and feek the roofs of bad report; 720
If by advice he might fubdue their pride,
And, taught truth's walk, their paffions might fub-
          fide.
So Zaccheus, Matthew, and a thoufand more
Forfook their former, for a better lore.
Our Chief was led by error, yet who thought   725
This practice charg'd as a contagious fault.
But he to minifter his healing aid
In fearch of patients thro' the city ftray'd ;
Weeping their ftate; from minds, offus'd with night,
He chas'd the clouds, and gave celeftial light. 730
A tafk moft pleafing to the Angel-choir ;
And to their God, the Angels' mighty Sire.
                                        For

For this, he left Olympus' blazing vault
And the glad anthems of the ſky he taught,
When any baſe immortal ſon of earth,   735
To whom the fouleſt crimes refer their birth,
Begins at juſtice's ſhrine, with awe to bend,
And virtuous deeds religiouſly defend;
Joy thrills thro' all the natives of the ſkies,
And Ether rings with their applauding cries. 740
The ſhepherd thus rich in a thouſand ſheep,
Before night ſeals his eyes in balmy ſleep;
Should he imprudent leave, the number told,
But one behind him, of the bleating fold!
Penſive returns, reviſits ev'ry glade,   745
And with his eyes pervades each latent ſhade.
At length he ſpies the fleecy wand'rer ſteal,
In queſt of food, thro' a ſequeſter'd vale.
Claſp'd in his arms forbids his charge to roam
A fugitive, forgetful of her home.   750
His ſweeteſt babes to kiſs their father burn,
And the houſe ſmiles at the loſt ſheep's return.
·Wherefore an ear to female tales he deigns;
For lately paſſing o'er Samaria's plains,
By chance he ſpies approaching him a dame 755
From Sichar's ancient walls to ſcoop the ſtream;
He ſues her ſuppliantly her vaſe to fill,
And taſtes the bounty of the limpid rill,
Who ſonorous rivers and the ſea domains,
And the vaſt globe bedews with copious rains;760
At whoſe command the thirſty crowd to ſave,
Rocks liquid grew and pour'd a bounteous wave.

· Mean

Mean while our wonder fwells, in thought conceal'd;
But, her admonifh'd, and her faults reveal'd,
The Lord delivers from profoundeft night,   765
And laves with beams of never-fading light.
The pious Sires full of parental care,
Oft brought their train of youths and virgins fair,
Their flowing locks with rofeat chaplets crown'd,
Or with foft fillets of green foliage bound ;   770
To have their hearts with love of virtue fir'd,
And their young minds with gen'rous thoughts
        infpir'd.
His infant audience placid he addrefs'd,
And with his touch fo purified the breaft,
That vice in vain might wear her magic charm,
                                        775
And hell, thro' all its reign, to crufh them, arm.

By words and acts he chiefly fhew'd the hate
He bore to minds with tow'ring pride elate :
I and my 'fociates, as our Chief we fought,
Reclin'd our weary limbs befide a grot,   78•
O'er whofe dark gate, an awful elm high weaves
An arch of branches and a wafte of leaves.
Confuming time, we mutually demand,
Who fhould fuperior be among our band ;
Who by our Hero was the moft approv'd,   785
The moft regarded and the beft belov'd :
Soon as he faw us at the grotto's gates
With knitted brows he bids us to relate
The fubject (ftrange to tell) of our difcourfe
And of our clam'rous ftrife the native fource. 790
                                        Our

Our pride subsiding, silent we remain,
So warm was our dispute, the theme so vain.
Then sudden in the midst he leads a child,
Void of ambition, and in desires mild;
None can, says he, ascend the happy skies,   795
But who scorn pride, the love of fame despise;
For them alone, the sky its gates displays,
Who like this child feel not the throbs of praise.
Sooner shall clouds dwell in the saline main,
And fishes live in every verdant plain;   800
In ether's limpid clime trees fix their root,
And in the blue immense their foliage shoot.
Still at my mother's pray'r my blood pale runs
The chiefest honours suing for her sons:
That when the mansions of the skies he gain'd 805
And with his mighty Sire coequal reign'd;
Then next him we on either side might stand.
One on his right, and one on his left hand
Not her, (a mother's fondness sure's no crime)
But us, he sudden views with looks sublime; 810
Justly reproves with better words and brows,
Who prompted with vain art such simple vows.
To crush the proud delights the Pow'r supreme;
So hateful is the love of praise and fame.
Altho' our Chief is equal to his Sire,   815
Since in external acts they both conspire,
Still when the muse to him her voice wou'd raise,
He to his Father paints the song of praise;
And owns, as man, he dares no enterprise,
Unless assisted by the lofty skies.   820

                         Hence

Hence thofe, whom from difeafes' pain he freed,
He often charg'd to hide the wond'rous deed.
Who by his nod the lepers fores could heal,
From publick praife his virtue to conceal,
Oft fent the patients to medic'nal ftreams,   825
To lave the tabid ulcers from their frames.
Shall I relate what people and what towns,
That ardent wifh'd he would accept their crowns,
Off'ring to him the royalties of empire,
The robe, the fceptre, and the facred-tire ?   830
He was by frequent pray'r urg'd by his band,
By arms to feize, and rule the Syrian land ;
Then all that ground the victor fhould obey,
Lafh'd with the furges of the ambient fea.
Soon then the broad-fpread earth new laws fhould
      own,   835
And ardent pay her homage to his throne.
To fhun the inftance of each fervent vow,
He flies and feeks the mountain's airy brow.
With livid envy yet and baleful hate,
They cruelly confpir'd our Hero's fate;   840
You know they drag'd him 'mid fuch furious cries,
As if their walls were fcal'd by enemies.
But, to obey his Sire, a painful ftore
Of bafeft infults he ferenely bore.
For he might 'fcape beneath night's friendly fhade ;
Yet to the fpies he twice himfelf betray'd :   845
Aw'd by his voice, I faw them bending prone;
And heard the ground by their proftration groan.

M

No

No honours from the temple he withdraws,
Nor rites defaces, nor diffolves their laws ;   850
Yet bids oblations ceafe of victims flain,
And from all fanguine off'rings to abftain.
For diff'rent rites are in the words defign'd ;
Then he unveils the Legiflator's mind.
What may furprife, they muft confefs and fay, 855
A bard fhould come and quaff this blaze of day,
Alone, who could for us unfold Heav'n's gates,
And waft juft fouls from night to ftarry feats.
For him they pant, once promis'd to their fires,
And in whofe praife the prophets ftrung their lyres.
860

Their ftate how wretched, how depriv'd of fight !
Who fee not radiance blazing thro' the night :
Their thirft how great ! who 'mid a copious ftream
Quench not the paffion of their parching flame.
Without a perverfe will, whom can't they charm, 865
Such virtue, merit, and fuch beauteous form ?
Soon as my ears inhal'd his vocal lays,
And eyes the love that o'er his perfon ftrays,
I left my fortune, mother, country, all,
As many have, nor grieve I at my call.   870
As from a fpark a mighty fire grows
And as it waftes itfelf the fiercer glows ;
So as my love each hour dominion gains,
My heart burns brighter with the pleafing pains:
For who are honour'd once his toils to fhare,   875
In ftrongeft bands for ever bound adhere.

He

He us'd no words nor promise to deceive,
Nor flatter'd us by fair rewards, believe;
But promis'd all things of the blackeft hue,
And the parade of our misfortunes drew.   880
Nor has his promise fail'd; condemn'd to roam,
We wander exiles, poor, without an home.
Such groves of ills bud low'ring on our eyes,
That new difafters on difafters rife.
One fhall (whoe'er he is) confign his breath   885
In peace, free folely from a cruel death.
But, for the reft of his obedient train,
A diverfe ftore of fanguine fates remain.
He bids, mean while, ourfelves and riches fcorn,
And aid the fick, the famifh'd and forlorn;   890
Dare to be poor, and, by long cuftom bold,
With focial arms adverfity infold.
Hence many did behold our bodies ftrewn
Along the fields, and fleep upon a ftone:
Or crop the teeming ears fatigu'd with toil,   895
And comfort hunger with the undrefs'd fpoil.
If any thirfty land a fountain gave,
We prone fcoop'd with our hands, and quaff'd the
          wave.
To fpeak inceffant if an hundred tongues
I had, join'd with the aid of brazen lungs,   900
I could not ftill, beneath our Chief, difclofe
What toils we calmly fuffer'd, or what woes.
For tho' unequal to our cares we ftood,
Our ftrength fome time confum'd for want of food,
          M 2   Above

Above the wealth of kings our souls still shin'd, 905
And tho' in body poor, yet rich in mind.

Nor less new crowds approach you may behold,
Ambitious in his train to be enroll'd.
Matrons with hoary Sires, the same's their will,
The same their certitude, his band to fill.   910
So if a potent King a war should wage,
Against some town, to make the battle rage,
Now points his weapons, now collects his host,
To ruin the town and massacre the coast.
Not sole his cohorts, and his muster'd bands,   915
But all assemble from the neighb'ring lands,
Who of dire wealth enamour'd have in view
The spoils of war, unask'd the camp pursue.
For crowds who follow of their own accord
Wide fields and roads too small a space afford. 920
Our Hero oft the pressing crowd evades,
To mountains flying and sequester'd shades.
Once trav'lling, I record, beside a coast,
The banks throng'd thick by an unusual host;
He seiz'd a boat, whose cord loos'd from the strand,

925
He launch'd to sea, an arrow's flight from land:
There stop'd, and ey'd the crowded shore and plains,
Addres'd the people in celestial strains,
The sacred walk of righteousness he shew'd,
And softly pointed out fair Ethicks road.   930
The captive throng on ev'ry accent hung
And list'ning drank the accent of his tongue.

The

The fea whofe waves, but now, wild beat the fhore,
Teaz'd with the winds, ceas'd, while he fpoke, to
    roar.
Groves, the bird's green cells, without motion ftand,
                                           935
Their branches fhading deep the winding ftrand.
But hoary dames, meantime the filence break,
Surpriz'd fuch facred truths to hear him fpeak:
With clam'rous joy pronounce his Mother bleft,
And bleft the moifture trickling from her breaft, 940
Bleffing the womb that gave him to our dawn
And the full breafts his infant lips had drawn.

    For man he taught, from earth and night to rear
The human foul to Ether's lofty fphere;
To view the ftreaming radiance of the fkies,   945
And all the fruitlefs cares of life defpife.
Then praifes peace; ye men fair peace purfue
With gentle vows, and haughty pride fubdue;
Humble of mind above the want of praife,
Honours contemn and riches flafhing blaze.   950
Known to misfortune and with little blefs'd
Suftain a life in poverty well vers'd.
Of rofy pleafure fleeting is the reign;
And nothing's permanent that is terrene.
This earth for you defigns no manfion-feat,   955
But plan'd for you more glorious regions wait.
From bodies free, your fouls fhall glad afpire
To better worlds, illum'd by my beft Sire:

                M 3   Where

Where plenty overflows, peace fmiles ferene,
Reft undifturb'd, and pleafures ever reign.   960
For fuch rewards how fhort's the longeft toil?
For me, who wouldn't leave this earthly foil?
For wealth fo true, for honours fo fublime,
Contend, above the wafte of chance or time.
Religious be, a mutual foftnefs fhew,   965
And feel with melting hearts each other's woe.
Forbid, by fuffering, wrath and hate to rife,
And the vague rumours of the throng defpife.
No wound for wound; 'tis nobler to expofe
The check once injur'd to repeated blows.   970
For praife therefore let others point the fteel,
And beauteous death by battles purchas'd feel;
To all benign, to foes foft peace proclaim,
So lightly hold the tranfient noife of fame.
But let the mind face death without affright   975
Nor force pervert it, obftinately right.
For tyrants may the mortal body flay;
And the limbs mangle, to the fword a prey;
Yet ftill the foul immortal fafe remains,
And death defies, fuperior to its pains.   980
The SIRE fhall bend, to guard you, from his fphere,
And none, without his will, dare pluck one hair.
Alone him fear; your pray'rs religious fhed,
And worthy of HIM your oblations fpread,
Whom feas obey, the land, and fields of air,   985
And the bright regions of Olympus fear:
The ground embrace in act of homage prone
And proftrate breathe your vows before his throne.
                                                    For,

For, after death, your fouls, if black with ftains,
He can commit to hell's infernal pains.   990
Dread not, when lions, loos'd againft you, roar,
And herds of fpeckled panthers thirft for gore ;
On the protection of my name rely,
And rufh intrepid 'mid the favage cry :
Soon fhall the bears, in pity, ceafe their founds, 995
And ftrive with lambent tongues to heal your wounds.
Of food alfo, mildly feclude the care,
Behold who crop the fields, and wing the air,
Nor arts them vex, nor future cares confound;
Yet they with garments and with food abound: 1000
Nature's great parent o'er creation ftands,
Dealing his aliment with foft'ring hands ;
Invefts the field with grafs, with flow'rs the mead,
With leaves the trees and mountains brows with
      fhade.
Impure defire expel, fraud and deceit,   1005
And view with mod'rate joy the well-fpread feaft.
All loit'ring leifure from your minds remove ;
Another's bed avoid, and lawlefs love.
Deprefs your hopes, forbidden heights to foar ;
And guide your vows, with moderation's lore. 1010
With your own ftore of wealth content, behold,
Without a bafe defire, another's gold.
I fhall not now the hateful tafk purfue,
Or draw th' influence of other faults to view ;
But what fhall I fay ? Mafk'd with virtue's veil, 1015
Foul thoughts, deceits, and fraudful hearts conceal.

M 4   .   From

From the polluted mind such pests erase,
On what's now latent, day shall pour a blaze.
Forbid also the wand'ring eye to roll
Nor, by spontaneous glances, wound the soul. 1020
Hence to indulge the love of speaking cease,
Destruction oft succeeds the guardless phrase.
Hence with no falsity your lips prophane;
But, with new morals crown'd, a life maintain.
Yet, should a trace remain of ancient blame, 1025
Lave the contagion in the sacred stream;
To the pure font, whence flows the plenteous rill,
Haste dames and thirsty fires and drink at will;
The surges of my font for all are roll'd;
Drink deeply then, the wave's not bought with gold.
1030

Thus shun death's walk, thus ether's mansion range,
Climes blaz'd with stars, obnoxious to no change.
These truths my Father told, the living source,
Whence all my words derive their native force.

This said, to heav'n's Monarch he turns the strain,
1035
Who's pleas'd no more with blood of cattle slain;
By pray'rs and vows, sweet peace from ether bear;
And, praying thus, he shews the mode of pray'r.

FATHER SUPREME! whose seat's the lucid skies,
To praise your holy name, bid nature rise: 1040
Let now, at length, the promis'd happy days
On the desiring nations dart their blaze:

Let

Let mortals homage to thy mandates pay,
As the bright tenants of the fky obey.
Our beings to fupport, benignly fhed,   1045
From ether's airy height, our daily bread.
O ever good ! let mercy on us flow,
As we forgive the malice of our foe.
Weak to refift, temptation from us chace,
And from all evils guard the·human race.   1050

    Into hereafter rapt, he pours his lays,
Now fhrouded deeply with obtufive rays.
This fun fhall vagrant from his ftation fly,
And drop his mien, the fplendor of the fky.
When night with hofts of light fhall deck her fhade,
                                                     1055
The dying moon fhall in an inftant fade ;
Ceafe on the world to pour her filver flood,
And fill her orb, diftain'd with gleaming blood.
The ftars, which now their deftin'd limits roll,
Shall then, diftracted, fhoot from either pole ; 1060
And the perpetual motion, which gives life
To the celeftial orbs, and hinders ftrife,
Ceafing fhall from its poles this world deduce,
And 'mid the chaos fet confufion loofe.
Our Chief, like thunder rattling thro' pure fpace,
                                              · 1065
Shall earth revifit, with an angel-race,
The lives of mankind ftrictly fhall review,
And all their crimes thro' ev'ry maze purfue.
When nature rages with the ambient flame,
The fiery tempeft fpreading thro' earth's frame ;1070
        3   On

On earth new fram'd and in a recent sky,
The shades defunct shall to their bodies fly :
Then shall the yawning tombs resign their dead,
Whose pious ghosts the subject stars shall tread,
Plac'd in Olympus those he shall enthrone,   1075
Whom, from creation, God foresaw his own:
A band of winged youths with piercing cries
Fill the arch'd windings of the ambient skies.
From the four winds they wake mankind in haste,
With clang'rous trumpets, to the judgment-seat.
                                                1080
The Judge, enthron'd sublime, with glory glows,
And his tremendous eyes around him throws,
Culls from the multitude the holy band,
And seats them glorified on his right hand :
But drives the guilty crowd, a num'rous host, 1085
On his left side without recov'ry lost.
So when the winter's raging storms subside,
And fields are vested with their vernal pride,
The smiling prospect bids the flock unfold,
And range the meadows verdant to behold.   1090
First for his sheep rich meads the shepherd notes,
But at a distance drives the smelling goats.
Then shall some men's transparent frames appear
Refulgent, shooting thro' the liquid air ;
Which once obnoxious to death's cruel pains,   1095
The mighty Sire shall purify from stains.
Then shall they flourish in a tranquil state,
Expos'd no more, the ills of life to taste.
Yet let none hope to have the human clay
Transfer'd to Heav'n's immense till the last day, 1100
                                        Except

Except a few, whom God, when he fhall rife,
From the dark tomb, fhall tranflate to the fkies.
This fublime ftation is alone confin'd,
Until that period, to the human mind :
While night and vengeance on the guilty wait, 1105
Of fin the painful and eternal ftate.
As we together the fame couch had prefs'd,
My drooping head reclining on his breaft ;
Our Chief all thefe ftrange fcenes had late difplay'd,
What time the night expands her deepeft fhade ;
                                          1110
For oft to catch his foothing words I ftrove,
And to him clung, the balm of penfive love.

His deeds perform'd along the Jordan's tide,
Or where Judea's hills in vales fubfide,
Shall I relate ? What crowds he oft addrefs'd ? 1115
His fpeech, now plain, and now in figures drefs'd.
Himfelf the firft and final caufe he fhews,
The path to tread, the fountain whence truth flows ;
The vital light, that gives mankind to fee,
And us now born, a happy progeny.   1120
Happy the age, that handed us to birth,
And thrice more happy is our natal earth,
Which grant his facred Perfon to embrace,
And of his tongue to drink each vocal grace.
This wond'rous favour, in fucceeding years, 1125
Shall be the envy of our pious heirs.

                                        Thus

Thus John rehears'd, while the admiring throng
Lift'ning inhal'd the feries of the fong:
When lo! rufh in a wicked Hebrew band,
And of their Chief the pris'ner's death demand.

1130

Jofeph and John to the great Mother fteal,
But the difafters of her Son conceal.

End of the Fourth Book.

ARGUMENT of the Fifth Book.

Pilate, to filence their clamours, defires the Jews to retire and choofe a fpeaker who may inform him of the crimes laid to the Prifoner's charge. While the Jews are deliberating, Judas, ftung with remorfe for his fin, enters the Council-chamber, declares the Prifoner's innocence and his own villainy, throws down before them the filver-money, the reward of his treachery; departs frantic with defpair, and hangs himfelf. On the Jews' return, Pilate re-afcends his judgment-feat, and harangues in favour of Chrift. He is anfwered by Annas in a fpeech replete with malice and falfhood. All then call for the difmiffion of Barabbas, the robber, and the crucifying of Chrift. Pilate, hereupon, fends the Prifoner to Herod, who fends him back to Pilate. Chrift is whip'd to appeafe the multitude, but to no purpofe. The wife of Pontius, frighted by a dream, defires her fpoufe not to fhed the blood of that innocent Man. Mean while Satan, to undo Pilate's refolution of faving the Lord, fends the Demon FEAR accompanied with SLOTH, whofe influence prevails on Pilate to give up Chrift to the fury of his enemies. Thefe, after many infults, lead him to be crucified. The Angels, fhocked at the barbarous treatment, prepare to refcue Chrift, but are hindered by the eternal Father. The Virgin Mary, hearing of her Son's difafters, repairs to Calvary where fhe fees her Son crucified between two thieves. Her lamentation. At length Chrift exhaufted with torments, while all nature fympathifes with his fate, expires in pain and agony.

THE

THE

CHRISTIAD.

BOOK V.

THE Roman Chief revolves, with ftudious care,
   The blameleſs Captive by ſome means to
   ſpare :
His virtue, beauty, and his fame combine
The tale to ftrengthen, and his birth divine :
Then cries ; (while tumults thro' the court ſpread
      wide)   5
Hebrews, depart, and bid your rage ſubſide :
Among your tribes, let one in order ſhew
The Priſoner's crime, that merits mortal woe.
Indignant they retire, with ſullen tread,
In mind reſolv'd to torment Chriſt 'till dead.   10

   Judas, who to the foe his King betray'd,
Now owns his perjur'd crime, by fear diſmay'd ;
How ready would the wretch the deed undo,
Which vengeful furies and remorſe purſue ?
His mind no reſt, his breaſt no comfort takes ; 15
Fair hope now ſleeps, and mad deſpair now wakes.
                                              The

The fum, that caus'd his pains, with rage he views,
Treafon's reward, once granted by the Jews ;
Brings to the Prieft's dire hall, then loudly cries,
Behold the wicked bribe, take back the prize. 20
O wretch undone, I fee, I bafely fold
God's Progeny, a God himfelf, for gold.
The fhades, that o'er my mind induc'd a night,
Fade now wide fcatter'd, and let in the light.

He faid; and cafts the coin before them wide; 25
But they his forrow and his tears deride.
Hence the unhappy, blind with fury, goes,
And more he thinks, the more augment his woes.
His heart corrodes to pining grief a prey ;
Nor he the Ether's convex dares furvey.   30
Then throwing round his baleful eyes, he cried,
How fhall unhappy I, alas ! decide ?
Shall ages, hid in the deep womb of time, -
Forget to tell the horror of my crime ?
Shall I go fuppliant, and my fault declare ?— 35
But's not in mercy fuch a fin to fpare—
Yet how addrefs, if to behold afraid,
Whom innocent and harmlefs I betray'd ?
Then fhall I go, as far as will can fly,
And live, unknown, beneath another fky.   40
Snatch me ye rapid whirl-winds from this coaft,
Where fading day (its round complete) is loft.
What place is fafe ? the Godhead's ev'ry-where,
And with his thunders fhakes this terrene fphere.
                                        Still

Still shall my guilty mind and cares attend,　45
Whether I traverse earth, or ships ascend.
Yet when, and where ?— but I in vain delay,
And on my mind let airy visions play.
Then earth yawn wide; receive within thy womb
A wretch who seeks to hide him in thy gloom.　50
Poor Judas, ah ! thy crimes bring on these woes,
Which you, in season, might their pest oppose.
Let thy spontaneous hand revenge thy deed,
And, shuning man and day, ignobly bleed.

Thus he exclaim'd ; resolv'd to find relief,　55
By drowning in his blood his mighty grief ;
Rashly supposing, by these desp'rate means,
His toil to finish, and corrosive pains.
And now he thinks the earth for him transpires,
Or himself wrap'd with Heav'n's consuming fires.60
So strongly fancy bids the Pris'ner rise,
In vivid paint, to his bewilder'd eyes.
His eyes with blood suffus'd, his face with gloom,
And trembling limbs announce impending doom.
Now darkness round him casts her ebon shade,　65
And to his visual orbs all nature fades.
Mad wretch who dares not his transgression own,
And call down pardon from the heav'nly throne ;
But thinks no vows can move the supreme SIRE,
Nor weeping penance quench his kindled ire,　70
But obstinately bad, and fix'd on fate,
He goes, and seeks a forest's deep retreat ;
Which, near the royal palace, wildly waves
A verdant tinctur'd waste of panting leaves.
　　　　　　　　　　　　　There

There trembling hesitates, in horrid strife,   75
By what destructive means to pour his life;
The mazes of his soul or to pervade,
And crimson in his breast the pointed blade :
Or headlong from a mountain's brow to fly,
And transfix'd on the subject rocks to die.   80
But the drear furies, his attendant train,
Soon guide the wretch seiz'd with the love of pain,
To his last scene, where quickly they entwine
A length of spreading boughs, which low recline;
About his fractur'd neck they bind the wreath, 85
Which stops the pores that give the soul to breathe.
Rewarded thus, his entrails burst their way,
And soon the with'ring body blots the day.

    The new-born day scarce blush'd in ether's space,
When near the palace rush the priestly race ;   90
The porches swell distended with the crowd,
And with vociferous tumults ecchoe loud.
Nor is it lawful (so by custom led)
On sacred days the profane court to tread.
At length the Roman comes, with youths embrac'd,
                                                           95
With flowing robes of purple proudly grac'd ;
Mounts at the gate his iv'ry throne sublime,
While nod the fasces of his native clime:
Each Father then his seat in order takes ;
Silence ensues ; and thus the Roman speaks: 100

                    N   Declare

Declare at length, the monftrous crime relate,
That fhould condemn the lovely youth to fate.
After ftrict fearch into his life and birth,
We could difcover nought, that merits death ;
But rather found, his won'drous deeds, the theme,
                                                    105
That burnifh'd bright the plumes of joyful fame.
The Prifoner fince I faw, and heard his phrafe ;
The fight, how melting ! how divine the lays !
His vifage, eyes, and language, all combine
To own him God, at leaft of race divine.   110
To him, therefore, your tribute-homage bring,
Nor, ignorantly proud, difown your King.

He faid; their lurking grief the Hebrews own,
By raging murmurs and a gen'ral groan.
Then fam'd for years, and fweet perfuafive tongue,
                                                    115
In the midft rofe Annas, and thus begun :

Roman, if ev'ry other proof fhould fail,
The Pris'ner's guilty conduct to reveal ;
This great affemblage of the city, led
To fee his perfon reckon'd with the dead,   120
At leaft might move thee, Leader, to proceed,
If no one elfe, to have the crim'nal bleed.
For this feducer, with an artful tongue,
Tip'd with fine words, has multitudes undone :
And wears, deceitful, virtue's honeft face,   125
While in his heart vice holds the fondeft place.
                                            Seeft

Seeft not, what can his new religion mean,
His orgies, nightly councils, that convene ?
Thro' Juda's towns, he lights fedition's flame,
And dares the empire of this great world claim; 130
Boafts God his Sire, who rules the ftarry vault,
And like the God abfolves who owns his fault ;
Withdraws the fear of vengeance after fate ;
Which crime, the laws ordain, with death to treat.
But from our ancient cuftoms he refrains,   135
While his falfe fram'd Godhead new laws ordains ;
New rites and offerings dares in towns proclaim ;
And lateft ages fhall obferve the fame.
Ev'n loudly threats, oh direful guilt ! to fpurn
Our facred altars, and our temple burn.   140
A temple by our fathers rear'd in air,
A coftly ftructure of laborious care ;
Will fhortly quench the fun with ebon dyes,
And charm the ftars from the inchanted fkies.
Nor long his breaft his vices latent bears ;   145
For to nefarious roofs he oft repairs,
Tho' interdicted, there affumes a feat,
While his vile band indulge the genial feaft.
Is there thro' all the town a wretch profane,
The greateft ruffian, of a ruffian-train;   150
With reftlefs joy, to him he fwiftly tends,
Nor ceafe his vifits, 'till they commence friends.
The love of vice appears to him fo fair :
And of his heart deceit holds fuch a fhare.—
On feftive days alfo when labours ceafe,   155
The fick he vifits, and expells difeafe.

How his Difciples roam, fhall I relate,
And live, unpunifh'd, on illicit meat :
By law unwarranted, and with fingers foul
The ftain'd bread handle, and inhale the bowl : 160
Shall for his fake the Sire fupreme withdraw
His holy rites and long-exifting law ?
Or in his mind can new refolves arife,
And fickle change reign in the conftant fkies ?
Give him to death, left, with his menac'd blow, 165
Our incens'd altars he fhould overthrow.
Give him to death, that none in future times
Shall dare effay to perpetrate fuch crimes.
Let him in pain, due to his vice, expire ;
And thus preferve our fhrines from profane fire. 170

He faid ; the throng roar out the fame demands ;
But with their cries unmov'd the Roman ftands.
Nor is the charge, againft the Pris'ner, new,
A work by hate compil'd, the Leader knew.
For Chrift's bright actions rous'd the Hebrews' ire,
175
And fet their facrilegious fouls on fire.
Fame fays, you charg'd him in thefe crimes, he
cry'd,
And he, with reafon ftrong, the charge deny'd.
Nor fears Jehovah's Son himfelf to own,
Who fhould, by promife, leave the Heav'n's bright
throne ;
To help weak mortals, his Sire's wrath appeafe, 180
And reconcile him to the Hebrew-race,

With

With his own pow'r to pay the parents faults,
So records tell, and fo your fathers taught.
For he, to prove the truth, through towns proceeds,
And the whole coafts gaze at his wond'rous deeds,
                                                    185
Which lie beyond the reach of human art,
Nor mortal genius can the fkill impart.
Many he call'd to drink the folar beam,
When death, pervading quite the human frame,
Diffolv'd the fprings, that granted life to roll, 190
And loos'd the body's commerce with the foul.
Ye wretched mortals, then, your hate fupprefs,
Ceafe your vain contefts, and your God confefs.

When he had faid, more fierce their fury glows,
                                                    195
More loud they urge their fuit, and tear their cloaths.
Not lefs impetuoufly their anger raves,
Than when broad Atevis or Padus' waves,
(The meadows fattening where their furges flow,
While fmiles the furface with a verdant glow) 200
Are by fome peafant, on a fudden, bound
Within ftrict limits by a rifing mound;
The river fwells more angry by delay,
The barrier breaks and victor rolls away.

Herod the King, and of a regal line,   205
Was then in town to fhare the rites divine:
For he part of his paternal realm fway'd,
And by Rome's bounty Galilee obey'd,

N 3

Of

Of whofe arrival, when the Roman heard,
From his ingrateful office to be freed ;   210
The Galilean bound he fends, and prays
The Galilean Chief with care to trace
The captive's crime, and with matureft thought
To deal a vengeance equal to the fault.
Chrift's name announc'd, joys in the Monarch wake,
                                                                         215
To fee the Pris'ner and to hear him fpeak.
Soon to the royal fight he ftood confefs'd,
Whom foon the King with various themes addrefs'd;
But to no theme he deign'd the leaft reply :
Nor from the lofty heav'ns caft down an eye.   220
Herod, admiring but a mortal born,
Reftor'd him to the Pretor-bands with fcorn :
And thus difmifs'd, tho' blamelefs, yet difgrac'd,
Returns to Pontius, with his charge difpleas'd.

My fainting mind fubfides, my fenfes fail   225
The treats of God's true offspring to detail :
Himfelf a God veil'd with a human frame,
And of the fkies the architect fupreme,
Whom neither ocean, earth, nor air's pure fpace,
Nor the bright tracts of ether can embrace.   230
All-potent GHOST, my drooping foul pervade :
Quit, Ghoft, the fky, and with thy God-head aid,
To paint this fcene, as oft as I effay,
O'er-caft with ebon tints all things decay :
The fun no more with rays the world bedews,   235
But fad-difcolour'd fade his rofy hues ;

While

While fparkling ftars are quench'd in fable dyes,
And pitying drops fall from the penfive fkies.
Offspring of God, of heav'n the light ferene,
Thyfelf a God, fent from Olympus' plain,   240
Can our diftrefs fuch pitying love excite
To fuffer pain, to make our pain more light ;
Suftain a load of evils not thy own,
And with the vengeance due to evils groan :
Oh fad reward ! for pitying much our ftate   245
To blot our crimes, with thy fpontaneous fate.
We cull'd the fruit of the forbidden tree :
Nail'd to the trunk, you bear the penal fee.
You, tho' a God, and God's undoubted feed,
Now bear the pains by mortal pow'r decreed,   250
Before a judgment-bench, ftand chain'd with awe,
Who fhall the world judge with your fupreme law.

The youth return'd in chains when Pontius faw,
Nor from the throne he can himfelf withdraw :
Toft in a fea of cares, and doubtful ftrife,   255
He tries each means to fave a Captive's life ;
Now wears a fuppliant, now a haughty air,
To move their minds, and hearts, untaught to fpare : —
But vain his threats, vain are his gentle lays,
The more he foothes, the more their furies blaze.
                                            260
At length, he cries ; the days their luftre fhed
When we (by your vain fathers' cuftom led)
Among the numbers in your gaols confin'd,
May one difmifs, and his fad chains unbind :

N 4   Do

Do you confent, that I this Pris'ner free ?   265
The blamelefs ought enjoy their liberty.
In you at large a feroce nature reigns,
While he already felt a ftore of pains ;
I'll free him then, or take him hence and flay,
Againft my will, to death a fpotlefs prey.   270

    His fpeech is broken by the cohort-crowd
Who forge new crimes and cry for vengeance loud.
About this time, the Prifon's gloomy round
Eccho'd with Barabbas, in fetters bound ;
Long time he waited death's eternal night,   275
No fafety dawning, as no hopes for flight ;
Than whom, none was more bafe in ev'ry crime,
Detefted by his Chiefs, and native clime.
The Roman afks, their anger to appeafe,
Whether this wretch or Chrift he fhould releafe ?
                                      280
With fury blind, and monftrous in their choice,
For Barabbas they beg with fuppliant voice :
While ftrenuoufly they urge Chrift's direful fate,
And with their pow'r the Rector's care fruftrate.

    The fcourge and rods (to weep who can forbear?)
                                      285
Chrift's facred frame by Pilate's order tear.
To quench their thirft of blood, by fuch vile arts,
Betrays, cries he, their unrelenting hearts ;
Perhaps the profpect of his mangled mien
Their glutted minds from gore and death will wean.
                                      290
                                      Now

Now blood from his disfigur'd body flows,
His limbs are tabid, and his neck with blows.
Flesh from his arms and neck in pieces bounds
While his bare sides glare with the lashes' wounds.
From his red lips spouts thick a sanguine stream, 295
His naked shoulders own the flagrant shame ;
His naked breast with black contusion swells,
And from his knees to feet a crimson wells.
In gore thus weltring, (drap'ry veil'd his waste)
He shews his figure bare with wounds disgrac'd. 300
Heav'n low'rs, the moon conceals her blunted light
Beneath the earth, and flies the bloody sight.
The stars, that us'd their twinkling orbs to roll,
Struck with amaze, now seem'd to shoot the pole.
Such various means to fail too sadly prove,   305
How hard's the task the Hebrews' hearts to move :
For bending vows can't calm their boist'rous ire,
Nor this blood-scene subdue their blood's desire.
But all catch fury from each other's breath
And low'ring urge the harmless suff'rer's death. 310
Now the court's vault is wounded with their cries,
And from profoundest hell the Furies rise ;
These shapeless phantoms hov'ring o'er the crowd,
New point their rage and them with darkness shroud.

Mean time the Roman's bride, with dreams half-
        dead,   315
Forbids her spouse the young man's blood to shed,
The portents of the Gods appear to threat
Th' hands polluted with the Pris'ner's fate.

                                    The

The youth's the fnowy lamb that rofe to view :
She cries, (for all my dreams are colour'd true) 320
Whofe mangled body barking dogs furround,
And fhepherd-throngs with ruftic weapons wound.
His cruel death foon all the paftures wail,
Each noted foreft and fequefter'd vale.
The Thund'rer now his vengeance fet on fire, 325
Again the murd'rers hurls from high his ire.
The heav'ns in pangs rufh down on ev'ry fide,
And hail beats on the woods and country wide.
Then foon this voice glides on the ftreams of air,
Crufh mortal rage : The God, O Roman, fpare. 330
I think this Youth (to you the marks muft fhine)
Derives his birth from a celeftial line.
To doom him then to death, my Lord, abftain,
Nor with his facred blood your hands prophane.
May the mild Gods thefe omens from us chace, 335
Attend the Jews alone, and threat their race.

The vifion heard, the Roman fiercer glows,
Refolv'd the Hebrews' fury to oppofe.
Now threat'ning acts, and with contracted brows
Bids them repeat, elfewhere, their cruel vows. 340
Now feems intent the Pris'ner's chains to loofe,
And from his ftore of cares himfelf fubduce.

The gloomy Chief of Erebus' dark ftate,
(His breaft corroded with eternal hate)
Views Pilate's fcheme with a fad heaving figh, 345
And his own plots 'gainft Chrift abortive lie.

                                                With-

Without delay, he fummons to his aid
The ghaftly monfter, Fear, from his drear fhade ;
Than whom no greater peft all hell confines,
The foe profefs'd to human bold defigns :   350
He brings pale coldnefs, ever of his train,
And floth, flow-moving with dejeded mien.
The Tyrant bids the monfter thence repair,
And wing his flight to day's fupernal air.
Where, her wild hills Phœnicia foft elates   355
And enter Solyma's extenfive gates :
To bend the Latian's mind with humbling views,
And, to deter him, his defign offufe.
He foon obeys ; the footy wings affumes
Of nightly birds, and vefts his limbs in plumes.
The obfcene bird arriv'd, before the eyes   360
Of purpled Pilate, importune oft flies ;
With dreadful howls, now frequent round him rings,
Now beats his breaft, and now his face with wings.
His heart is chill'd ; his eyes with wildnefs ftare, 365
His face grows pallid, and eredt his hair ;
Cold damps of horror thro' his body fteal ;
His knees fink languid, and his accents fail.
When thus diftrefs'd, foon as the crowd had feen
His faded cheeks, and his diftorted mien ;   370
Without delay, they feize the prefent hour,
And their addrefs thus with wild clamours pour :
Your captive dares of King affedt the name,
The fceptre wield, and regal honours claim.
If fuch offences are not big with doom,   375
Soon fhall feditious towns revolt from Rome.

All

All Syria foon fhall by his arts withdraw
A due fubmiffion to the Roman law.
If CÆSAR then, or Rome demand your care,
Forbid the peft to breathe this vital air ;   380
Due to his many crimes, the vengeance fhed,
Left the contagion thro' the land fhould fpread.

While with the ftubborn Jews the roofs thus ring,
The Roman trembles at the name of King,
The monfter Fear prevailing in his breaft,   385
Conquer'd at length he yields to their requeft;
His pow'r too weak their anger to affwage,
Becomes a flave to their vindictive rage.
So when the wind along the ocean roars,
Againft a fhip that fails with lab'ring oars ;   390
The pilot ftruggles, at the ftern plac'd high,
And fhouts his men the fervent oars to ply :
But when his views each element combin'd
His courfe to hinder, with the ftormy wind ;
Slack work the oars, his feat the pilot leaves,   395
And gives the fhip a prey to winds and waves.
I own your conqueft : He then furly cry'd
Since your bafe cruelty will not fubfide,
I fhall no longer your requeft deny,
Condemn'd for feign'd offences let him die.   400
With forrow pregnant, and without delay,
I hope a fatal forfeit you fhall pay,
Pains pour on you and on your race's head
Due to the captive's blood unjuftly fhed.

He

He faid, and bids the waiters quickly bring 405
A bowl crown'd with the current of a fpring;
And, while he laves his hands, he pours this ftrain:
As I thus purify my hands from ftain,
So I difclaim this blood unjuftly fpilt
And purge myfelf free of the bloody guilt;   410
When he had faid, the judgment-throne defcends,
And to his inmoft palace fwiftly tends.

The Hebrews thus: Let God, if pains are due,
Shed them on us, and on our race renew.

While in the porch before the palace-gate   415
Before the crowd this cafe was in debate:
The Leader's band within the fpacious court
With the mute Pris'ner barbaroufly fport.
As cities hail'd him King, he's now difgrac'd
With the mock-purple, and fublimely plac'd.   420
For the bright diadem, and crinal gold,
His bleeding temples pointed thorns infold:
And for the fceptre, which proud Monarchs wield,
They offer to his hands a river-reed.
The gates wide op'd, with glad applaufe they bring,
425

And, in the public view, falute him King.
Thus in their fports the little boys felect
One of their comrades. and their King elect:
Round their proud Monarch throng the fmiling bands,
And with glad fhouts perform his mock commands.
430

So

So in the hall the menial crew refort,
And pleas'd indulge themfelves in this bafe fport.
For with a veil they overcaft his fight,
And with their hands and reeds his vifage fmite.
Some pluck his beard, concreted with his blood;
                                                    435
Some from their filthy mouths emit a flood
Of falive moifture in his facred face;
While fome his beauteous frame with duft difgrace.
All bufy on him heap a ftore of pains;
Nor of the vile difhonour he complains.   440
A cruel vigil thefe barbarians keep,
Nor let his weary eye-lids clofe in fleep.
Oh heavy grief! how fhocking to be feen
Appears his mangled and inglorious mien!
To birds a refting-place woods give their leaves,
                                                    445
And mountains to the favage-kind their caves,
An hofpitable roof to reft at night,
And teeming bring their brute offspring to light.
But to Creation's Sire, whofe mighty fway,
The blazing manfions of the fky obey,   450
All earth denies a fpot, to reft his head,
And his exhaufted limbs in death to fpread.

    And now the Victor-Jews, among the ftore
Of direful pangs, the moft acute explore.
That death, attended with his tort'ring train, 455
May on the Pris'ner rufh with fharper pain,
                                            To

To fpread and nail him on a fatal tree,
And by flow pangs life wafte, the crowd agree ;
Of the fharp ax, the wood repeats each ftroke,
And foon falls rufhing down the ftately oak.   460
A Crofs is rear'd, of the cleft timber built,
A torture fram'd, to punifh heavy guilt.
Kings once this machine us'd, by loit'ring pain,
The condemn'd wretches' dying lives to drain.
Nor did this inftrument of horrid fame   465
A fpark of glory then or honour claim :
But, fince nail'd on the wood the Godhead lay,
A fuppliant rev'rence to the Crofs we pay :
Rear'd on our facred altars we behold
The tree inwrought with filver and with gold. 470
And the glad honours we to it decree
Relate to him, whofe death has blefs'd the tree.
The Crofs fhall, like a lamp, hang in the fkies,
And tinge the world with its refulgent dyes ;
When the laft day all creatures fhall entomb,   475
And a broad blaze all nature's works confume.

Earth'fcarce was cherifh'd with the morning's hue,
When the town pours her youth the fcene to view.
With tides of rufhing crowds the ways o'erflow,
And with wild tumult all things fervent glow. 480
Now fpoil'd of his mock purple robe of ftate,
They fhouting drag the Pris'ner to his fate :
Fetter'd amid the crowd, he's trembling led,
Gafh'd with noclurnal wounds and almoft dead :

On

On his weak fhoulders bears the Crofs's beam ; 485
(A knotted oak compos'd the fatal frame)
On which transfix'd, he leaves this nether air,
And by his death compleats his dol'rous care.
Around him throng a band in denfe array,
Whofe arms, and fhields, and fpears flafh on the
    day ;   490
Whofe helmets glow with crimfon plumage crown'd,
And brazen trumps in varied clangors found.
On foot fome follow, fome on lofty fteeds,
Whofe barb'rous fhouts each neighb'ring hill far
    fpeeds.
Still many weep, whom rectitude enflames ;   495
But chiefly tender maids and pious dames ;
To fee him climb the rough rock's airy height,
And 'gainft the ftones oft wound his naked feet.
While up the mount he drags the pond'rous oak,
Cries to his mourners with a penfive look,   500
Ye hoary Dames, tho' woes unjuft I bear,
Yet ceafe for me t'indulge the pious tear ;
To your impending pains your tears are due,
And to the wrath that fhall your race purfue.
Thus having faid, and, moving to his fate,   505
He leaves with tott'ring fteps the city's gate.

Mean while to be fpectator of the ftrife,
And view his Son exhale his mortal life ;
The Monarch of the fky afpires fublime
To the moft high tow'r of his heavenly clime. 510
                                          Befet :

Befet with troops of the Celeftials bright,
The plumy hoft of Heav'n attend his flight,
On mount Olympus, lucid to behold,
A temple ftands of gems and folid gold.
A mighty fabrick, the fupreme Sire's feat,   515
Which views the fubject ftars this world luftrate.
An adamantine cliff rears flowly fine,
In the mid, its head, like a taper'd pine.
On either fide the cliff, above the fkies,
Nine thrones arrang'd in various order rife.   520
Hither repair Olympus' native throng,
And round their King break forth in pomp of fong.
Then on their thrones reclin'd, the fparkling mound,
The thrice three choirs in myftic form furround.
For each's content, tho' different is their care;   525
Their pow'r unlike, yet happy in their fhare.
For, as with greater merit beams their mind,
So they more high are awfully enfhrin'd.
Thron'd in the midft, the potent Father fways,
And all creation with a glance furveys.   530
His lucid form diffufes floods of blaze,
And all things glow with his wide flafhing rays.
At length on Juda's land he drops his eyes,
Where the mount's brows with direful afpect rife.
The choirs view fad the mountain from their thrones,
                                                           535
Which on the town turns pale with human bones;
Where on offenders fatal pains attend,
And parch'd on trees, where livid corpfe fufpend.

                    O   Hither

Hither foon as our penfive Hero came,
Saw the fad tortures and the fatal beam ;   540
Around the hill his mournful eye he throws,
If he could find his friends among his foes :
But none could luftrate, but an hoftile band,
Whofe weapons flafh a fplendor o'er the land.
For all his friends, whom once he held fo dear, 545
Now fly him in diftrefs, difpers'd thro' fear.
So when the light'nings round fome fhepherd play,
Or in a vale he's kill'd by beaft of prey ;
Soon roam his fheep, affrighted with his fate,
And o'er the paftures wide their forrow bleat. 550

And now he mounts the Crofs, and hangs in air;
Now feems his Godhead to forget, and fears
This bitter kind of death ; now anxious roll
His drear difafters in his fainting foul ;
Sorrow fo fills his mind, that ev'ry pore   555
Emits fweat-drops deep ting'd with fable gore.
He now remembers oft his native fkies,
And, Ether viewing, thus breaks forth in fighs.
Why leave me, Mighty FATHER, in my woes ?
Where's fled the love, a Sire his offspring owes ?
                                                    560

The fad addrefs the potent parent hears,
The fad addrefs ftrikes deep the Angels' ears.
The caufe in his deep breaft revolves the God,
And finds the fcene is acted by his nod ;
The horrid pomp of tortures views ferene,   565
And ftills himfelf enflam'd with his Son's pain.
                                        But

But pow'r can't check the paffions that arife
In th'ambient crowd, wing'd natives of the fkies.
The fight thro' all a fudden grief diftills,
And indignation ev'ry breaft now fills.   570
And now refolv'd their Monarch's Son to aid,
And ftop the murder with the vengeful blade ;
An Angel, not the laft of the plum'd choir,
Than whom none can more loud the trump infpire,
To the high pole with fwift afcent now bounds, 575
And in the rofy fkies war's fignals founds :
Olympus ecchoes thro' his cryftal ftate,
And with unufual gleams the ftars vibrate.
If any Angel roams the lunar fphere,
The clangors foon affault his remote ear :   580
The brazen voice floats on the current wind,
And wounds the guardian fpirits of mankind :
While earth, thro' all her broad expanded plains,
Thrills with the valleys of the trumpet's ftrains.
Soon as the clangors reach the Angel hofts,   585
By ether's Monarch fent to various coafts,
They leave their charge imperfect, and repair
Above the polar heights thro' tracts of air.
And as the doves forfake their airy dome,
And love thro' meads, in fearch of food, to roam,
                                               590
Should a loud tempeft on a fudden rife,
And with expanfive clouds fuffufe the fkies,
On flutt'ring wings they foon fublime afpire,
And to their manfions from the fields retire.

O 2   Soon

Soon from Olympus' brow all glaring wheel, 595
And Heav'n fades horrid, with the flaſhing ſteel.
Arms and chariots return a brazen ſound,
And groaning wheels the ſtarry pavement wound :
Each pole the dreadful hurricane admires,
Ether's convulſive orbs, and flaſhing fires.   600
Tho' without body live theſe finer ſhades,
Whoſe purer natures to our ſenſes fade ;
Yet ſtill, whether to mortal climes conſign'd,
Or war, as once, againſt their rebel-kind ;
Each can aſſume a form of coarſer mould,   605
And their aerial limbs with wings infold.
In fictious bodies thus the Spirits dreſt,
Full to the viſual organ ſtand confeſs'd.
Now the celeſtials, in a circling flight,
Convene ; their bodies ruſhing on the ſight : 610
Long uſeleſs arms from Heav'n's braſs-columns
    ſeize,
Throwing about their forms a lambent blaze.
Celeſtial ſpoils, and wars victorious boaſt,
Gain'd o'er their brothers a defeated hoſt.
Now a javelin this holy Angel bears,   615
While this with ardor points the oaken ſpears.
Some graſp an arrow, ſome with fire-brands glow;
And o'er their ſhoulders caſt the lunar bow.
Others a ſtore of limpid whirl-bats hold,
And ſlings of temper'd tongs their hands infold ;
    620
While on their thighs ſuſtain the plumy hoſt,
The burniſh'd ſteel, in iv'ry ſheaths inclos'd.

                              Some

Some guide the chariots thro' the blue ferene,
The reft on painted.wings their frames fuftain.
Tho' wings to all the Angel choirs belong,   625
Unequal is the fwiftnefs of the throng :
With fluttering pinions fome each fhoulder .veil,
And with their plumage 'long the ether fail.
Some veft their feet with three-fold wings, and rear
Their foaring bodies to the Heav'nly air.   630
Their various flights with various looks are feen
So grac'd with diff'rent faces is their mien.
Nor is the painting of their plumes the fame ;
Some wreathe their feet with wings of rofy flame:
While from their fhoulders flafhing pinions rife,
                                        635
That emulate the luftre of the fkies:
Thofe fpread their plumage fplendent to the view,
Sheding the verdure of the em'rald's hue.
Thefe bathe their glofly backs with faffron rays :
While hundreds in the pride of colours blaze. 640
So when the fummer leaves the fultry fphere,
And beauteous autumn rules the fruitful year,
The trees improve the luftre of the fkies,
Bending with fruit bedrop'd with various dyes.

And now the hoft glide thro' the cryftal fpace,
                                        645
And, on their wings incumbent, Heav'n embrace.
So many mortals, fince creation's birth,
Ne'er trod at once the furface of the earth.
                O 3 .   In

In thrice three myriads rife the gen'ral band,
And thrice three chiefs the num'rous hoft command.
650

On Garganus' high brow, above the reft,
In weapons fam'd, a Leader fhines confefs'd:
The fame, whom once the battles' glorious toils
Sublimely rais'd, crown'd with victorious fpoils:
He ftalks triumphant 'mid the chiefs of fight, 655
With helmet, creft, and gems fuperbly bright.
The dragon's tawny hide he now difplays,
A fpoil, whofe fpires emit a horrid blaze.
The fpear transfix'd the monfter to the ground,
And his prefs'd back receives the mortal wound.
660

Wide blaze his arms; his fhield with radiance gleams;
And a bright jafper fets his fword in flames.

Come to the flaming portals of the fkies
With keener wrath the warrior fpirits rife.
Their fouls catch ardor from the glorious fight, 665
The famous enfigns of the former fight;
From lofty tow'rs they view the pendent cars,
On pofts hang arms, and darts, and fhields of wars,
Trophies, weapons, from the rebel fpirit-train,
Who dar'd with finful thoughts the fkies prophane.
670

Refolv'd Olympus with their nods to fhake
Elate with impotence, and fuperbly weak;
But to the hoft of purer minds they yield,
And, vanquifh'd, leave the fkies difputed field.
For

For by the fculptor's hand the gates unfold   675
The dreadful war engrav'd on polifhed gold.
In the pure fpace of the factitious air,
Each adverfe hoft in act of fight appear.
Now here, now there, a band of wand'rers fly
And with their wings obfcure the middle fky. 680
With blazing weapons now the troops engage :
Now war's confufion kindles into rage.
Some, wanting arms, feize by their locks the foe,
And whirling round thro' the blue ether throw.
At length urg'd ardent by the happy choir,   685
The rebel hoft with fullen fteps retire,
Now chas'd thro' heav'n, they fly with horror pale,
Swift as the rolling clouds, or whiftling gale ;
For the all-potent Sire feems, with his hand,
To dart his thunder 'gainft the routed band ; 690
Who urg'd with flames, and from Olympus hurl'd,
At once plunge deep into hell's gloomy world.
With former fpoils and figur'd fight elate,
They glow to rufh thro' ether's lofty gate.
Then down to earth had fhot the Angel hoft, 695
And fcatter'd flames along the guilty coaft :
Thy towns, Judea, had, already, lay,
For thy mifdeeds, to vengeful fire a prey,
Had not the Thund'rer from his ftarry tow'rs,
(Rous'd with the tumult of the heavenly pow'rs)
                                                    700
The ill-tim'd battle check'd and rafh effay,
With mandates harfh, and painful to obey :
                O 4   For

For mid the minftrels of the plumy bands,
Who act in virgin forms, the heav'n's commands,
Fair CLEMENCY of placid looks he fpies,   705
And to the chofen Angel thus he cries :

. Go, wing your chariot thro' the cryftal fphere,
And to your brothers thus my dictates bear :
To them belong neither the lore of Heav'n,
Nor the vaft empire of the world was giv'n,   710
That they fhou'd dare both fkies and earth con-
      found,
And flame the mind, with war's deftructive found ?
Let them appeas'd their bold defign forbear,
Lay down their arms, and hither fwift repair.

He faid : her chariot thro' Olympus rolls,   715
And fhe Ged's ire diffufes to the poles ;
Unlefs the hoft return, from weapons ceafe,
And their tumultuous minds fubfide in peace.
Fair HOPE and FAITH, on her attendant, rove,
And the mild parent of religious love,   720
With golden PEACE and PIETY join the band,
The candid olive noding in each hand.
Where'er they bend, the fky with weapons fhines,
The hoft grow mild, and ceafe from their defigns :
And now unarm'd, Olympus' martial band,   725
Before Jehovah's royal prefence ftand ;
Obedient to his word, each takes his feat,
According to his rank, and refts fedate.

                                         His

His eyes around the Thund'rer-father throws,
His head thrice nods, that bright with glory glows;
　　　　　　　　　　　　　　　　　　　　730
And thrice the poles with founds terrific fhake ;
When thus his words the awful filence break :

　Why let your rage againft my pleafure ftray,
Ah whither rufh ye mad Celeftials fay ?
On my affiftance can't my Son rely,　　　735
Or is my pow'r grown weaker in the fky ?
Then calm your minds, and lay afide your cares,
Thefe ills, my Son, with my permiffion, bears.
For know, man's crimes are blotted by his fate,
Thus heav'n, by our decree, unfolds its gate. 740
Therefore he lives on earth by labours worn,
The firft in woes, poor, wretched, and forlorn.
This day, big with his pain, fhall view him fpread
A willing bleeding victim, mid the dead.
Now willing horrors thro' his art'ries roll,　745
And death in profpect quite unmans his foul.
As if afide he had his God-head laid,
The armlefs mortal feels the painful blade.
For 'gainft his part divine mankind might low'r
In vain, and mortal weapons lofe their pow'r. 750
If fo my will, my virtue's not fo fmall,
But I might fave my Son in death to fall.
In vain all men might 'gainft him rife with rage,
That ever liv'd, or dy'd in any age.
My ftrength felt Babel, when her giants ftrove, 755
By edifice, to feize my realms above : v.
　　　　　　　　　　　　　　　　　　So

So ftrong, they could the lofty mountains tear
From their foundations, and whirl them in air.
Struck with my thunder ftill the ftructures fume,
And the drear ruins ferve them for a tomb :   760
Now reft the hoft of ftorms to nothing hurl'd,
Who cou'd unhinge the fabrick of this world.
I fhock'd the earth and ether's blue profound,
And all creation with the deluge drown'd.
The human race have feen my raging ire,   765
Now arm'd with thunder, and now clad with fire.
Thro' rocking orbs I oft in tempefts roar'd,
And mow'd down armies with the vengeful fword.
But wait ; a day fhall foon in ether reign
When that vile town fhall wifh, but wifh in vain,
                                    770
It ne'er had touch'd him, who can glorious trace
His origin divine from heav'n's high fpace.

    This faid, the trembling world feels deep his nod,
And ether's fanes fhake with the thund'ring God.
Their wrath and rage without delay retire,   775
And votive friendfhip melts the gen'ral choir :
So on the furface of a level'd plain,
In mimic fight, contend a youthful train :
A circled band of youths with wonder gaze
On the warm ftruggle for the voice of praife. 780
If one for toil unfit fhou'd fearful yield,
Or if, by cafual cadence, prefs the field :
Each true comrade the dire misfortune views,
To aid how willing !—but their laws refufe.
                                    Around

Around the fallen youth all ftand aghaft,   785
And with dire curfes the difafter blaft.
Without affiftance thus the Hero ftands,
On ev'ry fide befet with ruffian bands ;
And now the clam'rous crew, by furies led,
On a large tree his naked body fpread.   79●
Stretch'd to each margin of the tranfverfe beam,
His hands by fteel transfix'd with crimfon ftream.
His gufhing feet the fame fharp weapons bore ;
While the crofs blufhes with the copious gore.
All call forth their ftrength ; with blows groans the
        oak,   795
And the fupine hill ecchoes with each ftroke.
Words, o'er his head, in diff'rent tongues, relate
His country, name, and caufe of his dire fate.
Then, one on either hand, two croffes rear
Two focial fuff'rers, hanging in the air ;   8●●
Whom for their crimes the rig'rous laws refign
To awful equity and pains condign.
HIM, in the mid, a loftier crofs fublimes,
As if the firft in bafenefs and in crimes.
Unhappy Solyma, unhappy feat,   805
Rear'd on the faithlefs plains of Juda's ftate ;
To men of pious mind thou direful bane,
And even treach'rous to the Prophet-train.
Is this the feat, is this the royal bed,
And this the feaft for ether's King you fpread ? 8 10
Such honours and affociates you prepare
For him, who left for man the lucid fphere ;
                                    Who

Who dwelt ſpontaneous on the globe terrene,
Beneath the image of a human mien. . . .
Who led from Egypt's coaſt your harmleſs race,
          815
Thro' the wild realms of the briny ſpace ;
Bade the rough ſurge to a ſmooth way ſubſide,
And ſtop'd the progreſs of the headlong tide :
Who, with your labours touch'd, thro' dreary waſtes
From high Olympus ſhed celeſtial feaſts : . 820
And, when the fonts to pour their torrents fail'd,
The rocks with guſhing rills your thirſt allay'd.
Your ſtate moſt lov'd of all he wou'd enthrone
Above the ſtars by merits all his own.
Are theſe the homage-gifts your patron ſhares, 825
And thus rewarded are his tender cares !
Can't Prophets' lays, nor wonders faith impart ;
And with the preſent God glows not the heart ?
What criminal ever felt ſuch dreadful woe,
And who prepar'd ſuch tortures for a foe ? 830

  Now hanging on the Croſs all ſilent wait,
To ſee ſome wonder in his hour of fate :
What hope can now the Victim entertain,
In what, confide deliv'rance from his pain ?
But he long time unmov'd with torments hung,
          835
Nor drop'd a plaintive accent from his tongue,
Nor from his looks yet fled each roſy grace :
Nor ceas'd his eyes to ſhed a ſacred blaze.
         But

But blood and dufty fweat his cheeks bedew,
And his teeth blufh diftain'd with fanguine hue.
                                              840
So Lucifer, bath'd in the azure waves,
The ftarry firmament with luftre laves.
Shou'd o'er the world's bright fpace arife a cloud,
And the pale ether on a fudden fhroud ;
His looks are beauteous, while his glories fade ;
                                              845
And his beams gufh tranflucent thro' the fhade.

Mean while, his Mother, led by vagrant fame,
With hafte, to the great city lately came.
But now fhe hears her Son endures his fate,
(By treach'ry feiz'd) without the city-gate.   850
With the dire news, her looks grow fadly pale,
And her ftiff lips, to pour their accents, fail.
For tho' fhe knew this fcene receiv'd the nod
Of her Son's God-head, and his Father God :
Still o'er her mind fuch floods of forrow flow, 855
That down fhe finks a victim to her woe.
The houfe founds plaintive with her female train,
Who ftrive to foothe her forrow fhed in vain.
And now fhe roams the town now here and there,
Seeking the fatal place with toilfome care :   860
Now ftops, now gazes round, now opes her ear,
To view the tumult, or their clamours hear.
At eve, fo, when the doe from fertile lawns,
Or mountain's brow, returns to her lov'd fawns,
                                              Her

Her tender care in their known haunts not found,
                                              865
But ftain'd with fanguine drops the vicine ground,
Wildly fhe throws about her prying eyes,
And thro' the foreft roams with heaving fighs.
If fhe the raging lion's fteps can trace,
Or mark the wolf's along the woody fpace :   870
Thro' devious mazes fhe inceffant roves,
Marking with cloven feet the noding groves.
The Mother views the mount, which olives crown,
And which projects its fhadows o'er the town ;
Jav'lins and fhields rufh blazing on her eyes,   875
And copious hofts of foot and horfemen rife :
Thro' preffing multitudes fhe cuts her way,
And leaves the city-walls without delay :
Her flight the matrons from their porches fee,
Or lofty windows, feel her mifery :   880
Now thefe, now others, fhe outftrips in fpeed :
Tho often wounded by the running fteed.
John with his mother, virgin Martha, came ;
Her fifter, Salome, attends the dame ;
Cleophas' weak fpoufe joins the fad parade,   885
Their temples fhrouded with a fable fhade.

Now near the hill, fhe views the ftanding tree,
Ladders, and other figns of agony :
And, tho' their ufe was yet to her unknown,   890
Howe'er their fight extunds a fearful groan.
Her hands thrice fmite her gen'rous breaft, and tear
The head's, fair ornament, her flowing hair.
                                        Alas !

Alas ! within her mind fhe thus debates,
What mean thefe tools, what ills this machine
    threats ?   895
The raging Jews, I know, an odious foe,
Would on us fhed, long fince, unworthy woe.
This vifion, furely, hover'd o'er my head,
When I, one fleeplefs night, comprefs'd my bed.
I thought the Jews, with a lamb's ritual gore,
Each man befmear'd the threfhold of his door,900
What time thro' labours and a long exile,
They ftole, admonifh'd, from the realms of Nile.

    Thus having thought, fhe goes without delay,
Burfting thro' condens'd troops and arms her way.
The troops each paffage with their fhields inclofe,
                        905
And her fwift progrefs with their force oppofe.
On the hill's brow, the knotted Crofs appears,
And the huge rough engine confirms her fears.
But when fhe fees her Son's tormenting ftate,
Fix'd to the Crofs, convulfive with his fate ;   910
His hands and feet pierc'd with the jav'lin's
    wound ;
His temples with a bleeding chaplet crown'd ;
Bedew'd with death's fad drops, his languid eyes ;
His beard and treffes ftain'd with fanguine dyes ;
Drop'd on one fhoulder his dejefted head ;   915
And o'er his form death's pallid tinfture fpread ;
The wretched Mother ftiffens as the rock,
Which, on the Alps, contemns the tempeft's
    fhock ;

                            The

The triple thunder's direful force defies,
And the perpetual deluge of the skies :   920
Hoary with frost, it roughly stands sublime,
And unchang'd triumphs o'er the wrecks of time.
Touch'd with her sorrow each gazing mountain
             mourns,
And distant rivers pour their weeping urns :
The lofty cedars, on the mountain's brows   925
Distill their sacred grief from bending boughs.

When from the tree the Son his Mother spy'd,
Her mental torments thro' his bosom glide :
But on her soon he rests his dying sight,
And from this loving glance results delight.   930
To soothe her mind opprest with her distress :
At length he pours this sad and last address.
I suffer'd mute, 'till now, without relief;
Nor, woman, be a prey to gnawing grief,
Since Heav'n's great Sire permits this group of pains
                                    935
Who with his nod o'er boundless nature reigns.
Woman, this youth (for John stood weeping near)
Behold, hereafter, as your Son most dear ;
Then soon to John his words he thus applies :
This Woman always view with filial eyes :   940
Guard her abandon'd state, I dying sue,
And pay the love, to a fond Mother due.

With wounded minds the foes lament his pains,
And the fierce host grow soften'd with his strains.

                                    At

At length the Mother her fad filence breaks,   945
While a deep groan her throbbing bofom fhakes.
Lav'd with her forrow, fhe the Crofs contains
Within her clafping arms, and thus complains :

　My Son, of all creation's works the pride,
To your fad Mother how your charms fublide!95ɔ
Why can't my love forbid you undergo
The cruel agony of mortal woe,
For others' crimes the pangs of tortures feel,
And pierce my bofom with the bleeding fteel ?
But, fay, is this your face, on which I gaze, 955
That once fhone milder than the morning blaze ?
Are your's thefe languid eyes ?—Who dar'd pro-
　　　phane
Their fhining fluices with a fading ftain ?—
Ah! how from him chang'd, whom the youthful
　　　throng
Hail'd coming to the town, in feftive fong! 960
Whofe way the choir with rofy chaplets ftrow'd ;
Beneath whofe feet the purple carpets glow'd.
All own'd you King, and all a God confefs'd :
Why are you with fuch gems and purple drefs'd ?
An Angel me, with virgin tremors chill'd,   965
Once with a far more pleafing promife fill'd.
Am I thus happier than the happieft fair ;
And move I thus the Queen of ether's fphere ?
Are thefe the glories playing round my head,
And thefe the honours on my ftation fhed ?   970
After my throes, their gifts why Kings beftow'd,
And from Ce'eftials why foft anthems flow'd ?
　　　　　　　P　　　　　　　　　　If

If fuch a cruel lot remain'd for me,
And fpun out life this bloody fcene to fee.
Thrice happy dames,. whofe fons the King with
         rage   975
Depriv'd of life in their foft infant age;
Oh had you 'mid the deluge loft thy breath,
Which pannic-ftruck he fhed to give thee death !
The Sage foretold my woes, in horrid founds,
My breaft fhould welter by the poniard's wounds.
                                                       980
Stop, paffengers, your fteps and fee my ftate,
And join me to my Son, to fhare his fate.
For ev'ry joy of life is fled away,
And who can be to grief a greater prey ?
Then to his Crofs, if pity in you reigns,   985
Transfix my body, focial of his pains.
At leaft ye mountains wild, whofe verdant brows
Are now full fated with my plaintive vows,
Benignly hear, and fuccour my diftrefs,
And hear a wretched Mother's fad addrefs.   990
Rufh fudden now from your aerial height,
And end my forrows with your tumbling weight.

   The weeping Maid thus pour'd the fadd'ning
        ftrain :
Nor could her friends remove her from the fcene.
The troops their fcoffs now on the Suff'rer fpend,
                                                       995
(To a hard foe, a foe in war's a friend)
                                                    With

With laughter-noding heads the Crofs furround,
And the fky's concave with thefe infults wound.
Lo! who our city threaten'd and our fanes;
And faid, he fhot from Ether's cryftal plains:1000
His lineage drawing from the Sire fupreme,
And falfely dar'd himfelf a God proclaim.
What homage now is to his Godhead paid,
Since God difowns him by refufing aid?
Who many fnatch'd defcending to the grave, 1005
From his own groupe of woes, himfelf can't fave.
Let him now break, to fhew his Deity,
His captive-chains, and fly the gracelefs tree.
Then fhall we own, by fuch a wond'rous fign,
The fkies his manfion, and his race divine.   1010

On the fad fuff'rer in his dying hour,
Their bafe derifion thus the foldiers fhow'r:
But, with a mind unconquer'd and ferene,
He paffive bears their infolent difdain,
Implores with too much clemency his Sire,   1015
To fpare their ignorance and darkfome ire.

Mean while two youths, nail'd to a tranfverfe
        beam,
The fame their theft, and punifhment the fame!
Among themfelves are heard in warm debate,
Tho' writhing with the pains of inftant fate. 1020
One mad with ling'ring woes thus dares deride
The dying Chief, with words elate with pride:

Deſtroy our temple built with toilſome care,
And, in three days, the ſacred ſtructure rear.
If, as you ſay, from Ether comes your line,   1025
And great Jehovah is your Sire divine :
To free us and yourſelf is in your pow'r,
From the ſad train of woes, that on us low'r.
But torments now your race divine belie,
Tho' ſpread thro' towns, compell'd with us to die.
                                        1030

Who on the Chief's right hand in torment hung,
In reprimands employs his dying tongue.
What madneſs rules your mind, ah wretch ! declare
The vengeance due to our offence we bear.
But he without offence is drag'd to fate,   1035
The harmleſs victim of outrageous hate.
Ought we not then our horrid deeds confeſs,
Implore his pardon, and for peace addreſs.
This having ſaid, to God he turns his eyes,
View me, you God's true offspring, thus he cries,
                                        1040

And, ſince the lofty ſtars your coming wait,
Be gracious preſent in my dying ſtate.
The God aſſents, and thus vouchſafes to ſay :
You ſhall my praiſe and glories ſhare to-day :
The realms, which me, ſhall happy you receive ;
                                        1045
Then, from this hour, the ſkies in mind conceive.

                                        With

With pain he fpoke ; the ftream of life fubfides ;
While death from the pang'd foul the frame divides.
A boiling fweat now from his body flows,
And his parch'd mouth with thirfty drynefs glows.
                                                1050
At length, he rais'd his eyes with death opprefs'd,
And call'd to quaff the ftream, his laft requeft.
Ty'd to the margin of an ofier-pole,
To his pale thirfty lips they move a bowl
Crown'd with the juice of vinegar and gall ; 1055
Loathfome ingredients! which the tafte appall.
From the touch'd juice his poifon'd tongue refrains,
And a long time the bitter fenfe retains.

Mean while the bands with loud diforder rife,
With ardor ftriving to divide the prize.   1060
The Suffer'r's robe is the contefted fpoil,
Which once his Mother wove with pious toil.
But, as the Tunick without feam appears,
It can't be dealt among the bands in fhares:
Wherefore in fortune all their hopes confide, 1065
By lot to carry what they can't divide.
This once, the facred Prophets told in lays,
Their throbbing bofoms big with future days.

His middle courfe now Sol had almoft made,
When on a fudden clouds his radiance fhade. 1070
And in meridian blaze, (a fearful fight)
On earth incumbent broods a fable night.
The fkies lie wrap'd in clouds of mournful hue,
And ev'ry profpect flies the mortal view.
                    P 3   In

In the high Heav'ns fuch figns of grief appear, 1075
(If grief had place in the celeftial fphere)
One might believe Jehovah heav'd with fighs,
And turn'd from wicked earth his ftarry eyes.
The lightnings flafh ; fparkle the confcious poles,
And fhaking thunder thro' Olympus rolls.   1080
Such murmurs rattle thro' the blue profound,
That the world's fabrick cracks, and feems unbound.
Earth's centre roars, his waves vaft ocean fpreads,
Reel the high domes, and turrets nod their heads.
A chilling horror thro' the nation ftreams,   1085
And cities ftructur'd on the world's extremes.
The caufe unknown, tho' ftrange the fcenes appear,
And heav'ns and earth a night perpetual fear.
But browner horrors on the Hebrews frown,
And a pale pannic hovers o'er their town.   1090
A gen'ral groan afcends the heav'nly climes ;
Each mind deep-wounded with its confcious crimes.
Chafte dames in long proceffion feek the fane,
With youths attended and a virgin-train :
With adoration at the altar fall,   1095
And on fair Peace with hofts and incenfe call.
A fignal threat burfts from the thund'ring Sire,
And on the temple falls the vengeful ire :
The broad expanded veil, from vulgar view,
Which once the facred myftic rites withdrew, 1100
Gapes, a wide fciffure, while the columns nod,
Cracking beneath the temple of the God.
And now the dying God's laft accents wound
The penfive air with vehemence of found.

                                   Lo!

Lo! all is confummated, Father deign   1105
Receive this foul without a guilty ftain:
Thus having faid, he faints, from life retires,
And, bowing down his languid head, expires.

End of the Fifth Book.

P 4   ARGU-

ARGUMENT to the Sixth Book.

Joseph of Arimathea requests Pilate to grant him the body of Christ. This favour obtained, conjointly with Nicodemus, he takes it down from the Cross, and lays it in a sepulchre he had newly erected for himself. Here a band of soldiers are made to watch to hinder the body being stolen by the Disciples. In the mean time the soul of Christ descends into that part of Hell, where the souls of the righteous were. Their joy at the sight of Him is described, and their deliverance from their prison. Early the third morn after the crucifixion, Mary Magdalen and the other Marys come to embalm the body, but, instead of it, find an Angel sitting in the sepulchre, who announces the Resurrection of the Lord, and his going before them into Galilee. This report was regarded by the Apostles and others, as the work of female fancy; but they were soon convinced of the contrary, by his many apparitions, and the wonders he had wrought among them, whilst he conversed with, and instructed them for forty days together in their several Apostolical duties. This Work now draws to a conclusion by Christ's Ascension into Heaven, preceded by the instruments of his passion borne by Angels. Next ensues the Descent of the Holy Ghost; the wonderful change wrought in the Disciples by His descent, and the miracles performed by them from his inspiration. Lastly is set forth the departure of the Apostles to diverse parts of the world for preaching faith in Jesus and the blessings attending his reign.   THE

THE

CHRISTIAD.

BOOK VI.

NOW Vefper haftes to mount the gloomy fky,
    While the dead bodies unfepulchr'd lie :
Remain unwept on the mount's hoary height,
Trees fuftaining ftill their mortal weight.
Jofephus, from Arimathean tow'rs,   5
On the bafe treat with indignation low'rs :
His foul refin'd with ev'ry mental grace,
And beauty fmiling in his youthful face :
In the contended field of battle bold ;
Rich in expanfe of land and copious gold.   10
He, by the Hero's wond'rous actions fway'd,
A glad attendant, his commands obey'd ;
While others then by fear to forefts hafte,
Or hide in cav'rns or range fome dreary wafte ;
Without delay the nation's Chief he feeks,   15
And thus, endow'd with youth and courage, fpeaks :
Thou beft of Romans, whom, with plaufive breath,
Fame fings unftain'd with our dear Hero's death ;
Who, by your pow'r, tho' oft withdrawn from fate,
Still fell a victim to our nation's hate.   20

Stung

Stung with his words to their offences due,
Tho' free they feiz'd him, and tho' guiltlefs flew,
Grant then, at leaft, the body to inter,
The only comfort thou canft now confer.
I fhall repofe his relicks in the tomb   25
Which late I rear'd, full of my future doom.

    Pontius to this replies with foften'd voice,
To grant him living, how wou'd I rejoice !
For I atteft you, Gods, whom truth delights,
(And Gods and FAITH are worfhip'd with our rites)
                                                30
How often I revolv'd in mind each fcheme,
From death to free him, who was free from blame.
But vain I footh'd the city with my pray'r,
Their rage deftroying, whom I wifh'd to fpare.
Go then, his body honour with an urn,   35
And with due obfequies his fun'ral mourn.

    This faid : Jofephus bends his ardent way,
And feeks the mountain's brow without delay,
By Nicodemus join'd, who climbs the height,
His mind deep wounded with the Hero's fate.   40
And now they both the mountain's brow purfue,
Whence the drear place full rufhes to the view ;
When lo ! bright weapons flafh along the ground,
And cohorts arm'd the mountain's cliff furround.
The town forbids the trees the corfe difplay,   45
Or with the carnage blot their feftive day.

                                        The

The malefactors by the Scribes' commands
For burial then are loos'd by weapon'd bands:
But the tormented thieves are found alive,
Who fond of death their tortures still survive.   50
Wherefore they break with iron tools their bones,
And the mount ecchoes with their piteous groans.
Their deaths thus haft'n'd, the bodies they depose,
And swiftly in the yawning grave inclose:
But when they saw HIM dead, who bore our pains,
                                                    55

To abuse the sightless corse their rage abstains;
They all admire his vitals' sudden fail,
His nervelefs limbs, and visage wond'rous pale.
'Tis fam'd the youthful natives of the sky,
Their vestures blushing with a crimson dye,   60
Were seen with wings to beat the airy space,
And in a cluft'ring orb the cross embrace,
Catch the bless'd moisture gushing from the wound,
And bear the chalice to the bright profound.
The base Longinus dares alone to hide   65
His profane weapon in his sacred side;
The spear grows tepid, and imbibes the blood,
Which gurgles like a parti-colour'd flood;
For water stain'd with gore wells from the wound,
Purpling the grass, and drenching deep the ground.
                                                    70

Josephus rushes thro' the guarding train,
Ascends the cross, lets down his Master slain;
                                            Far

Far from the din of arms the corfe conveys,
And with the cloth, bought for that ufe, arrays.
Ye heav'n's young throng, your prefence hither
      bring,   75
Charg'd with the honours of eternal fpring ;
Narciffus, hyacinths, and vi'lets pour,
And bathe the body with the rofy fhow'r.
The hills and woods refound with female cries,
And earth laments his death in ftreaming fighs. 80
The wretch'd Mother, with difhevell'd hair,
Pines on a rock, her heart diftrefs'd with care :
Holds in her lap her Son, with blood deep dy'd,
His eye-lids kiffes, and his wounded fide.
And now nor tears nor fight her grief confefs ;   85
Too great for utt'rance is her deep diftrefs ;
Chill'd with her fear, and ftupid with her moan,
She grows as filent as the fenfelefs ftone.
Smiting their throbbing breafts fome dames deplore ;
With tepid ftreams fome lave the corfe from gore :
                                     90

Some, with the textur'd off 'ring of a fhroud,
The fqualid members of the corfe infold.
This matron bending drops the penfive tear,
And dries his knees with her diforder'd hair :
While this one kiffes, with a fobbing breath,   95
His hands and feet, ftiff with the cold of death.
The ftreaming forrow flows from all their eyes,
And the mount ecchoes with their difmal cries.
The men, while larger drops their cheeks diftain,
Scarce from the corfe remove the female train. 100
      3   At

At length the matrons, footh'd, retire with pain,
And in his tomb the men repose the flain.
The obsequies perform'd, they all recede,
And to her dome th' unhappy Mother lead.

Nor anxious care is from the Hebrews fled, 105
Their hearts ftill fear HIM, tho' among the dead.
For oft they heard HIM promife (while his train
Dreaded the profpect of the hoftile pain)
He fhould arife the third day from the dead,
And facred bards the fame have loudly faid.   110
Full of this fear, they fend, without delay,
A band, to guard the buft both night and day :
Left any fhould, by night, withdraw the flain,
And with falfe fame the city entertain ;
That the fepulchr'd treads this terrene fphere, 115
Inhales the folar beams and vital air.

Come Holy GHOST proceeding from the Sire,
Thou, ether's God, thou, joy of ether's choir,
Whatever veftiges of woe remain,
Caught from the treatment of our Hero flain, 120
Blot from my mind ; and let thy God-head roll
A foft infufion thro' my placid foul.
Such liquid gladnefs in my breaft infufe,
As the blefs'd natives of the fkies bedews,
Where joy in copious torrents pours its tide, 125
And ftreaming without limits pleafures glide.
The fcene is fhifted : Joy begins its reign ;
And nature now affumes a better mien.

And

And now the God from darknefs to tranflate
The holy Bards and Bands to ether's feat,   130
Free from his body's chain his foul invades
(The realm of filent ghofts) the deepeft fhades:
Thro' darkfome labyrinths, and craggy ways,
Impervious to the fun's tranfpiercing rays;
A place imbofom'd in eternal gloom,   135
Of groping fear the horror-brooding dome :
The brother ghofts, who thro' night's horror ftray,
Affembled here, hold their imprifon'd fway;
Whom the Supreme caft from the ftarry climes,
Shedding his wrath on their ideal crimes.   140
Plung'd in Tartarean gulphs the wretched train
Too late deplore their direful luft of reign.
Thefe tyrants yet torment the fhadowy hoft
Confin'd and fetter'd on the fable coaft.
The fouls, found cruel, while they breath'd this air,
                                               145
In hell's abyfs by Styx inclos'd, repair;
Them plung'd alive, in vaults replete with fume,
Eternal fires and growing flames confume.

The Righteous feats, remote, but next in place,
Their turrets raife in a wide ambient fpace.   150
No burning here in flames vindictive glows,
But eafe inglorious and a dead repofe.
Confin'd, the blamelefs ghofts live in this clime,
Not for their own, but their firft parent's crime.
From pain exempt, they envy not our rays,   155
But thofe that round Olympus' tenants blaze.

                                            Here

Here dwell the patriarchs, an ancient race ;
Their lives by no laws fquar'd, but native grace ;
Thro' untill'd fields, with flocks they fpent their
　　time,
Obfervant of the cuftoms of their clime :　　160
Without compulfion by ftrict juftice fway'd,
Their homage to pure rectitude they paid.
Here breathe the bards, who with the God-head
　　fraught,
Boldly, thro' towns, future contingents taught ;
Here Chiefs, who once the world with mandates
　　fway'd ;　　　　　　　　　　　　　　165
And thofe, who freely their decrees obey'd :
Here fages, matrons, babes, a manfion claim,
The fame's their love, their wifh of Heav'n the
　　fame.

And now, by chance, the ghofts revolve in mind
The circling years, for their releafe confign'd ;　170
Thinking the period of their ills draws near, ·
With gladnefs thus they foothe their common care.
Behold, the welcome day impends on high,
When we may drink the light, and view the fky.
Jehovah once this gladfome day confefs'd,　　175
Gliding from ether's blaze into our breaft,
Leaving to after ages to behold
The faving luftre we have once foretold.
But, foft, attend, our light fhall quickly blaze ;
On us fhall God's true offspring fhed his rays :　180
　　　　　　　　　　　　　　　　　The

The fame, who in a Lion's fierceft mien
Confefs'd himfelf, our eyes o'ercaft with ftain.
Who fhould, for many, feel the pangs of woe,
And, for us dying, triumph o'er our foe.
At length the Lion conquers; Io's fing;   185
The blood of Judah, David's great offspring!
Ye happy mortals wide your Peans ftream ;
Ye fhapelefs ghofts with fhouts your joy proclaim.
Hark ! Heav'n now calls : For us the ftarry fpheres
Difplay their portals, bar'd for many years.   190
As promis'd in our ftrains the hour's advance,
When lofty mountains fhall with gladnefs dance, .
When hills with pleafure fhall exulting bound,
Their beauteous brows with pampine chaplets
          crown'd.

So frequent in the fields exult the rams ;   195
Hid in rich paftures play the tender lambs :
Or, lift'ning to their fleecy parent's bleat,
Afcend with playful fteps the mountain's height;
With liquid honey fhall the fountains glow ;
With liquid honey fhall the rivers flow :   200
Or fnowy milk their filver beds fhall fill,
And from the purling rocks the nectar rill.

While thefe prophetic ftrains they raptur'd fing,
The vaulted roofs with their applaufes ring.
Thus when the natives of a town fuftain   205
A tedious fiege watch'd by a hoftile train ;
With ambient trenches fafe the city ftands,
And the bar'd gates defy the martial bands.

                                    Who

Who round the walls with clam'rous fury fwarm,
And ftrive with miffive bombs the town to ftorm.
                                                    210

But if from lofty tow'rs, afar they eye
Auxiliar troops to their affiftance fly,
Their hopes revive ; and with rejoicing cries
They pierce the convex of the ftarry fkies.

  Sudden the great avenger ftands confefs'd   215
Within the door, with holy radiance drefs'd.
A huge confronting gate remains ftill clos'd,
Its broad expanfe of folid brafs compos'd ;
A hundred tow'ring columns bear the frame,
Which mocks the force of fteel and crackling flame.
                                                    220

Here ftops the God, and thunders at the gate ;
Th' earth's foundations, fhock'd with the blow, vi-
        brate :
The vagrant ftars roll trembling in their fpheres ;
And hell, thro' all its caverns groaning, fears.
The tribes, who hate the light, a trembling fwarm,
                                                    225

From deepeft vales emerge at the alarm :
They to the knees in human form appear,
Beneath, a dragon's hideous figure wear.
Loud fhrieks and direful flames fpout from their
        throats,
And fumed darknefs thro' the palace floats.   230
Sudden the gate difplays its valves abroad,
And flies the hinges of its own accord,

                    Q.   The

The dome's confus'd, when night begins to fade,
And from the prefence of the God recede ;
Whofe eyes with holy radiance fo bedew   235
The horrible abyfs of liv'd hue,
As when a gem, bright rival of the day,
Streams thro' the fable night a living ray,
With flames victorious deluges the gloom,
Or vefts with crimfon rays fome regal room.   240

But when the demons faw the God invade,
And own'd his prefence in their dreary fhade,
And with the fulgence that his form embrace,
And all the glories darting from his face,
With tremors chill'd, they fly the heav'nly fight 245
And caft themfelves into the deepeft night,
Licking their tails that round their bodies rowl,
And from their dens afcends an hideous howl.
Such roaring ftorms, when eaftern tempefts blow,
The half wild Alpine natives undergo ;   250
If from their cots, by chance they view the fight
Of Roman troops, with flafhing weapons bright ;
Soon from their fmoaky huts, they trembling fly,
Seeking, along the Alps, an higher fky :
There feated on fome diftant rock, admire   255
The marching Roman Leaders' rich attire.

But the chafte ghofts, once lambent with his blaze,
Their fupine hands to high Olympus raife :

                           With

With joy they fhout, with joy their tears they pour,
And with their eyes and minds his fight devour.
                                                    260
Now round the Victor throng the airy train,
And all falute him in this gen'ral ftrain :
How welcome is thy prefence to our eyes !
Thou fplendent glory of the ferene fkies !
By thee, the gifts, (nor have we hop'd in vain) 265
By our firft parent loft, his feed regain.
In its old ftate you now the world replace,
And ope a walk unknown to ether's fpace.
You come at length bright as the lamp of day,
Effulging on our eyes a living ray.   270
Why worn with woe you come thro' tempefts hurl'd ?
(For Fame defcends into our fhady world.)
Who has with wounds your facred frame deform'd,
Or in your gufhing blood his weapon warm'd ?
Shall earth fuch crimes upon her furface bear, 275
While, ocean, you embrace with fhores her fphere ?
Where have you loiter'd, in what cave retir'd,
While your Creator in fuch pain expir'd ?
Then all mankind fhould perifh in your tide,
And guilty earth beneath your waves fubfide.   280
But fay, true offspring of the heav'nly King,
Could nothing, but your blood, falvation bring?
For our redemption, from th' infernal ftate,
Was once not valu'd at fo high a rate.
Love fix'd the price which you to mortals bear,
                                                    285
Dear to the human race, to Angels dear :
                    Q 2   We

We rais'd the supreme arm with thunder red,
And, with the pain due to our crimes, you bled.

Such language flow'd along the dreary coast :
Now from their cells fly forth the joyous host ; 290
The happy souls the Victor-god pursue
Thro' ether's convex op'ning on the view,
To live for ever on the starry soil,
Secure from danger and exempt from toil.
The Sire of men first seeks the starry clime,   295
Nor rears his head as conscious of his crime.
The patriarchs succeed, an hoary band,
Who once were rulers in their native land :
Next come the bards, whose breasts with future
           glow,
Their temples bound with fillets white as snow. 300
But those unhappy shades, whose crimes detain,
Condemn'd to languish in eternal pain,
'Mid ambient flames in deepest caverns dwell,
And madly groan to find no end of hell.
But, chief, the King of the sad realms below, 305
First of the Demons, and the first in woe,
His heart with fury stung, and big with sighs,
Envies the happy his forsaken skies.
But the blest souls, along the tender air,
With gladness seek the promis'd crystal sphere,
                                   310
With vocal harmony salute their King,
Who crowns their lives with an immortal spring :
                                   Wrap'd

Wrap'd in repofe, they drink eternal day ;
And death no more his portals fhall difplay.
The plaufive air their ftarry paffage hails :   315
Clouds fly the ether and fubfide the gales :
With placid motion, the fmiling world glides ;
And ftars roll fmiling thro' Olympus' wilds.
To light the ghofts Aurora early wakes
With choral birds, and Vefper ether ftreaks.   320

While in the blue immenfe fuch wonders rife,
The third day blufhes in the eaftern fkies :
The Sire fupreme his Son with radiance wreaths,
And on his limbs immortal beauty breathes.
His frame once mortal, and to wounds a prey, 325
Is now immortal, glorious as the ray
Which polar ftars fhed on the clear ferene,
Or golden Sol in his meridian reign.
So, while a fire's with afhes overfpread,
No flames along the houfe a luftre fhed ;   330
But fed with fuel, and waken'd with a blaft,
The houfe with fudden flames is overcaft :
And thus exhaufted with revolving years,
Sole of his fpecies, the glad Phœnix rears,
Upon fome lofty mountain's airy brow,   335
His fun'ral pile, of every od'rous bough.
Along the balmy tow'ring pile now fpread,
(The pile, his tomb at once, and natal bed)
His age he buries in the blazing flame,
Survives himfelf, another and the fame;   340
In

In bloom of youth, from his own afhes fprings,
Effulgent with his creft, and crimfon wings.
With wonder, round him throng a feather'd hoft,
Viewing his flight to his Egyptian coaft.

Thefe wond'rous vifions floating in the fkies, 345
Diffolve the pannic nations with furprize.
And now the fun his orient beams difplays,
The night retiring from the gufhing blaze.
Now Magdalena, with a weeping train,
Transfix'd with forrow, for her Hero flain,   350
Brings in her lap, when Sol in ether dawns,
The fcented herbage of Arabia's lawns,
The balfam, fpikenard, and the myrrh's perfume;
The ritual honours, offered at the tomb.
As thro' the fields the dames with forrow go, 355
Each mutual fpeaks the dictates of her woe.
Unhappy we, the penfive matrons cry'd,
That have not with our piteous Hero dy'd !—
But how fhall we the watchful guard deceive,
Or the huge ftone from the tomb's entrance heave,
                                                360
To pay, at leaft, our duty to the dead,
And in the dreary tomb our off'ring fpread ?

While thus complaining, near the tomb they
    drew,
Throwing, on ev'ry fide, a piercing view,
Void of all guards the mountain's orb behold, 365
And the great rock from the fepulchre roll'd.
                                        But

But the tomb finding, empty of the corfe,
With thoughts the flain was ftolen by the foes,
From Magdalena drops the balmy ftore
Of fun'ral gifts, fhe to the body bore.   370
The hills and groves with fighs lament the fair,
With forrow tearing her difhevell'd hair.
But foon a youth, with purple wings, they eye,
With drap'ry white, a native of the fky.
To the fad train he pays this foft addrefs :   375
Whom feek ye Dames ; why pine ye with diftrefs?
Let fear, in future, in your minds fubfide,
And trickling gladnefs in your bofoms glide.
Since he, whofe cruel torments you deplore,
Staining for you the gibbet with his gore :   380
Since he, whofe fole fpontaneous death alone
Could, for the fins of all mankind, atone :
Triumphant o'er the King of Hell's retreat,
Revifits, from the fhades, this lucid ftate ;
Inhales, at prefent, this fupernal day ;   385
His refin'd frame, no more, to death a prey.

This faid, in air his melted figure glides ;
But doubt, before the prefent fcene fubfides,
Pierc'd with delay her mind, with love her heart ;
The Maid admires the tomb, and builder's art: 390
For on the tomb a fculptur'd fhore is fpread,
Where lies a fifh, whofe jaws a deluge fhed :
Such is the tyrant of the fea, a whale,
Whofe bulk's a dread to them who near it fail :

From whose voracious mouth the Prophet roll'd,
                                              395
To reinhale this air, and day behold.
This scene (she cries) confirms the Angel's strain;
Nor ancient types drew future things in vain.
For as the bard lay in the monster's womb,
Three nights and days involv'd with ambient gloom,
                                              400
So God by friends and skies deplor'd, when dead,
Amid the darkness of the tomb was spread,
A Victor from the empty vault should rise,
And now (as he foretold) asserts his skies.

But soon the God, in rustic vest array'd,   405
Moves to the tomb, where sits the musing Maid.
Pensive she eyes him : But his speech betrays
The God bedew'd with newly painted rays.
She falls, and holds his knees in close embrace,
Her eyes roll round him, and devour his face. 410
His placid looks soon soothe her pining love,
And from her breast her plaintive grief remove.
Her colour ripens ; but the turgid tear
Flows from her eyes, and, down her neck, her hair.
So hangs the rose her head of blushing hue,   415
Her purple foliage charg'd with nightly dew ;
But should the sun ascend the cloudless skies,
And vest the fields with his refulgent dyes :
She rears her head, and suddenly displays
Her damask bosom to his golden rays.   420

As

As fades her grief, in charms the Maid fo grows ;
And with her King and God to converfe glows.
And while fhe pants what language to purfue,
Wrap'd in a cloud, he vanifhes from view.

While, thro' the towns of Paleftina, Fame   425
Scatters, without delay, the wond'rous theme :
Congeal'd with fear, the priefts attempt each means
To ftop her progrefs, and condemn her ftrains.
But chief, the troops, who fpread the firft report,
Guards of the buft, by golden bribes they court
                                            430
To fing, that his Difciples ftole the flain,
While, o'er the fleeping world, night held its reign.
But vain's the tafk to tame truth's mighty force ;
For more the priefts contend to ftop the courfe
Of Fame, with higher flights fhe prunes her wings,
                                            435
And on remoter coafts the wonders fings.
Some boldly own they faw the tombs difplay
Their gates, fpontaneous, and admit the day :
Pale fhades ftalk ghaftly in the glare of light,
Whofe bones earth fhrouded with her central night.
                                            440

Mean time the Hero's friends, a penfive band,
Wither'd with fear, are fcatter'd o'er the land;
Fancy the fun fhall ne'er the fkies illume,
And, he extinct, the world fhall fade with gloom.
                                            At

At length, beneath the roof, they fad convene,445
Which oft the Hero honour'd with his train ;
To them, their King alive, a fweet retreat ;
But, flain, appears a folitary feat.
The dome no more fhall feaft the Hero-gueft,
Or, with his looks, his focial friends be blefs'd :450
No more his name fhall fill the raptur'd ear,
Or his foft eye out-blaze the ftarry fphere.
Such fick'ning thoughts the fad affembly fhade,
And nature feems with black defpair to fade.
The fhepherd thus, whom lucre taught to pore, 455
A hive leaves empty of its waxen ftore ;
The fadd'ning bees furround the hollow oak,
Tho' thence expell'd with gales of fulph'rous fmoak.
Robb'd of their harveft, ftill they view the hives,
Cull'd to fupport, in winter's reign, their lives.460
In vain they rang'd the fields with bufy toil,
And fip'd the flow'rs, to form the honey-fpoil.

Behold the matrons to the dome repair,
Where the affembly lay in fad defpair ;
Amaz'd report they faw an Angel-choir ;   465
The King, himfelf, new drefs'd with beams of fire ;
Befides, the tomb of it's dead-charge refign'd,
And all the fun'ral drap'ry left behind.
Some climb the mountain's crown with breathlefs
        hafte,
And find the tomb an empty, dreary wafte.   470
Thefe wond'rous vifions ftill to fome appear
The work of fancy, and of female fear.

                                        As

As in our dreams we fancy to behold,
Or abſent looks or 'mong the dead enroll'd.
But lo! when Veſper rul'd the cryſtal plain,   475
The Hero ſtands before his conven'd train ;
His well known form and voice the God confeſs
Laying aſide his blaze, and ſunny dreſs.

Then Didymus was abſent from the dome,
Impell'd by fear (the Hero ſlain) to roam ;   480
To ſee his 'ſociates to the town repairs,
Who lay in wonder loſt, and mute with fears :
So when fierce lightnings, burſting from a cloud,
In flames ſome temple or proud ſtructure ſhroud ;
Within the walls the frighted burghers gaze,   485
And view the manſion, veſted with the blaze.
A thrilling horror thro' their boſoms glides,
Racking their hearts before the pain ſubſides.
With ardor Didymus, the ſcene unknown,
His 'ſociates ſues, the wond'rous cauſe to own :490
Peter, while tears bedew his hoary cheeks,
After a cloſe embrace, at length thus ſpeaks:
Heav'n's Monarch lives ; whom death ſnatch'd from
            our ſight ;
He lives, thrice happy we, and quaffs this light.
Thus having ſaid, his joys ſo tow'ring riſe,   495
That, in his mind, he ſeems to tread the ſkies.

But Didymus ſtill doubts and thus replies :
Say, is't the King, himſelf, who breathes theſe ſkies ?
                                    Or,

Or, rather, say, a creature of the brain,
Who, to deceive your eyes, assumes his mien? 500

Peter returns : 'Tis he, the very same ;
Our eyes have view'd, and hands have felt his frame.
Survey'd the gaping scissure of his wounds,
And air celestial that his form surrounds.

What time, bright Vesper sways Olympus' state,
                                                505
The windows clos'd, and clos'd the massy gate,
Beneath this roof, we lay dissolved with fear,
And pensive press'd our seats the feast to share.
In this clos'd hall our Chief invades our sight,
Whose sparkling looks amaze us and delight : 510
With chilling horror we astonish'd gaze ;
While the walls vested with his lustre blaze.
But soon he checks our fear and vain surprise ;
And interdicts us from the board to rise.
'Tis I ; be peaceful ; and your fears subdue ; 515
Here feel my frame, and my five wounds now view:
Nor did he scorn besides, to take a seat,
And humbly social share our frugal feast ;
The last and noted words deign'd to repeat,
Which from him sadly flow'd, when near his fate.
                                                520
Then willing, from our sight, to disappear,
His body softly fades to liquid air.
Scarce had the Sage pronounc'd the wond'rous scene
Approv'd and clamour'd by the present train,
            5   When

When enters Cleophas with gladſome mind,   525
(Whom to his Apoſtles the Chief once join'd)
He lives ; diſmiſs your fears, my friends, he cries :
Our Monarch lives ; to death no more a prize.
Theſe very eyes devour'd his beauteous face;
Theſe very ears inhal'd his well-known phraſe :53●
My fellow-traveller drunk the vocal tide ;
Pointing to Amon, who then preſs'd his ſide.
For as we travell'd with our ſorrows pale,
Where Emaus' hills ſubſide into a vale ;
With us the way an unknown travell'r preſs'd ;535
His perſon ſtrange, and in ſtrange garments dreſs'd.
While he deceiv'd, with varied ſpeech, the road,
Tears from our eyes, ſighs from our boſoms flow'd :
With ſoothing words he ſought to give relief,
And oft enquir'd the ſubject of our grief.   540
Our Hero's cruel fate, to him, we ſigh'd,
In whoſe ſad death, our comfort alſo dy'd.
How all his words and deeds our hope inſpir'd ;
And with his life our flatter'd hope retir'd.
Unable longer our complaints to hear,   545
He thus replies, with reprimands ſevere :
O ſhameleſs race, offus'd with mental gloom !
Have not your bards foretold your Leader's doom ?
His bloody fall your ancient records taught!
Which you diſcredit, tho' with juſtice fraught :
                                            550
That he ſhould ſole, to calm his Father's ire,
For all mankind, ſpontaneouſly expire,

                                            His

His gushing wounds should streak, with crimson
    dyes,
His rapid progress to his native skies.
A diff'rent doctrine for his friends he chose,   555
By op'ning, long before his fate, his woes:
For in the town, I know it, he display'd
His future passion, cast in mystic shade.
Now all things shine transparent and serene,
Nor have your hopes, the clouds expell'd, prov'd
    vain.   560
Behold the King, who plants with vines his ground,
'Gainst spoiler beasts and men, well fenc'd around,
From town he sends a train to guard the same ;
The rustic ruffians kill them without blame.
At length his Son consents the fields to tread, 565
And by the same is counted with the dead.
The Sire supreme, his sacred Prophets slain,
Thus bids his Son descend the starry plain.
But lo ! the Palestines, with fury blind,
Their Master's Son to cruel death consign'd :   570
But soon the King their City shall subdue :
And pour the vengeance to the murder due ;
Set slaughter loose, among the barb'rous swains;
And foreign hands shall dress the vintage plains.
This said ; the Bards' dark dictates he displays,575
And on the Sages' off'rings pours the blaze :
Evincing by his proofs their rites and strains
Were pregnant with the Saviour's future pains :
The bloody ransom, that could draw, from night,
Each human soul, that ever breath'd this light.580

As

As he evolv'd the rites, how darknefs fled!
What light on the prophetic leaves was fpread!
What thrilling fweetnefs thro' our fenfes flow'd :
And, in our breafts, what loving ardor glow'd!
So brafs refigns its rigour in the flames ;   585
And ice diffolves before the folar beams.
So blind we were, he ftill remain'd unknown,
'Till we arriv'd to Emaus' little town,
Where feigning to proceed a longer way,
We humbly fu'd beneath the roof to ftay.   590
To ceafe his journey, Vefper might perfuade,
Expanding over earth a fable fhade.
He foon obeys ; deigning to take a feat,
And with us fhare our poor and frugal feaft.
No fooner had he touch'd the wheaten bread   595
And broke, as by his ancient cuftom led ;
Soon night departs, our eyes inhale the day ;
We own the God, and adoration pay.
But into air, like fume, he fudden fades,
And, grown too fine for fenfe, our fight evades. 600
The truth of Cleophas not one refifts
But Didymus ; whofe error ftill exifts :
None fhall perfuade me that he lives (he cries)
Unlefs he ftands confpicuous to my eyes ;
Unlefs I feel the wounds his body bore,   605
Once welling out in rills his vital gore.
This faid : The windows bar'd, and door remain,
Chrift ftands with rays bedew'd, amid his train.
Thus, thro' the glafs impervious to the winds,
The fun a paffage for his fplendor finds ;   610

Diffufes

Diffuses wide his glory thro' the room,
His lustre shedding on the horrid gloom.
No vestige, thro' the unhurt glass, betrays,
The golden flux and reflux of his rays.
All prostrate press the earth without delay,   615
And on adoring knees their homage pay.
When Dydimus beheld the display'd wounds,
And heard himself address'd by vocal sounds,
Instant he tumbles prone, with horror shakes,
And angry with himself at length thus speaks: 620
Convinc'd I own the features of your face;
And the true tokens of your God-head trace.
I little thought, (I own) that, after death,
You could inhale this light and earthly breath.
Madly forgetful of your supreme lays,   625
You should your body, on the third light, raise.
Nor strange: When oft you bade some frames
        repair,
Tho' four days buried, to this vital air.
When present at such deeds, could I refrain
My faith, unless distemper'd was my brain?   630
Perhaps my error flows from your decree,
That others may believe, who shall not see;
May not demand to feel your mortal mien,
Left spectres to deceive your frame should feign.
While thus he pray'd, the blazing God retires, 635
And with pure zeal each of his train inspires;
Nor from the earth he trod Olympus' way,
'Till, in the east, emerg'd the four-tenth day.

                                Now

Now Peter and his friends had plough'd the main
And fiſh'd, to gain their bread, all night in vain.
                                        640
Drench'd with the billows and fatigu'd with toil,
Collect their fruitleſs nets uncrown'd with ſpoil,
When lo! a youth of beauteous form they ey'd,
Beholding from the ſhore the briny tide.
Nor ſtood the Godhead to their fight reveal'd, 645
His ſacred frame with mortal limbs conceal'd.
At length he thus addreſs'd the fiſher-band,
Deſiſt not men, but turn the ſtern to land ;
'Tis granted, ſailing to the pebbled ſhore,
To crown your labours with a ſcaly ſtore.   650
Their courſe revers'd, they inſtantly obey ;
And with their out-caſt nets ferments the ſea.
A ſign of his vaſt prey ſoon Peter made,
And call'd his friends, by geſture, to his aid.
The loaded net all ſcarce with labour heave ; 655
While leap the fiſhes, panting for the wave :
John ſoon the God diſcovers, and thus cries,
Our Chief is here, I know him in diſguiſe.
See how his body glows with heav'nly grace !
What ſmiles guſh radiant from his beauteous face !
                                        660
No ſooner Peter had his Hero ey'd,
But from his ſhip he plunges in the tide,
Ardent to hail his Chief, the firſt on ſhore,
Tho' trembling at the ſurges' ſtormy roar.
The reſt, with fervent oars purſue the ſands   665
In haſt'ning veſſels, where the Hero ſtands.
                    R

And now the fishers, at the Chief's desire,
Prepare the repast which their toils require.
With wheaten cakes, some load the board in haste.
Some broil the fish upon the sandy waste.   670
While some inspire the kindling flames to rise,
Whose gloomy light meanders to the skies.
Hunger expell'd, the King, without delay,
Thus cries, his God-head blazing on the day :

    Mortals with ardent vows pursue fair peace, 675
And court fair peace with softest songs of praise.
And now, my friends, we must for ever part ;
Farewell for ever ; let me share the heart :
For high Olympus, thro' its splendent seats,
Displays its portals and my presence waits.   680
To be above the reach of frowning care
For suff'ring ev'ry ill your minds prepare :
Fear not to go before majestic pow'r,
But strictest truth in Tyrants ears dare show'r :
Too rich to covet what this light displays,   685
Look down on thrones, nor dread the sceptre's
      rays ;
Nor be too anxious to remark what hour
Or the best method your advice to pour.
I shall be present with you in my aid,
Shedding a tide of words, with grace array'd. 690
The Heav'ns themselves shall in your cause con-
      spire,
To nerve your strength, and comfort to inspire :
                  When

When the tenth day fhall veft with blaze the poles,
My Sire fhall waft his Spirit in your fouls.
Beneath whofe guardian care, you fhall proclaim,
695
Boldly, before the Lords of earth, my name.
A holy progeny fhall fhortly rife,
Brightly diffufive to the golden fkies.
The lufcious vines their unfhorn boughs thus
fhoot,
Teeming at once with foliage and with fruit; 700
But on this world when the laft day fhall fhine;
And yawning tombs their human bones refign:
When all the dead, who in earth's bofom lay,
Shall rife again, emerging to the day;
When Sages, Matrons, and an infant band, 705
Shall throng thefe mountains and the fubject land;
When I fhall fit in judgment in the vale,
And death and life to all mankind fhall deal:
Ye twelve fhall, each, affume his lofty feat,
Shedding, with me, on man, or life, or fate. 710
Ifr'el's twelve tribes from you their lot fhall hear,
And nature wonder at the ftate you fhare.
Peter, mean-time, (in zeal to none you yield,
The world's great key and fceptre you fhall wield:
Prefide o'er all, who willing fill my train; 715
Such honours I confer, you fhall maintain.
To you is giv'n the world's imperial lore,
Your reign be legal, and humane your pow'r.
The fmiles of Peace on the religious fhed,
And your juft anger let rebellion dread. 720

Shall

Shall any wretch, with dire offences bafe,
And deaf to reprimands your vengeance raife?
From human commerce chas'd and facred fanes,
Shall alfo be expell'd the heav'nly plains.
He'll hope, in vain, to tread the ftarry climes,

                                    725

'Till, purg'd by penance, you abfolve his crimes.
To you fuch fway is giv'n o'er human clay,
To fhut the gates of ether or difplay.

    Such mandates he pronounc'd, before his flight
From this expanded earth and human fight.   730
Thus the fage fhepherd, in his dying hour,
Refigns his fheep and fold to his fon's pow'r,
Shews the rapacious wolves' each furtive fnare;
And the fields hurtful to the bleating care.
The Marin'r thus, grown hoary on the waves, 735
The veffel's helm to his companions leaves:
Inftructs the younger in the var'ous ftrands,
The dang'rous Syrens, and voracious fands.

    This having faid: Refplendent lights furround
The mountain's airy brows, with palms imbrown'd:

                                    740

The lengthen'd fhores, fequeft'ring in a maze,
Are richly gilded with refulgent rays.
Dreft with frefh fmiles mean time, Olympus rings
With plaufive hands, and parti-colour'd wings:
To form a choir, convene an heav'nly throng, 745
And ether's vaulted roofs refound with fong.

                                    To

To the bright battlements with joy foon fly,
And cluft'ring crown the fummit of the fky ;
Some from the portals rufh abroad difplay'd,
And, poiz'd in air, with wings Olympus fhade,
                                              750
Some touch the mellow flute, fome ftrike the lyre.
While fome the twifted cornet loud infpire :
Some the hoarfe clangors of the trumpet blow,
And bid foft mufic thro' the cymbals flow.
Before Jehovah's throne the choir advance,   755
Thrice lightly tread the mazes of the dance ;
Thrice meafure the long length of ether's court,
The trodden poles refounding with the fport.
Thus joy the plumy hoft, in meafur'd bounds,
While mufic ftreams abroad in varied founds,
                                              760
Before the walls of Remus proftrate lay,
When Tarpeian turrets rear'd their fronts to day ;
When beauteous Rome the world's great emprefs,
        fway'd,
And fubject nations her commands obey'd ;
The Conful thus, triumphant from the war,   765
Bends to the capital his victor-car.
Jehovah's offspring thus afcends fublime,
The clouds difperfing, to the ftarry clime.
But left mankind's offences fhould inflame,
And roufe to vengeful ire the Sire fupreme ;   770
To ftop the fury of the direful blow,
He brings the enfigns of his deadly woe.

R 3   And,

And, firſt, ſome Angels with the croſs precede;
Some with the rods ſucceed in the parade.
Some bear the direful ſcourges which he bore, 775
Whoſe ſwelling knots bluſh crimſon with his gore.
The column ſome ſuſtain, to which cloſe-bound
His body yawn'd, by ſtripes, one gen'ral wound.
This Angel brandiſhes the pointed ſpear :
And this the pole, which waves the bowl in air.
                                                    780

With the three nails ſome ſeek Olympus' ſeat,
Which once transfix'd the Hero's hands and feet.
The thorny chaplet, which his temples crown'd,
Soars with an Angel to the blue profound.
This bears his title high, which Rome decreed ;
                                                    785

And one the lanthorn waving on a reed.
This travels gladly with the broken wand ;
Which, for a ſceptre, bore the Monarch's hand.
Before the Hero, thus his pomp of pain
Is brought to ether by an Angel-train.   790
The men behold, in admiration loſt,
The azure ſpace throng'd with a plumy hoſt ;
Their Monarch view, ſmooth gliding up the air,
With hands erect beyond the ſolar ſphere.
But hark ! a noiſe from op'ning clouds deſcends,
                                                    795

And in their ears theſe liquid accents ſpends :
Why gaze ye, trembling, on this ſtarry plain ?
Here, with his Sire, the God reſumes his reign.

With-

Without delay, Olympus' dome refounds
With vocal ftrains and inftrumental founds :   800
Their joys, alternate, the Apoftles fing ;
To heav'n their eyes and fpirits on the wing.
Rejoice ye nations, and with hymns attend ;
Behold the God the tow'ring fkies afcend.
Ye beafts exult, who tread the verdant way ; 805
Ye birds with clapping wings your joys difplay ;
Ye fcaly herd, who thro' the waters glide,
And praife him, earth, who fpreads your furface
    wide.
Let tow'ring mountains from their centers bound ;
And with their tides their gladnefs rivers found.
                                        810
Your God, with vocal rills, ye fountains praife,
And winding earth ; his glory roar, ye feas.
Let nature, in her works, her Author own,
And, with a gen'ral fong, addrefs his throne.
Before time born, Jehovah's great increafe, 815
Shall always reign, whofe God-head fills all fpace;
Who call'd to being all things from no-where,
The foaming ocean, earth, and ether's fphere :
From nothing gave to all with life to rife,
That move beneath the convex of the fkies ; 820
Divided heav'n from earth, the earth from feas,
Vefting Olympus' domes with fheets of blaze ;
Pencil'd the earth with herbs of various hue ;
Swell'd fields with corn and vines with rofy dew.
From you life flows; the heav'ns proclaim your
    fway ;   825
And heav'n-defcending rains your nod obey.
                R 4   With

With awe the clouds and winds your mandates
      hear,
And morn and eve revolve each on its fphere.
Replete with monftrous births the azure main
With its obedience fpeaks your juft domain. 830
Once balancing the earth your hand embrac'd,
And launch'd the globe into the airy wafte:
Each element in its due place you bound,
And bade it feek the center in its round:
Thro' the pure void on whirlwinds wings you fly,
                  835

And fhrin'd in clouds you dart from fky to fky.
The fleeting hours, indocile of delay,
At your command their winged courfers ftay.
To you duration bears no varied name;
Time, prefent, paft, and future, is the fame. 840
You bade the fun forbear his fwift career,
Shedding his beams on the meridian fphere.
The filver moon, whofe horns began to bud,
And wand'ring ftars to you obedient ftood.
The fire's confuming rage your mandate tam'd,
                  845

Which round the children innocently flam'd;
Who, 'mid the fiery furnace, tun'd your praife,
And ether bent attentive to the lays.
Like cryftal walls, you rear'd, on either hand,
The feas, while Ifrael fafely trod the fand. 850
You chang'd the current of the headlong tide,
Which all the banks with admiration ey'd.
                  From

From the ftruck rocks foft trickling ftreams diftill;
While fonts and rivers ftagnate at your will :
Earth, at your afpect, fhakes with trembling fear,
                                              855
And with your touch the mountains blaze in air.
Kings, at your feet, their arms and fceptres lay,
And to your God-head adoration pay.
Sounds on the deaf, rays on the blind, you ftream,
Health on the fick, and motion on the lame.   860
You hand to life frames fading in the tomb,
And long extinguifh'd fenfes you refume.
Nor was you with your early death difmay'd,
Nor with hell's regions, which with horror fade ;
For the grim Tyrant of the dreary coaft,   865
Chill'd at your prefence, with his baleful hoft,
Dreading the havock of his fhadowy reign,
Lurk'd in a cavern, with the fiery-train.
While you victorious, and your ghoftly prey,
Emerg'd from darknefs to eternal day ;   870
Where now you rule the fenate of the fkies,
And from your goodnefs better ages rife.
Hail nature's Lord! this world's great Saviour,
        hail !
With fmiles behold us, and with mercy deal ;
Your death difplays Olympus' portals wide,   875
And foothes your Father's anger to fubfide.

    Thus hymn'd the eleven Sages on the ftrand,
Beneath a rock, join'd by a youthful band.
                                          Yet,

Yet, 'mid such joy, with panic fear they chill'd,
Nor with the Spirit-God their hearts were fill'd; 880
The Desart's dreary wilds they often sought,
And, trembling, plung'd into some shaggy grot.
So when the hawk bears from her cell away,
And tears with crooked beak his cooing prey,
The other doves disperse, and in some tow'r, 885
Safe from the foe, their blended sorrow pour.
With no less horror, at their Monarch's doom,
Their fears conduct them to a close-bar'd room,
The promise of their Hero where they wait,
The God-head gliding from Olympus' seat. 890

    Now dawns the promis'd day, for darkness flies
The tenth day's lustre, beaming in the skies;
The Sire supreme, in the celestial space,
The stars now kindles with a purer blaze:
'Mid his Celestials, where he sits sublime,   895
His compacts filling, and dispensing time.
To whom his Son stands splendidly confess'd,
(His mortal limbs in liquid glory dress'd)
And pours his vows, before the sacred shrine;
In accents softly breathing love divine,   900

    My collegues, Father, now demand your aid;
Who, since their Leader's death, with horror fade:
In terror lost, they rove from place to place,
Such is the weakness of the mortal race.
Their fear expel, strength to their breasts bestow,
                                                 905
To front all dangers and subdue the foe.

                                        Now

Now Solyma and Judah's realm confpire
With guile to feize, or 'gainft them dart their ire,
You promis'd, Sire, (nor is your promife vain)
Equal to ev'ry noble act, my train   910
Shall, far as ocean girts this world, proclaim,
Thro' ev'ry land, my never-fading name.
Inftruct the nations to refpect my law,
And by new myftic rites to homage draw:
And, fince you grant them in the fkies a place, 915
I, oft, relying on your tender grace,
Their fainting fpirits rais'd; wak'd with the
        thought,
That aid would foon defcend the ftarry vault.
Thus help'd, they'd fcorn a Tyrant's cruel fway,
And all his wicked mandates difobey;   920
With joy, the pangs of death fpontaneous prove,
And victims fall to true Religion's love.

    This faid, his transfix'd feet and hands he fhews,
And with the wound his fide that crimfon glows,
The thorny chaplet that embrac'd his head,   925
When to the Crofs he was a victim led.
His arms wreath'd round his Son, the mighty
        Sire,
Thus, full of love, affents to his defire:
Your vows are heard; ceafe, Son, your hands to
        tend,
To your collegues, the Sacred Ghoft we'll fend, 930
And others, whom you will, we fhall infpire,
And in their breafts illume our holy fire.
                                    Wafte-

Wasteful of life, they shall not dread the steel,
Nor flames, nor beasts, nor the sharp-dented
    wheel.
Who tremble now, at Zephyr's softest sigh,   935
Shall, for your love, to certain dangers fly.
Then death contemning, and with virtuous pride,
Their souls shall issue in a sanguine tide.
No seasons shall delay their rapid course,
Nor summer's heats, nor winter's stormy force; 940
The yawning ground when sultry Sol shall cleave,
Or Boreas bind with icy chains the wave.
Farther than Bactra's walls, and Ganges' sands,
The mountain Ismarus, and Thracia's lands,
Shall wond'ring view the progress of their toil,
                   945
With Gades' island and rich India's soil.
Their lays shall eccho on Britannia's shore,
Round which the ocean's azure surges roar.
The world thus roam'd and mended by their strains,
Shall to your honour rear aspiring fanes.   950
Reformed realms to homage you shall haste,
And isles environ'd with the wat'ry waste.
An age of gold once promised, as you know,
Shall, on the tutor'd world from ether glow.
Not only for the just, condemn'd to fade,   955
By guilt primeval, in the realm of shade;
But also many more; whose actual crimes
Should have for ever clos'd the starry climes.
Your wounds have op'd the gates of Ether wide,
Such force and virtue in your death reside.   960
                       Let

Let then the groupe of faults, fince time was born,
To the laft blaze that fhall light up the morn,
Advance ; the fmalleft fluid of your veins
Shall chace the myriads and erafe their ftains,
What time the Sun in his career fhall round, 965
Near fifteen hundred years, the bright profound.
Then Bards fhall rife, with love of truth infpir'd,
Regardlefs of the tales by Greece admir'd ;
Thro' nations pour your murder in their lays,
And towns fhall eccho with your facred praife.
                                          970
But, chief, Hefperia's coaft fhall found your name,
Where wand'ring Addus fpreads his gentle ftream ;
Where Sirius, lucent as the cryftal, laves
The moffy margin with his winding waves :
Or, Po, the chief of floods, his torrents pours, 975
Roaring befide Cremona's mould'ring towers :
Whofe foaming fhore with rufhing billows threats
A deluge often to the nodding feats.
Sweet as the fwans, who ether rapid foar,
A band of youths, upon the pebbled fhore,   980
In concert aided by a virgin-throng,
Shall pour your glory in the chafteft fong :
Or in the meads contend who beft can raife
The fofteft numbers to your facred praife :
Infants in bands fhall their firft accents frame, 985
By lifping tenderly your faving name :
Such deathlefs glory fhall around you fhine :
He faid, and on him breath'd his love divine.
                                          Fancy,

Fancy, mean while, prefenting to their view
The traytor Judas' crime of odious hue,   990
The collegues for the miffion now prepare,
And 'mong themfelves divide the terrene fphere,
Where each fhall in his bounds new ethics deal,
And to the nations novel rites reveal ;
One for the facred Senate to provide,   995
That twelve might ftill o'er all the reft prefide ;
And now by lot, from the difciple-train,
To fill the vacant fee, they one obtain :
The lot, Matthias, in a happy hour,
Defcends and vefts you with the holy pow'r ; 1000
In merit wealthy, and in fortune poor ;
In title fplendent, and in birth obfcure.

While the fame grief on every vifage low'rs,
The fame addrefs the whole affembly pours :
Would the Almighty Ghoft from ether's fphere
        1005
By infpiration to our hearts repair ;
For oft the Lord to his affociates faid
The Spirit-God would come to give us aid.
Truth always crown'd our Chiefs' prophetic ftrains ;
This promife only incomplete remains.   1010

But hark ! thro' ether thunder founds hoarfe
        peals,
And heav'n defcends to earth's fequefter'd vales.
Unufual lightnings flafh acrofs the eyes,
And clouds diftain'd with fire defcend the fkies.

                                Torrents

Torents of fire gufh forth in parted rays,   1015
And all the dome is delug'd with the blaze.
Flames falling on their heads their temples bind,
And radiance fets on fire the fultry wind.
So when the fteel upon the anvil burns,
The lufty artifts raife their arms by turns :   1020
By turns, pour down their fturdy blows in
        throngs,
Turning the tortur'd ore with tranfvers'd tongs.
For God the Sire, and his coeval heir,
The Spirit jointly waft from Ether's fphere.
Now lo! the Spirit God Olympus leaves,   1025
And in the men infus'd the God-head heaves.
Cold fear retires, while facred fury rolls
Thro' the deep mazes of the raptur'd fouls :
Impatient of delay, they feel no reft,
Their bofoms throbbing with the Spirit-gueft. 1030
Thrice round them rays with awful fplendor fhine,
Thrice rapt in air, they flame with love divine.
In ev'ry mind a gufhing radiance glows,
And their hearts labour with infpiring throes.
Now free from terror, the Difciple-throng   1035
Declare God's wond'rous deeds in wond'rous fong,
While the fame words (who can believe the lay ?)
To ftranger crowds the cleareft truths convey :
For of the num'rous hoft each foreign'r hears
His native language, founding in his ears.   1040
From diff'rent climes, now various tribes repair
To view the town or facred rites to fhare ;

                            Thefe

These rites begin, when fifty days are paft,
After the paſchal lamb's religious feaſt.
Who 'mid the myriads, ſprung from Lybian
   ground,   1045
Hear th'Apoſtles their proper idiom ſound.
Admiring Gauls and Romans catch their notes ;
While to the Parthian ears their language floats.
Their natal accents lift'ning Scythians hear,
And Thracians numb'd beneath their icy ſphere.
          1050
Crete, Africa, Phrygia hearken with ſurprize ;
And thoſe who breathe Arabia's happy ſkies.
The tribes ſtand aw'd, who till fair India's lands ;
And Garamantes who roam thro' wilds of ſands.
Each band admire to hear their country phraſe :
         1055
And on themſelves with admirtion gaze.
The man abſorpt, their ſouls now wing the ſphere,
And the bleſt converſe of Etherials ſhare.

 And now their lips hereafters loud proclaim ;
For, lo! the God, with his celeſtial flame, 1060
Expels the night, that on their ſenſes reſts,
And damps the riſing ardor of their breaſts,
Whom, once, each noiſe with trembling horror
   fill'd,
And chas'd to dens, with death's baſe proſpect
   chill'd ;
Now free from cowardice they walk in day, 1065
And, careleſs of mankind, their thoughts diſplay ;
           Nor

Nor now the point of the deftructive fpear,
Nor favage beafts, nor fheets of flame they fear ;
But own the fkies to be his natal clime,
Who late was flaughter'd, pure of any crime. 1070
With fhame's deep blufhes now their faces glow,
That e'er they trembled at their Monarch's foe.
Their fouls inhale the God with eager breath,
Who in them wakes the hope of glorious death.
So when, in chinks, the thirfty meadow lies, 1075
The herbage withers and each beauty dies;
But let the fkies defcend in foft'ring rains,
The profpect fmiles and colours paint the plains.

And now difpers'd thro' various climes each
     ftrays,
The Leader's deeds their fong; his name their praife:
                                               1080
So that, as ancient Bards foretold, their ftrains
Sound on this earthly globe's remoteft plains.
If any pant, where earth deferted lies
Beneath the radiance of the torrid fkies ;
Or dwell, where ocean's billows wildly roar, 1085
Circling the extreme world's expanded fhore.
Their words they hear : While towns with awe
     attend
Their facred rites and to their mandates bend.
The ftain of ancient fin all nations lave,
And fpotlefs rife from the baptifmal wave.   1090
A new religion in the world appears,
And for her awful rites new altars rears :

S   The

The band are Chriſtians ſoon proclaim'd by fame,
So call'd from Chriſt, their mighty Hero's name.
On earth a golden age beams from the ſkies,
And beauteous years in fair ſucceſſion riſe.   1096

F I N I S.

I N-

I N D E X.

*The Roman Numbers shew the Book; the common
Numbers the Verse.*

Christ

INDEX.

Lamen-

www.ingramcontent.com/pod-product-compliance
Lightning Source LLC
Chambersburg PA
CBHW021050030726
47496CB00006B/1764